Kessy Lane

Kessy Lane

by

Don R. Goebel

A Novel Page Production
P.O. Box 26064
St. Louis Park, MN, 55426

ISBN-13: 978-0-99614-510-7
LCCN: 2016954159

Distributed by Itasca Books

Cover by Darrick Lyons
Edited by Heather Indelicato and Pam Nordberg
Author photo by Amy Rondeau Photography

Printed in the United States of America

For my brother Mike.

Chapter 1

A squeezing hand on his shoulder startled Jon awake.

"Come back up the path with me. Kessy's still gone."

Looking up at his cousin Josh, whose tired red eyes suggested he hadn't slept all night, made Jon feel as though he'd closed his own eyes only moments ago. The realization that he'd fallen asleep in the cabin's basement before Josh's sister Kessy returned to the cabin stabbed him with guilt.

Josh bit his nails as Jon sat up on the couch pushing his fingers through his scalp and through his short, dark hair. The news was like a jolt of adrenaline. He'd fallen asleep on the couch in his blue jeans And black Slipknot Iowa record hoodie at some point last night after everyone had returned to the cabin.

As his fingers reached the back of his head, he stared down at the fine layer of dirt that dusted the record cover goat's head graphic on his chest. It reminded him that their group had been running around the cabin what felt like hours ago, Friday evening upon arrival. Brushing his hand down his chest, taking some of the dirt off the image of a goat's head and the words 'Slipknot Iowa'.

His muscles felt stiff as he held himself up. Making fists on the old grey cushions, he tried to find his bearings as Josh headed for the stairs and the outside path.

"How long has she been gone, Josh?"

Jon rubbed his eyes, trying to alleviate the burn. He hoped Josh would answer his question so he would have a minute to get himself together. He shoved his shoes on quickly as Josh disappeared up the small staircase without him.

As he pressed to his feet, feeling the muscles strain in his legs, he heard the creak of Josh's feet pounding on the old boards. A voice in the kitchen sounded like Dan, saying something about going back up. Dan, a twenty-seven-year-old midlevel manager at an auto shop back in the Cities, was a guy Josh knew better than he did. Jon was a year younger than Dan, a graduate with an English degree. He remembered what Dan had said to him the previous night when they were trying to find Kessy.

"Jon! Go check the lake."

As these words swam back to mind, the thought of meeting eyes with the guy irritated him. "Going to check the lake" now felt like Dan's desire to leave Jon there as the rest of them left the area. The notion made him fume as he glided through the kitchen and outside without a glance at Dan.

Running over the gravel to catch up with Josh, displacing the dew that gently coated each stone as it crunched beneath his feet, Jon breathed in the cool morning air. The fog from the previous night had lifted considerably, leaving only a light brushing through the forest in the distance.

Turning briefly to see if Dan or any of the others had followed, Jon got his first impression of the tiny cabin they'd rented for their weekend getaway. A pretty location found advertised in a magazine was Kessy's idea. Old, weathered grey cedar boards ran along the front of it under a dark brown shingle roof littered with pine needles and leaves. The appearance matched the photo of spring in the north woods of Minnesota.

But when he saw Dan's dark blue jeans, grey, slightly worn shop shirt with racing flags waving on his chest, and thin face with the long, fixed stare through the rain-and-dirt-dusted glass, it made his nerves twist.

Dan followed Jon as far as the door.

He's not gonna follow after Josh? Or "manage me" and tell me to go check the lake again, is he?

Josh and Jon reached the edge of the path where the ground turned to dirt again. Jon listened for the crunch of Dan's shoes as the sound of their own steps softened. When he didn't hear anything, Jon rubbed the dark circles under his eyes and glanced at Josh. His cousin was his same age and also a recent grad, with similar uncertainty for his future. He had the same five o'clock shadow on the cheeks of his round face as Jon. Josh's curly dark brown hair was a mess from a night of running around their cabin in the dense fog. Wearing the same grey U of M hoodie and blue jeans as on their van ride up Friday night, Josh continued to bite his nails, his brown eyes heavy with dark circles as he fixed his attention on the path.

Last night seemed so long ago. As they hurried back up the path, Josh's fast pace fueled Jon's feeling that he'd missed something. He tried to remember when he'd last seen Kessy.

They had searched for her around the cabin, calling out to her through the fog. He remembered screaming her name through the woods.

He remembered with a sense of irritation having to track down his cousin on her twenty-first birthday. The feeling was the same, not quite knowing what was going on. Then, it had been the screen of her cell phone. He remembered seeing it light up on the bar counter, then repeatedly scanning the area for her and hoping to see her nearby. But this time there was no phone and no coverage this far north of the Twin Cities.

Being surrounded by towering pine trees near the Boundary Waters and screaming Kessy's name into the late spring, lake-effect fog had felt like trying to yell for her over the music in that bar. He remembered thinking that if the bartender could just turn it the fuck down for just a second, she might hear them. But when they couldn't find her, he and Josh had reluctantly left the bar. The idea that she might have left without telling anyone was a scary notion after she'd been celebrating so enthusiastically. The memory of Josh venting his worry and relief by scolding Kessy after they'd found her, sat in Jon's mind. Having been drawn to the bright lights and bass heavy dance music from a concert venue down the block from the bar they were in, Kessy stood just inside, transfixed until Josh spotted her. After fearing the worst and being forced to yell over the music to get her attention, Josh felt forced to be parental with her. After the way

Josh woke him and the two of them made their way up the path, it felt familiar but he wasn't as worried as he was during her twenty-first, somehow the isolation aspect of the north woods didn't feel as vulnerable.

"God this is annoying . . ."

Pulled out of his thoughts, Jon glanced at Josh. "What? What Dan said just now?"

"No." Josh's gaze stayed on the path as he spoke. "Leaving the house yesterday, my fucking dad told me to 'look after Kessy.'"

"I heard that too," he said, shaking his head. "She's twenty-one; she's grown.

"That's why he said it. She's still Daddy's little girl to him, like she can do no wrong. But the idea of her drinking is upsetting enough, like she needs to be babysat."

Is his attitude toward Kessy escalating because his dad called him Jr. yesterday morning?

"Did he actually call you Jr. as you were leaving?"

Josh shook his head. "Naw, Kessy was giving me a hard time 'cause she heard him tell me to look after her."

"Did you talk to her about this last night? Did she find another cabin that gave her a drink?"

Josh shook his head as his gaze returned to the path for a moment. "No."

Jon glanced at him. "No? What did Dan say to you just now in the kitchen?"

"I don't know. We were at the door at the other cabin and Tracy was talking to those guys. He was trying to describe Kessy to them, but . . ." Josh shook his head as he thought about it. "There was music playing, so even if she didn't hear Tracy at the door, she should have seen those people racing out when we were leaving because everyone was yelling when Tracy almost got into a fight with the guy." Josh went back to biting his nails.

Jon searched up the path as he thought about this, waiting for more. What Josh was speaking of was a part of Friday evening that Jon had not been involved in.

The first part began with burning off the lagging energy in their legs after the long ride from the Cities to the Boundary Waters. Adrenaline energized them as they ran around the cabin surrounded in fog until they landed, one by one, in the den of the cabin. When Kessy didn't appear on the staircase, smiling, out of breath, and dripping sweat like the rest of them had, they became concerned that she'd gotten turned around in the fog.

Kessy's brother Josh made his way out of the den first with Cristy, whom Kessy had raced through the fog. As Josh and Cristy retraced the girls' path, Jon and the others followed. When they didn't find her, Dan took a calm approach by calling her name into the fog-brushed woods. The calm shifted into panic when Jon began yelling her name. Dan told Jon to check the lake, and when Jon returned, the rest of the group was gone.

Jon felt ditched and that Dan had purposely left him out of the next part of the evening. He wondered why Dan wasn't more worried about Kessy getting dangerously turned around in the fog to the degree that she could not hear their calling and his yelling.

Josh shook his head. "Kessy's heard Dan yell before. She should have known we were there for her when she heard him telling everyone to leave!"

The image of Tracy and Dan getting into a fight at some other cabin was being pieced together in Jon's mind. The thought that Dan finally lost his cool made him feel better about his having ditched him at the lake. But it didn't sound as though Kessy had been a part of it.

Jon turned to Josh. "So you guys did get into a fight last night with another cabin! Did you see Kessy in the cabin? Was she involved?"

"No, there was a crowd of people in the clearing because a guy threw a bottle at Tracy, and Dan was yelling for everyone to leave. We had to get out of there."

Jon thought about this, but it made no sense to him, so he asked again, "Was Kessy involved in any of this or not?"

He stood, waiting for a response to the only important question that there wasn't a clear answer to. But as Josh didn't respond—the question seemed to embarrass him—Jon backed off. The image of fifteen to twenty people in a clearing and Dan yelling as they left sat in his mind. But from what he understood, it didn't sound as though Kessy had been a part of this altercation.

Is Josh sure Kessy's in this other cabin?

He'd missed Tracy and Dan getting into a fight with the people in some other cabin because Dan had told him to go check the lake after he kept screaming Kessy's name into the forest. *He got rid of me for screaming, then he and Tracy got into a fight with another cabin? Nice.* It made him wonder what Dan's expression would have been, had he glanced over to him sitting at the table as he'd made his way out of the kitchen.

The anger he'd felt, believing that Dan had "managed him" to get rid of him like he might at the shop back in the Cities, lifted. His muscles relaxed, and the antagonism that fogged his thoughts slowly eased up. He tried to remember what Kessy was wearing. Remembering this would put more of the night's events into place.

He thought he remembered her wearing a pink hoodie. But with his anxiety and lack of sleep, he had trouble thinking about her appearance beyond what Dan barked at Tracy.

In the distance sat another cabin, like theirs but bigger with cedar siding and a brown shingle roof, covered in a gentle haze of fog left over from the previous night. Trucks were parked at the edge of the clearing, but its grounds were bare of people. Only the spent yellow torches, stuck in the ground across the clearing behind the cabin, suggested additional activity.

Jon's attention flitted over the trucks. *Is anyone in these trucks?* He turned to Josh. "This is where you guys were last night?"

Josh took a deep breath as he nodded and squeezed his shaking hands several times.

Hearing about Dan and Tracy's altercation after the fact hadn't felt quite real to him until he saw the location. Seeing such a large cabin and a clearing littered with trucks, the density of people present the previous night, filling these trucks and their beds, was a bit intimidating.

They came around the corner, and Jon's pace slowed as Josh went to the nearest window. He cupped his hands against the glass and leaned in. When Josh left the window, Jon debated doing the same.

Had he seen someone?

The temptation to take his turn at the glass was dampened by a thought that he had to voice, however quietly.

"Are the people that you guys encountered in this cabin gonna recognize you?"

Jon's concern for Kessy was outweighed by the image of twenty to thirty people flooding into this clearing, waiting for a fight to blossom. He hoped Josh didn't knock on the door or barge in.

"What are you gonna do?" He felt a slight quiver in his voice. He wasn't sure if anything Josh described had involved Kessy and, as a result, could only assume she was in this cabin. Josh got to the screen door. The idea of their getting involved made his heart race as the nerves in his voice traveled into his arms. It intimidated and excited him as he followed Josh over to the door.

Josh hesitated at the door. The question remained in his mind. *Are you sure she's here?*

He was prepared to follow Josh in. Josh leaned into the screen, his left hand squeezing the handle. The door opened with an awful screech. Jon saw the dark brown walls and thin carpet inside this cabin, similar to theirs.

Josh's slow steps made little sound. Jon followed for several yards before wondering, *Are they gonna recognize him?*

Guilty by association, he rehearsed the words "*looking for his sister, Kessy*" in case they were confronted. Jon fixated on the back of Josh's hoodie as he followed him into a living room area where they could see people resting.

The smell of cigarettes hung in the air. He glanced at each couch, reminded that it was still early in the morning; Josh had woken him before the sun emerged, and most everyone was still asleep. The guys on either side of the couch had their heads resting in their hands with their arms propped on the armrests. Jon wondered if either of them had been involved in the confrontation.

The gentle sound of feet shifting over gravel pulled his attention to the screen door at the back. His blood rushed for a moment, and Josh's attention appeared to waver but not because of the sound outside. As Josh stared into space for a moment, Jon spoke softly, "Are you sure she's in this cabin?"

Josh was silent, continuing to stare into space, like fixating on a thought.

If he was sure, he would be looking for her now.

He noticed a kitchen littered with bottles. Maybe Kessy had had her drink and ended up sleeping it off in one of the rooms.

"Josh, did you see Kessy here last night?"

If the answer was no, then Josh's sister was still lost in the woods. If yes, she might be passed out in one of the rooms of the cabin. With Josh's hesitation, Jon began to think the answer was no. Jon saw a hall off the kitchen with several doors. It felt awkward to start searching for Josh's sister on the floor or on one of the beds of these rooms, but he didn't know what else Josh knew or was planning on doing.

Gotta be something he's not telling me.

He turned back to Josh.

"Josh, if you don't tell me what you're thinking, I can't help you." Josh still stared off, so Jon pushed further, "If you think she's in here, why aren't you looking for her? Why aren't you yelling her name?"

Josh finally seemed to snap out of it as he pushed away. Jon wasn't sure if he was finally going to do something after barging into this cabin or if he didn't want to hear Jon's questions. Either way, Jon felt a wave of guilt for what he'd said.

He was letting his irritation about Dan, and Josh's guarded behavior, get to him. In a heartbeat he decided to follow, back the way they'd come. Josh appeared to be heading toward a staircase in the corner. Jon's nerves twisted for a moment, thinking they would finally run into someone.

Jon debated speaking or moving around to face him first. "Josh . . ."

Josh's head dropped.

Did you see Kessy here last night? These words drifted through his mind, but he couldn't bring himself to say them. Josh was pale like a sheet as sweat streamed down his forehead.

Jon's next words felt wrong, but his cousin appeared ready to either throw up or pass out. "We gotta get outta here."

He threw his arm around Josh, pulling him to stand up straight and guiding him out. The desire to call out for Kessy, or to bring Josh outside then go back in and call her, was fleeting. But he didn't know if Josh had seen his sister in that cabin the previous night. He felt like yelling at the guy like he'd yelled for Kessy last night.

Give me somethin', man! What had or had not happened to Josh's sister that Josh only felt comfortable bringing Jon back up with him?

"Give me something, Josh. You're pale as a sheet, man. Why?"

Josh shifted his direction back toward the path entrance, and Jon followed. Jon would get nothing out of Josh because he was so thoroughly preoccupied by his encounter with that cabin the previous night.

"What did Kessy do last night?"

Chapter 2

Saying the words, "I didn't see Kessy in that cabin" would only beg the question why Josh thought she would be there. This was a path Josh didn't want to go down. The insinuation that Kessy had done something or had been involved in the confrontation made what had occurred difficult to put into words. He didn't want to be the one that tried to explain it. Tracy had done the talking last night, so Josh wanted to get back to the cabin and have him or Dan explain what had happened. Why had they left the area in front of their cabin to begin with? *It was because Cristy had wondered whether they had neighbors in the area.*

They were hopeful when they found a neighboring cabin the previous evening. He still felt heartbroken at the lack of concern they'd encountered. He remembered so little of the actual back and forth. Tracy had tried to explain to the people at the other cabin that Josh's sister was in the area.

It seemed like Tracy had tried to make his way in past those guys at their front door. After Jon had been screaming her name, a frantic energy had been created that swiftly caused a panic.

Josh could not remember exactly what had happened, and this was why he hadn't answered Jon. He didn't feel like trying to answer the follow-up question of exactly what had been said. It had happened so fast, and all he could think was that when they were discussing Kessy at their front door, the guys there had tried to convince Tracy that she was fine. But he didn't actually remember this being said.

He was desperately trying to remember it so he could justify wanting to go back to the cabin as he had with Jon. Telling Jon this felt like it was giving them both more reason to worry. *If she's wasn't up there at all, she could be lying unconscious somewhere in the forest.* He didn't want to put into words how the possibility of either one made his stomach twist. When he answered Jon, he told him what he knew.

"Tracy did the talking."

It was little to go on, especially highlighted by the fact that Tracy was the one bleeding when they were trotting back down the path. *Dan knows we went back up there, he probably told Tracy, and they're gonna ask what happened when we got there.* Anticipating a slew of questions while approaching the screen door, he waited to see someone. He was ready for someone to notice them.

It took about ten feet of walking on the noisy gravel before Cristy appeared through the dirt-dusted glass wearing the grey zip-up over light blue jeans she'd had on last night. An attractive girl, her fair skin stood out against the deep colors of the cabin. With her face so visible, her shoulder-length brunette hair had to be in a ponytail. As they got closer, Josh could see the worry in her soft blue eyes.

She was undoubtedly desperate to ask whether they'd been back up the path and spoke with Kessy. The question was answered. Those questions were answered when she saw it was still just the two of them.

***

The two had paired up as the group ran around the cabin the previous night. Cristy, at twenty-four, was only a few years older than Kessy, who was freshly twenty-one. They were friends who'd met at college, and because Kessy had invited her, Cristy felt a need to keep Kessy close. So when Kessy hadn't returned to the den, Josh had followed Cristy back outside to retrace her steps. When she had nothing more to trace, the guys had begun calling into the fog for her.

Cristy felt like she'd let Josh down, as she was the last person who'd seen Kessy. So while Friday had bled into Saturday, when she discovered Josh was gone and Jon with him before sunrise, she hoped that this steady worry would end. But when they returned, Kessy wasn't with them.

She waited for them to sit down at the kitchen table and for Josh to say his sister to know what was going on with Kessy, but he said nothing. They settled into their seats, as Josh's eyes seemed lost in rumination over the table.

"Did you talk to her?"

Josh's attention stayed on the table, acknowledging the question, but before he could answer, the sound of feet on the carpet in the den swiftly making their way up the stairs from the den to the kitchen pulled everyone's attention.

Tracy emerged. A neighborhood friend of Josh's as well as Dan's, at twenty-seven he'd graduated with Dan a few years ahead of Jon and Josh, majoring in psychology. He was a stocky man at six feet with dark, wavy hair that was thinning on top and a five o'clock shadow. Wearing the same black jeans, he'd changed into his grey gym shirt with black barbells forming an X over his chest, one that didn't quite cover a black band tattoo that wrapped beneath his elbow on his left bicep. He had a distinct red-and-black mark above his nose and on part of his cheek. He asked Josh pointedly, as if to say, *you're gonna answer*. "Did you talk to her?"

"I didn't see her."

"What do you mean, *you didn't see her?*"

"I looked in the windows and I didn't see her. I went inside and looked around, because she's my sister, and I didn't see her."

An uncomfortable quiet settled in the room. Tracy's attention stayed on Josh. "Did you check the bedrooms?"

"I checked the whole area."

"Did you check the bedrooms? You went up early enough. They're all still asleep. They probably gave her a bed for the night."

"I didn't see her."

Tracy waited on Josh to give him something more as he refused to make eye contact with him, his gaze not leaving the table. Jon glanced at Josh; his own behavior began to mirror

Josh's, as he knew the guy was partially lying to Tracy, but he knew the words "they gave her a bed for the night" were not ones Josh wanted to think about.

He's suggesting Kessy was in a bed. Makes sense, but it's gonna sound to Josh like she spent the evening with someone. Shaking his head gently, he thought, *That might be why he didn't search for her; he didn't want to find her like that.* Glancing at Josh as this realization formed like embarrassment in his mind, his cheeks and forehead turned red.

Another sound came from the den. It sounded like the springs stretching in the couch, followed by more feet on the floor. The swift pace made Jon a bit nervous as Dan emerged from the stairway.

The same age as Tracy, Dan had a thinner frame than him and a more oval face. His dark blonde hair, a mess on his head, was accented by a few days of growth on his face. Entering the kitchen, a box of cigarettes in hand, he pulled one out and paused to glare at Tracy.

Dan demanded, "Why don't you explain to Josh why you took a swing at that guy last night? That's what you're really pissed about. Kessy will be back when she's back, her and Trevor both."

"I did not take a shot at him! He was spilling his drink and I pushed him away so he wouldn't—"

Dan interrupted, lighting up as he barked, "I was standing right there!" He spread his arms, a cigarette in one hand and the box in the other. The dirt that dusted his arm stuck to a layer of dried sweat, causing a white scar from working at the auto shop to be more visible on the back of his left hand—a jagged white trail, one that ran from the knuckle of his middle finger down the back of his hand and past his wrist.

Tracy quickly got up and leaned against the counter, arms crossed, glowering at Dan. Dan stood in the middle of the room as he began to highlight the previous night's encounter.

"You fucking shoved the guy then yelled at everyone to get out of there! I can't even remember what you said about Kessy, but it sounded weird to me, so it had to have sounded weird to them! *'This is Josh. His sister, Kessy Lane, is not at our cabin. Is she here?'* is what you should have fucking said!" He glanced at his lighter before shaking his head and spreading his arms again, bewildered as to take Tracy's behavior to task. "You said 'area' a bunch of times like—"

"I did not shove that guy!"

"Then why the fuck did he try and break a glass bottle into your face? That's not a normal occurrence when he's a smaller guy, and you, at least six inches taller and fifty pounds heavier, are barking at him!"

"I explained that Kessy might be in the area—"

"Why the fuck didn't you just say: attractive brunette, pink hoodie? Then those guys would have known exactly who you were talking about!" He put a cigarette on his lips.

"I didn't think of that at the time! I tried to give them the facts. I told them her name and they started laughing."

"Yeah, why the hell did you shove him for that?"

"I didn't. The guy with the bottle started laughing about her name or something, and he started spilling his drink. That's when I pushed him back."

"Exactly. You shoved him!" Dan took the cigarette off to bark again, lighter and box in one hand, cigarette in the other.

"You know what the difference is between pushing someone's arm away and shoving a guy? If I had shoved that guy, he wouldn't have been standing!" Tracy added, defensively.

"You got confrontational with the guy! That's exactly what it looked like, and that's exactly how they responded! You should have backed up if he was spilling on you! Back up, wipe it off, then ask them again and say: 'cute brunette, pink hoodie.' Then you shut up and wait for them to respond!"

"That is what I said!"

"I heard you! You said the word 'area' like three times or something! The facts were: brunette, pink hoodie, and the last half hour! If the girl was within hearing distance, she might have heard you from whatever room she was in, and left!"

"I said, 'pink hoodie.' I know I said that. I told them she might be in the area. I told them her name. That's when they lost it, at least the one guy did. I don't know why."

Cristy spoke quietly, "It sounded like he said Kissy Kissy. He was drunk. Anything like that could be funny when you're drunk."

Tracy turned to her. "What?"

Dan glanced at her, then back to Tracy, and continued, "The thing is, you didn't explain why the hell we were there, but you did shove the guy with the outline of a marijuana leaf on his shirt, and the guy fucking snapped. He needed to prove how tough he was, and you gave him a reason to do just that, so he tried to break his bottle in your face.

"Did you hear those guys when we were leaving and you were bleeding all over? They were celebrating that shit! They kept asking, 'Cory, what'd you do?' and the guy was grinning ear to ear!"

Dan paused to light his cigarette. He took a drag and blew it at the screen door. Then pointing at Tracy with it between his fingers, he said, "The thing is, if you go back up there, they'll recognize you. You're just a hothead as far as they're concerned."

"I'm a hothead? I'm the one who walked away, not the one who needed to prove how tough he was and followed after us for about thirty feet. And the other guy is just reacting?"

"Yeah, he is. And if you go back up there, he's gonna recognize you. The only one they won't recognize is Jon. He can go up there and see if he can find Kessy in her pink hoodie. There're enough people up there; they wouldn't know the difference." Shoving the screen door open with a screech, he stepped outside.

***

It was quiet for some time; the points made by both sides had painted a vague picture of what had happened. Jon had almost forgotten about Trevor until Dan had mentioned him. He'd invited the guy up to the cabin himself but realized now that he hadn't seen him since he'd gone to check the lake.

Dan's suggestion made sense. But after what they'd described, Jon didn't want to go into that atmosphere alone, much less go asking around for a girl in a pink hoodie.

It surprised him that Josh had done what he'd done that morning, after what Dan had described. It sounded to Jon like a lot of people had witnessed Tracy bleeding and filled the clearing after it happened. The fact that Josh had gone right in, and he'd followed, was unnerving.

Chapter 3

"The only one they won't recognize is Jon. He can go up there and see if he can find his cousin." Dan's words sat with Jon.

Tracy seemed fairly unaffected by Dan's words. Despite all the blame Dan had hurled at him, Tracy was still confident about what he'd done. Tracy and Jon met eyes, acknowledging Dan's suggestion.

"She'll be back this morning."

Josh turned toward Tracy hopefully. "You think so?"

Tracy turned away, almost like he regretted what he'd just said.

Jon stared at Tracy, waiting for him to respond. *He doesn't know and he's trying to avoid the thought of having to go back to that cabin. But he's flat out lying to Josh!*

"What do you think she's doing up there?" Tracy stared at Jon after he asked the question. Jon studied the black-and-blue mark over the crown of Tracy's nose, where it appeared as though the bottle had hit his face.

Tracy turned away again, and then his gaze settled on the floor. "If she's not back by this afternoon, head up, and get her."

With that, he pushed off the counter and went outside.

***

Tracy's comment about Kessy returning on her own kept Jon, Josh, and Cristy waiting for just that. While none of this meant that anything had happened to Kessy, for Jon the thought that Kessy had behaved similarly at that cabin as she had on her twenty first. Leaving her friends and wandering from the bar to find a nightclub nearby full of loud music, drinks, and strangers. This time she'd found another cabin where Jon imagined her tipping bottles back until she had to sleep off her drunken stupor wherever she landed. Jon believed this memory was the reason for Josh's annoyance that morning, driven by Kessy's rude behavior. But after listening to Dan and Tracy argue about the behavior that sounded as though it had led to Tracy's bloody nose, he had a difficult time not picturing Kessy somewhere inside that other cabin, drink in hand, watching in horror.

If the communication between the cabins was truly as bad as Dan said it was and a fight resulted, if I were Kessy I'd be real embarrassed and want nothing to do with us. Especially if she saw what I saw—Tracy holding one of her hoodies against his face after having a bottle thrown at him.

Jon remembered how annoyed Josh had been on the path and how unresponsive he'd been in the cabin, and it reminded him that he'd missed the whole scene.

Gosh, if I'd been there last night and seen that fight and crowd I might feel differently thinking about Kessy being around that scene surrounded by a bunch of strangers. But it feels like the only people with anything to answer for are the ones who started shoving within minutes of encountering those same strangers.

As he stood up from the table, Jon caught Cristy's eye. She seemed as ready to get out of the cabin as he was; she stood to follow him out. He had a desire to voice his thoughts to her, away from Josh and the rest of the guys. He understood parts of what had happened at that other cabin, but he wanted to know what any of it had to do with Kessy besides her hoodie being used to cauterize a bleeding nose.

As they got around the back of the cabin toward the lake, he glanced to the edge of the clearing where Dan and Tracy now stood.

Are they waiting for Kessy?

He wondered if they would confront Kessy about her being there and then deciding to stay. The same mood of unresolved energy that had started with his yelling into the woods hung in the air.

"If I had been involved with the encounter with that other cabin last night, I might feel differently about it."

"What are you talking about?"

"They're over waiting for her, for Kessy to appear on the path. Or at least that's what it looks like."

Cristy glanced back at them but didn't say a word.

"What do you think she did when she saw you guys?"

"What?"

"Kessy at that other cabin, when all that shoving was going on. I saw her watching in horror as that broke out."

She shook her head.

"Especially if they caused as much of a crowd . . ." he trailed off.

Jon felt like Cristy disagreed.

"What are you thinking?" Jon asked.

"After you went to check the lake last night, I suggested we check other cabins, the possibility that we might have a neighbor farther up the path."

He studied her face as he waited for more, pulled into the blues of her eyes and then the heavy bags under them. Her cheeks and forehead, dotted with specks of dirt, glowed in the afternoon sun under a layer of dried sweat.

"I feel bad about that," Cristy explained.

"I started screaming; that's why Dan got rid of me."

"Yeah . . ."

They were within view of the lake, staring at the section of the shore he'd paused at Friday night, when they stopped.

"You said you thought Kessy was *watching* last night?" Cristy asked.

"Ah yeah, that's what I see happening after the crowd formed."

"I was looking for her the whole time!"

Cristy continued, "There was a big crowd. I checked back when we were leaving; I expected to see her pink hoodie after Tracy mentioned it. If she had heard that crowd, then seen us, she would not have stayed."

"You don't think she would have been embarrassed by the attention from the crowd when she saw what was going on, how Tracy and Dan . . ."

Cristy shook her head as he trailed off again.

"What?"

"If Kessy got turned around in the fog and was far enough out that she couldn't hear you yelling, if she made her way up to that cabin, she should have been in the immediate area. She wouldn't have stayed after that happened."

Her tone reminded him of Josh's earlier.

"What do you think she did?"

Cristy shook her head "I don't know. But I'm worried. This doesn't feel like her twenty-first when she was drinking and went off on her own. If she were in the woods, I think she would have heard you. She'd be scared after being turned around in the fog, and as soon as she heard Dan and Tracy, she should've left that second."

Jon had only a vague understanding of what had happened, but both Josh and Cristy spoke with a similar concern for Kessy yet with little to go on. They each only had a feeling after she hadn't shown her face at the other cabin. Because of the argument between Tracy and Dan, he had a sense that something else had happened.

"What do you wanna do?"

She hugged her arms into the pockets of her hoodie, shivering gently in the cool afternoon air. He wondered if he'd pushed her the way he had Josh. He wondered if he'd pushed her the way he had Josh when her head dropped.

"So many people saw that argument. The guy with the marijuana shirt and all his friends from the frat saw it."

With the little sleep she'd gotten, the red hairline veins that surrounded her blue eyes had rings under them. Jon felt as though if he asked anything further he would push her to tears.

"If you want to go up, I'll go with you."

Saying this to her, acknowledging her concern for Kessy, seemed to take some of the pressure off as she looked up at the lake and took a deep breath.

"You wanna go up right now?" he offered.

She stared at the lake. "I kinda wanna get the cops involved. That way when we go back up those people wouldn't be able to stop us at the front door!"

"*What! Why?*" Her standoffish tone made Jon jump as an exasperated two-word response shot through his mind like growing towers before he reacted with panic, "D—Do you think that's necessary?"

Her gaze didn't leave the lake and Jon shook his head, wondering, *Are these the same thoughts Josh had after we left that cabin? They are really upset that Kessy didn't show her face!* Cristy, sounding desperate for police involvement, created a more callous vision of the guys in that other cabin.

What the hell did I miss? Tracy and Dan are pissed! Trevor is up there with Kessy, Josh doesn't want to hear that his sister might be shacking up, and Cristy wants to involve the cops! What the fuck happened last night?

"What are their names?" Frustration gripped Jon's words.

"Who?"

"The guys that you ran into last night, the ones you want the cops to talk to, what are their names?"

"When we were leaving, some guys kept yelling, 'Cory, what'd you do?'"

"Who's Cory?"

"He threw his bottle at Tracy after he shoved him, that's what caused a crowd. He was grinning ear to ear, him and his—"

"What's he look like?"

"Trevor's height, about five-foot-seven, short red hair, outline of a pot leaf on his shirt." As soon as Cristy gave him just a few details on Cory, Jon chewed on the thought that a guy was somehow responsible for Kessy not showing her face. While this hadn't been explicitly stated, he envisioned a shoving match breaking out at a front door while Kessy was inside, surrounded by strangers, trying to warm up. When the bottle was thrown and the yelling and screaming followed, a mass exodus happened. Jon saw Kessy in her pink hoodie seeing all of this, too scared to get closer to the door.

Fuck, if I'd been there, I might feel differently!

Cristy had described Kessy as being scared before she found her way to that cabin, and then assumed she'd heard Tracy arguing and decided to stay.

After hearing secondhand from the lot of them, then being in the cabin with Josh and seeing nothing of consequence besides a number of people sleeping, one question struck him. *The only group that is being a jerk right now is ours. Does Kessy even realize it was her group at the door?*

While he'd voiced some of this, his perspective only seemed to baffle Cristy and draw them into a stunted conversation. Though she hadn't actually given him an answer, he was ready to follow her lead if she pulled the trigger on his offer.

As he turned toward their cabin, he wondered if Dan and Tracy were still at the edge of the clearing waiting for Kessy. "I want to know what they would say to Kessy if they saw her on the path right now."

These words distracted Cristy out of her thoughts. She turned to him then followed his gaze.

***

Dan flicked the end of his cigarette with his thumb, glancing at Tracy as he appeared preoccupied with the path. "You actually worried about Kessy? She'll be back. She and Trevor have class Monday, the rest of us have work commitments; they know that." Dan took a drag, continuing, "And if you mentioned her pink hoodie like you thought you did, they'll find her and kick her out based on your behavior alone."

Tracy shook his head and touched the mark on his face.

"What, are you still angry that Cory threw a bottle at you? You didn't give him the reaction he wanted, but the sight of blood was enough to set them off. Tracy, you don't think you have anything in common with their behavior, but it's an excitable crowd. That's why it appealed to Kessy and Trevor; just like her twenty-first."

Dan took another drag off his cigarette, flicking its end, as Tracy stared at the path. "Imagine how it would have gone if Jon had been there, the way he was carrying on. He would have been neurotic and screaming in their face. *He'd* have been slugged instead . . ." Dan trailed off when he saw Tracy shaking his head. "Yeah, you're still angry. Tracy, you're tryin' to read into the encounter 'cause you majored in psych; you got their attention when you banged on their door, but you believed they wouldn't be any help when you saw they'd been drinking.

"As soon as that Cory guy started laughing at Kessy's name, you knew you wouldn't get anywhere. But when he threw his bottle because you shoved him and a crowd formed, it just confirmed your opin—"

Tracy cut him off. "You know why I lost their attention the moment they opened the door? You know why Cory reacted that way?"

"Why?"

Tracy turned to him finally. "They were relieved I wasn't the DNR."

"Yeah?"

He turned back and crossed his arms. "What we should have done was just go inside, find Kessy, and leave. Banging on the door created an expectation. Those guys were running around out of breath and drinking; they wouldn't have known the difference had we just gone in."

"And by the way, Jon isn't neurotic. He was panicked because he knew someone he cares about was lost in the fog."

Dan shook his head and then pointed at their cabin. "Tracy, keep in mind that's a rental." Then he pointed up the path. "Up there, with all those trucks and vans we saw in the clearing, I'm willing to bet one of those guys owns that cabin, so they're used to renters. They probably know some of the regulars during the season." Dan took a drag then continued "Probably the same guy who yelled at Cory. The one I was trying to explain the situation to. We never learned his name, but I think he knows the owner; he was the only one who wasn't excited like the rest were."

"The guy in the UFC shirt who was horrified after the bottle was thrown? If that were the case, I can't believe he would stand by the way he did." Tracy cut into his conversation..

"The one with the smokers voice, Trace!" Dan declared, annoyed. "The one who yelled 'Cory!' Cory was the one with the pot leaf on his shirt who pitched his bottle and the guy who was upset with him was the same one we were talking to."

Tracy interrupted, "I remember I was right there!"

Dan continued, "His gravelly voice cut through the others. I heard him through all their excitement over my bleeding face, and you did too. His growl was distinct when he raised his voice. He was real upset! Why else would he be that upset unless he had some connection with that cabin?"

"He was angry and horrified because I was!" Tracy barked.

"And they know where we're staying!" Dan said "They know we're probably staying in the cabin down the path, and they realize they don't know us because we're not regulars. So barging in like you suggested is not an option."

"Josh went up with Jon this morning!" Tracy countered. Dan stared at him. "He didn't really search for his sister from the sounds of it. I think because he didn't want to find her in bed with some guy, probably Trevor. But he went up with Jon and I'm willing to bet the guys that answered the door last night didn't notice, you know why?"

"Because it's early?"

"You got it! Early in the morning, sun isn't up, they're still passed out from last night. They don't know the difference

between someone collecting their sister to someone going outside for a cigarette."

"Jeez, Tracy, you learn that in psychology of frat class?" Dan
shook his head. "This doesn't require a bachelor's degree to figure
out. That's all it is up there. They're having a party all weekend.

"Think about it! It's the perfect time to go into that cabin,
knowing what they were doing the night before, or hours ago
in this case. It makes sense!"

"You know what you could do, though the thought would
never cross your mind."

"What?" Tracy asked.

"Go up, squash your beef, and apologize for being so
confrontational."

Tracy mumbled something, shaking his head.

Dan continued, "Not to the one who threw the bottle, the
one whose cabin that is. The guy with the gravelly voice you
were going on about appearing horrified. If he feels the way you
think he does, he's gonna know why you're there."

Tracy's head dropped as Dan said this.

"He knows we're down here, we got a few more days left up
here ourselves, we might want to get along while we're here. It
would be the civil thing to do."

Tracy's head came up as he pressed his fingers together by his
chest. "If what you're suggesting is the case; If I'm the guy who
owns that cabin and within hours of arriving I see a drunken
idiot throw a bottle at a complete stranger's face after minutes of
attempted conversation, that's now a confrontation. When that
stranger walks away bleeding, if that somehow doesn't bother
me, I am either thoroughly fucking clueless or totally embarrassed and want to appear on that path and apologize the first
chance I get!"

"*You're* waiting for an apology? Tracy, I'd bet they believe
you were high based on your behavior! Again, you said the guy
was horrified, but his reaction was informed by yours because
you were throwing questions at him just before you hit Cory

for laughing at you. I highly doubt he will be as contrite as you want him to." Dan pointed up the path again. "The guy in that cabin isn't going out of his way to be around you again."

Tracy shook his head, glaring. Dan took another drag off his cigarette, his eyes shifting to Tracy's tattoo.

"If nothing else, he'll remember you for your tattoo. You heard him yell after Cory. I heard them identify you by your tattoo, calling you 'the guy with the tattoo.' He glanced at it several times while you were carrying on.

"If I were the owner of that cabin, I would leave the guy with the tattoo the fuck alone unless he comes back."

Dan took another drag off his cigarette. "Someone comes into the shop and snaps, as a manager you remember that. If it happens again, it's strength in numbers. These are the basics, Tracy. That's how people behave, and they rarely apologize."

***

Tracy wants an apology? Josh shook his head as he leaned against the sink, peering through the waves in the aged glass, having eavesdropped on Dan and Tracy's conversation. *If Kessy was kicked out, she'd be back by now, and the fact that she isn't doesn't seem to bother them.*

But hearing Tracy affirm him visiting that cabin this morning gave Jon encouragement until he heard the comment about finding Kessy in bed with Trevor.

***

As the sun began to set, and neither Kessy nor Trevor was back, Josh bit his nails until he ran out of white sections. As he debated going up alone, he considered asking Jon and Cristy for company, believing they shared his concern, as Tracy and Dan had eventually left the clearing and gone down to the lake.

As the air cooled, a haze of fog began to form in the atmosphere and the environment felt familiar. If both Kessy and Trevor were ready to head back, soon it would be as difficult to navigate as it had been the previous evening.

As Tracy and Dan wandered back into the kitchen, Tracy wondered aloud if the guy who owned that cabin had been at the door last night and whether he was disappointed at the lack of an apology. Tracy asked as he leaned against the sink, "You think Kessy would want to stay around a guy like that? A guy that has no problem standing by while a fight breaks out?"

Josh sat at the table, growing tired of listening to Tracy. Feeling put on the spot by Tracy's questioning his sister's choice to not return that afternoon created a desire to defend her somehow. *Is he judging her for staying?*

This thought grinded on Josh as he peered out the window at the fog. As he spoke, fear for her well-being crept into his voice. "The fog is forming again. It feels like it's gonna happen again."

"No it won't. Jon and Cristy are going up to get Kessy now." Dan said this as though he were delivering mail.

This surprised Josh as he sat back in his chair. "Why didn't . . ."

Dan held a drink in his hand as he turned to Josh, leaning against the counter with Tracy. "Since Tracy didn't get the apology he was waiting for, my guess is that the story of what happened will have circulated through the whole cabin. I think it set a tone for them that we don't need to put ourselves into. They'll remember us. I don't think they'll remember Cristy and they don't know Jon."

"When did they leave?" Josh shot back.

"They'll remember you." Dan cut him off.

Josh looked at the table. He had the desire to follow but felt shut down again and sunk in his seat. *I wasn't asking permission!*

He heard a *pff* as they opened their bottles and the clinks as the caps bounced over the counter. Josh imagined the both of them tossing their caps behind them without a care as he fumed in his chair, gaze fixed on the wood grain in the table as his desire to follow Jon and Cristy was crippled. It took time for Dan's perspective to sink in, for him to be convinced to stay put.

They aren't worried about her at all after they described the environment that she's been around all day.

"Josh, they'll likely be right back with her," Tracy offered.

Josh felt his eyes welling as he spoke, "Who do you trust up there?" He let his words linger for a second. "'Cause I fucking hate everyone in that cabin right now!"

"They probably feel the same way about us!" Dan said, eyes still fixed on Tracy. "And you said pink hoodie a lot!" With this Josh pushed out of his chair and headed for the door.

"Josh!"

"I'm goin' to the lake!"

***

Jon glanced back at their cabin, waiting to see Josh storm out of it to follow after them. He was ready for it after Dan and Tracy went back in. But it didn't happen.

"Gotta imagine they'll tell Josh and we'll hear him burst out the door."

Cristy thought about this. "Before they started laughing at Kessy's name, Tracy pointed Josh out to them. Even if they didn't remember that moment, he'd feel familiar to those guys because it was last night."

"You don't think they'll remember you?"

"I was in back; as soon as the shoving started, the attention was on Tracy."

With Cristy at his side, Jon wondered if they'd hear yelling and see a crowd as had been described. As the other cabin slowly became visible through the trees, the subtle sounds of conversation and laughter drifted to their ears. He couldn't make out anything, but he saw people outside. He wanted to see Cory, the guy who had thrown a bottle at Tracy. Cristy had described him as short and with a leaf on his shirt.

They saw the back of the cabin and the people as he and Cristy got closer to the end of the path. He heard a girl's voice. Briefly thinking it might be Kessy, though knowing it wasn't, he picked up his pace.

As they crunched over the rocks, people turned and glanced at him, but they mostly noticed Cristy. He stared at a dozen people standing outside the cabin, darting from face to face for someone that fit Cristy's description of Cory.

They slowed their pace through the clearing as Jon glanced back at Cristy. "Recognize anyone?"

She didn't give him a second glance. She was here for Kessy. He realized she was heading for the back door.

He felt a rush as they walked past these people, side by side, until they reached the screen door. Jon pulled it open with an awful screech, hearing music on inside.

A voice inside said, "Do it! It's not on!"

As they stepped into the kitchen, Jon saw the back of the guy who'd spoken. He had short red hair, was wearing a black shirt that covered a thin build, and held a video camera in his hand.

"The glass is full now! Do it!"

A guy leaning against the counter yelled over the music at a girl whose back was toward them. He was damn near berating her to do something. Jon wondered what the hell they'd shown up to witness.

"Do it! Come on, deep throat!"

His eyes widened, wondering if something was going to happen in front of a crowd of people. All eyes were on this girl just a few feet from them. Jon's eyes darted from a girl with short, straight bottle-blonde hair whom they had their eyes on, to the brunette and the two other guys staring at her with smirks on their faces. He didn't quite know what they wanted from her until she gave in to the pressure.

Leaning forward until it appeared as though her nose could have been touching the table, she appeared to maneuver her head. The three at the table lowered their heads to get a better view of what she was doing as the camera did the same thing. Jon grabbed Cristy, getting them out of the frame. The girl was maneuvering her lips around and over what appeared to be a shot glass, down to its base, touching her lips to the table before cocking her head back. She appeared to have taken the entire glass into her mouth. Pursing her lips near its base to keep it there, she leaned back and pulled up her top. She wasn't wearing a bra.

Her onlookers went wild. Jon turned to Cristy, who was still taking it in. He glanced back as the shot glass was placed back on the table with a bang. The guy with the camera appeared to adjust its display. Cristy peered at the camera, and Jon leaned in, speaking to her quietly.

"What the hell did we just come into?"

"It's called 'deep throating' a drink. It helps if a girl is really drunk."

"How . . . ?"

"I heard about it in college. Guys try to get a reaction by explaining it to a girl."

"Is lifting her shirt part of it?"

"That's why it helps for a girl to be really drunk."

"And the guy filming it?"

Before she responded, one of the guys against the counter asked, "Cory, did you film that?"

"What the fuck!" The girl at the table was trying to give the impression she was upset.

Hearing the guy's name, things clicked for Jon. *The one with the camera is the same one who pitched a bottle into Tracy's face.*

They began yelling, "Who's next? Who's next?"

Jon felt hatred for them as they demanded more. He stared at this Cory guy, with his camera and pug face. *Ugly little shit.* Jon envisioned a similar scenario inside here before Tracy had pounded on their door. *This guy was probably interrupted from this last night, too.*

It felt like a drinking activity with tremendous expectations. When one girl did it, there would be fanfare for more to follow suit.

He imagined Kessy, in this cabin after being turned around in the fog, trying to make herself small when they called upon her to join in the action. *She would have been told to relax with a drink poured for her by this fucking guy, while he held his camera at his side, waiting for just the moment to put her on the spot. Then she would react out of fear under their berating and do what she was told.*

Nothing good could result from such a game—being several drinks in and pressured into such an action with so many guys around . . . and then a video camera to "perform" for. And if it didn't happen . . . he could see a disappointed crowd being just as vocal.

Though not present last night, Jon felt involved as he envisioned this scenario. He instinctually went to a small steel tub in the kitchen, taking note of the quantity of glass bottles in the container.

He turned and stared at Cory. He hoped the guy would notice the attention and be pulled from his playback to find him glaring. But Cory was enthralled with his camera. Jon turned back to the tub and pulled out two glass bottles. He crept back past Cory, eyeballing him.

***

"You think he filmed Kessy?"

Cristy stared at Jon for a moment. *The guy standing behind them could have easily heard him.* Jon saw her expression and froze. They waited, expecting the cameraman to react. When he didn't, they saw the screen door open, and Jon searched for the direction he'd gone.

He has no reason to think that Kessy was in any sort of similar position or that she has been on film, but the possibility's there, and Jon has latched on to it.

The energy the camera created was unsettling. She didn't know what was going to happen next. Cristy continued to stare at Jon, waiting for him to make a decision, whatever it may be.

Chapter 4

It was just a notion with no proof, but Jon had to know. Witnessing the atmosphere and assuming the worst made him think of Tracy's question about the bedrooms. Now he'd witnessed some of what went on in this cabin.

He had to put together a plan, though he couldn't just leave Cristy. When he held out one of the bottles for her, she reluctantly took it.

"The areas Tracy mentioned—"

"Yeah."

***

Jon wanted her to check the bedrooms, this much Cristy gathered, but she didn't need the bottle he'd handed her. He'd picked it up so they could travel freely throughout the cabin. He was worried about blending in, but she wasn't.

Find Kessy and get out. This was all that mattered to her, not some footage that may or may not exist. If Kessy was pressured into a similar drinking game, Cristy knew it would result in a hangover that would land Kessy in a bedroom. At the thought of finding Kessy and leaving, she took a drink.

She stood there as Jon took a swig from his bottle then went back outside and in the same direction Cory had gone. She didn't know what Jon was planning on doing when he found the guy, and it irritated her, thinking that ultimately he was putting more importance on Cory than on Kessy.

But, she was going to do what he wanted. She took another drink, readying herself to start opening doors, when she heard a voice. "Why don't you sit down?"

Her heart jumped into her throat as she stared at the guy. He wore the same sleeveless white Señor Frog's shirt and light blue jeans that he'd worn when he had stood, laughing to himself, next to Cory, calling, "Kissy, Kissy." She thought he might have recognized her from the previous night. His eyes were a bit glazed over as though he'd been drinking. She turned quickly to the girl at the table who knew what was happening, but avoided eye contact.

"You wanna sit down?" he asked again.

Cristy attempted to dissuade the attention. "I'm waiting for a friend of mine."

"They won't be able to find you if you're sitting?"

He was friendly when he wanted something from her, but she was sure he'd had a few and was feeling brave to volunteer a girl to sit at the table. That Cory guy wasn't around. If this guy was going for a repeat filming, he would have to bring Cory back first. Jon had gone out after him, so they would be back soon.

His hand gripped her arm, moving her from the edge of the kitchen. She glanced at the table, still trying to make eye contact with the girl sitting there. The guy worked to get her to the table, like there was some kind of shared understanding of expectations. Like sitting in the center of the room meant she was next.

When she realized the onlookers in the room were either checking her out from the corners of their eyes or doing their best to ignore her, tending to the bottles in their hands, she panicked. She wanted to yell in hopes that Jon would hear her. But she didn't want to scream. If she did, she would start crying, and there was no way to wander the cabin looking for a girl after doing that.

In that moment, thinking of Kessy gave her an idea. "L-let me find my girlfriend first!" Her voice quivered over her words. "Let me find my girlfriend; then I'll sit down."

Those in the kitchen raised their heads. She tipped her bottle back, taking as big a swig as she could, one that would thoroughly convince them of her intentions and to ease the possibility of what might happen between the girls.

Now she had to do something, fast. *Find Kessy, fast. Then what?* She didn't know. She didn't know how she was going to "find her girlfriend." Moving aimlessly about the cabin would feel like she was leading them on, but it was the only option she'd given herself. It felt insane and brilliant at the same time.

"What's she look like?"

She stared at him. The thought that he might help her was unnerving. Trying to locate Jon would likely escalate things. If she called out for Kessy, it would be what he was expecting.

He paused as she took another long swig from her drink.

One of the guys leaning against the counter said, "You gonna help her look, Chris?"

The name felt familiar, like Cory had possibly said it the previous night. She couldn't remember if he had been one of the ones intent on seeing the blood on the rocks.

If she called, "Kessy Lane!" she feared she would get no response. *She's not just gonna appear the way they're expecting. Nothing is gonna happen.* The heavy feeling in her stomach and the position of her heart constricted tighter. She would go to the rooms down the nearest hall. Staggering past Chris, she felt him ogling her, but the attention of the others seemed to be fleeting. They would care again if she returned with another female.

It brought a feeling of foreboding, knowing the guys in the cabin had mental images and tremendous expectation for the search. The bottle began slipping between her fingers. She gripped it with both hands as she reached the last door in the short hallway. The bottle slipped from her hand as she reached for the knob, catching her thumb and pointer finger on its lip. It made a soft impact on the carpeted floor beneath her.

Chris's hand gripped her arm again. He easily turned her around, but she lost her footing as he held her against the door. The wooden door made an awful cracking sound, popping and snapping under the pressure of their weight.

The fabric on her top stretched and ripped, as his free arm went up for a firm grip of her breast. Her entire left shoulder was totally exposed. The dry skin of the fingers that had been gripping her arm grabbed down over the bottom of her nose and mashed her lips over her teeth. Tears rolled down her cheeks.

She felt fists repeatedly striking the other side of the door. She moaned as a muffled voice from the room behind her yelled, "Hey! Hey!"

A girl's voice. Cristy could feel the knob jerking. Someone was trying to twist it open. Chris eased up for a second. With her toes touching the floor, Cristy pushed all her energy into his chest, and the door swung open. She fell back and hit her head on the floor with a thud.

Chapter 5

Jon proceeded out the door and began scanning the faces in the clearing, but did not see Cory's. Trying to keep up a pace, he moved out of the clearing, toward the path they'd walked up. He glanced at the path before making his way around the corner of the cabin, assuming Cory's direction.

As he got around to the front, near the door, he thought of how Cory had pitched a bottle at Tracy. Jon paused, scanning the rocks in front for evidence of a broken bottle. He saw nothing and headed back inside.

The guy already filmed a girl in the kitchen. He's gonna go to a different location. He saw some stairs going down. *A den would be a good start.* The layout was similar to the den in their cabin. When he got downstairs, he found himself scanning for Trevor, of all people. He remembered that Trevor was apparently still around here somewhere.

I forgot all about him. He stayed. Probably saw this environment and wanted to save Kessy from it. Probably thought he was being a hero when everyone left. No one seemed all that concerned that he'd stayed. *He and I are buddies, but Dan doesn't really like him and Josh is leery of him because he has a thing for Kessy, which is why he stayed. Kessy's the vulnerable one; she's new to drinking. Trevor is like an afterthought to the guys.*

He settled at the side of the staircase, leaning against the wall. The people on two dark brown couches facing each other glanced up at him and then continued their conversations. When Jon kept staring in their direction, they were compelled to notice him.

He'd made up his mind about their character and was rather OK with making them uncomfortable.

Though he knew none of the people in the room, he felt content until a brunette girl on the couch facing him started simply, "Are you looking for someone?"

He felt a hint of bravado. There was no harm in some partial honesty. "Meeting Cory down here," he said, staring her dead in the eye, not friendly. He felt the energy of the guy in the kitchen with the camera.

She squinted at him, confused as her attention lowered to the image on his chest.

"Is that a goat?"

Her question pulled the attention of others on the couch. Before Jon could answer, a guy beside her glancing at the image spoke.

"That's Slipknot. Their Iowa record cover."

"It looks like an angry goat." Her tone was sarcastic.

A few more heads turned. Somehow he felt like he was getting somewhere in locating Kessy.

His energy gradually shifted into nerves. He was beginning to second-guess his feelings of bravery. He was still hoping to run into Cory, but he had no real connection to make it happen.

Minutes dragged by, and his goal felt rash and unnecessary. But the thought of Cristy upstairs going room to room was enough to justify staying where he was.

He had to know what was on that tape. Cory might post the video online. He couldn't let that happen to Kessy.

Chapter 6

When Cory, with two others who seemed just as interested in his exploits caught on film, emerged from the stairs, Jon fixed his gaze on the floor.

The girl on the couch had her eyes on Jon, who was still leaning against the wall, when the playback of the footage caught his attention. Suddenly he was worried that she would remark to Cory that some guy was here for him, but the volume and footage distracted the two guys enough to not notice her.

Jon considered his options. He considered heaving the bottle, but simply observing along with the group felt like the most subtle way to find out what was on the tape. The girl on the couch eyed him as he slid slowly over the wall.

Not quite brave enough to stand behind the two, he settled against a nearby wall.

Now he could clearly hear some excitement going on. It wasn't applause, like in the kitchen. It sounded like a much larger group reacting to something more harshly dissonant. There was too much noise to make out what was going on without an image to correlate it with. He thought of Tracy in front of the cabin, a bottle thrown at his face before it spilled and clinked over the rocks.

"This happened last night?"

Cory had indeed caught the encounter on tape.

"Yup!"

"Play it again?"

Jon thought of Tracy's blood falling on to the rocks. If this had been caught on tape, it would explain why they wanted to see it again.

"Yeah . . . play it again." But their tone didn't have enough excitement in it for them to have just seen something they liked. The request sounded as though they'd missed something.

They were quiet during a second playback. Jon tried to listen but found himself waiting for their reaction. He lifted his bottle to his lips. When he could finally get a glance at the image, the display was closed.

"Was that a fight?"

"Is there more?"

Cory had a snide smile on his face, like he might have been about to divulge something, when he saw Jon.

Jon squeezed the bottle in his hand and envisioned pitching it into Cory's face. Cory's smile faded as his eyes grew. They maintained eye contact until the other guys noticed and promptly turned to Jon. Jon's focus remained on Cory for another second before one of them addressed him.

"What the fuck is your problem?"

The bottle with its condensation slid through Jon's fingers as this question was thrown at him; he turned back toward the couches, doing his best to not let it slip from his anxious grip. The question had swiftly pushed away other conversations. All eyes were on him, they waited for his response.

The same girl on the couch, with a slightly confused expression, asked again, "I thought you said you were looking for Cory?"

He squeezed the bottle as their persistence pulled over his nerves like sandpaper. Feeling like something would finally go down, he felt his free hand shake at the possibility. Without further thought, he skipped up the staircase with long strides.

He heard a guy's voice behind him in the den, "What the fuck was that?"

"The guy with the bottle was here for Cory?"

He got to the landing and glanced toward the kitchen where Cristy had stood, but didn't think much when she was gone.

She's finding Kessy. He saw the stairway to the attic up ahead, through the living room, and headed that way.

Chapter 7

Cristy held herself against the wall to her left in this new room she intended to look for Kessy in. She now sat on the floor, eyes squeezed shut, and felt the impact through the floor of the person who'd opened the door and the one who'd attacked her.

Chris was at the front door last night! He came at me seconds after Jon left my side! Jon could have turned around and seen him! Chris must have seen me the moment we walked in. He saw Jon leave, while that shot was being done. What had felt like a way to avoid sitting at the table and a chance to find Kessy had only served to fuel Chris's interest.

Fucking wrong! The way I carried on when he offered me a seat was so fucking wrong! It was like I was asking to be attacked! And I made Kessy a part of it! That suspended further thought, filling her mind with blame that coursed throughout the rest of her body.

She felt the raw skin on her chest where Chris's hand had gripped. Her top was torn; she was still exposed, but it didn't register. Her arms covered her chest, and her hands hid her face. As the minutes dragged by, she began breathing regularly again.

She could hear heavy breathing on the other side of the room. Feeling that presence made her want to cover up. Her hands trembled as she uncovered her face, opening her eyes; she blinked through several tears and tried to pull herself together. She wasn't going to acknowledge the other person in the room, though when she opened her eyes, the sprayed white texture on the other girl's jeans caught Cristy's eye.

"You were here last night!" said the other girl. "Are you stayin' in the cabin down the path?"

She recognized me! Fuck! It scared Cristy, like she'd been caught. Waiting, Cristy closed her eyes.

The energy in the room had shifted with the girl's recollection. "I remember you guys leaving!"

Chapter 8

Jon had a feeling of guilt, wondering where Cristy had gone. He wanted to believe that nothing could have happened to Cristy in such a short amount of time.

The attic was a small room, like another den in the cabin. It smelled a bit like stale weed. Though the sun hadn't set yet, he noticed through a small window off to his right that the light was being choked out by the thickening fog outside.

This left a single incandescent lamp in the far left corner to cast a dim light over a table and two couches. He couldn't see who was in the room. As he stood, waiting for his eyes to adjust, he sensed other people in the room.

"Cory!"

"That's not Cory."

"I want him to film this!"

"I know. But that's not him."

Jon wanted to know what was going to happen. His eyes had adjusted, so when an open spot on a couch off to his right appeared, he went over to it.

He sat in the corner, on what felt like a mess of papers. They popped and contorted beneath him as he tried to sit quietly. He was able to hear music and conversations as they drifted up the stairs and into the room. He waited.

He shifted, and the papers contorted and popped again. It made him nervous, not wanting to draw any more attention to himself before Cory stomped up the steps. Shoving his hand beneath his seat, he gripped whatever he could and pulled it to his lap.

"Cory! Cory! You missed it!"

Jon's hands shook as he mashed the paper in his hands in anticipation. At the sound of feet coming up the steps, he regretted leaving his bottle on the floor. Cory burst into the room, slamming the door behind him and cutting off the noise from downstairs.

"Dark in here!"

Jon stared at his lap as the light on the camera glided through the room. He covered his whole mouth with his hand in an effort to not be recognized. Staring down at the papers in his hand, he angled them as though what the guy was doing with the camera was not taking his attention.

Cory and his two buddies stood on the other side of a coffee table.

"Which one?" Cory asked.

"Blue shirt."

"You mean the one sitting next to the angry goat."

"What?"

Cory didn't clarify. Jon's anxiety grew as he glanced at the image on his hoodie. As the glow of the light glided over the table, allowing him a glimpse of the items on it before it stopped over the person next to him on the couch wearing a blue shirt. He leaned away from the light, closing his eyes, too scared to breathe. Then they started talking.

"You find your girl, man?" The guy next to Cory spoke.

"You were getting up in my boy's face, asking if he was involved with your girl. You find her?" said the guy next to him.

"He said he was gonna do something. You swore to God." The guy next to Cory again.

They're talking about Kessy. Trevor must be here too. Jon was too scared to check even from the corner of his eye, afraid he would be caught by the camera light. Instead, he stared down at the papers in his hand, waiting for something to happen.

"Why are you so quiet, man? You were real upset yesterday. Nothing to say now?"

He saw the white edges in his hand brought into view by the light. From the top of his eye, he saw a guy next to the camera lean into view. He was unable to see what he was doing, but he heard a scrape over the carpet. He pulled the papers to his waist as the muscles in his legs clenched like a wringing bar towel against the front of the couch when the table was forced at him.

It struck his right leg and both of the person's next to him before the guy who'd shoved it lunged. Jon's leg jolted with the sharp, shooting pain, kicking over the bottle he'd placed on the floor. His eyes squeezed shut. His teeth gnashed. He curled the pile in his hand. The paper's edges sliced into his fingers. The person next to him was lifted off the couch and thrown to the floor with a thud.

The striking sounds felt distant through his pain. He couldn't register this three-on-one onslaught of film and fists until his pulse stopped hammering in his head and he could take a breath.

Chapter 9

The pain was sharp. Jon's grip slowly let up. The papers in his hand slid to his lap.

If I open my eyes I'm going to see the guy lying on the floor, somewhere nearby. I'll recognize the clothing, his blue Blink shirt. I know it's going to be Trevor.

Jon wanted to pretend that it couldn't have been Trevor sitting next to him on the couch. *It could've been someone else they pulled off the couch, someone else they beat until he must be unconscious.*

Hearing the sound of more feet climbing the stairs, and believing Cory and the two attackers were returning, he suddenly saw Cristy. At least he thought it was her. She turned away the moment she saw a body on the floor. By the time he was moving his arm out to wave at her, anything to get her attention, she'd already gone back down the steps.

He leaned forward, putting pressure on his legs to stand. The throbbing spiked. He gripped the pile of papers again, grinding his teeth. He realized he was going to have a limp as he squeezed the pile again, pushing through the pain.

As he stood, he felt something sharp on his finger. He glanced again at the pile in his hand and saw a bunch of Polaroid photos. He must have slid his thumb into the back of one of them when a sliced edge on another had cut into his finger and he'd bled over all of them. He shifted them in his hand to avoid the sharp edge.

As he made his way out, he recognized Trevor's blue shirt and black jeans but couldn't stop to help him. He wanted to know what was on the photos, especially the one he'd cut himself on, but first he had to catch up to Cristy.

***

Cristy turned the second she saw someone lying on the floor. She saw the clothing and thought she recognized it, but she didn't move any closer to confirm. It was dark in the attic, but someone appeared hunched over on a couch. She thought the one on the couch had turned her direction. *This was a bad idea.* She couldn't get away fast enough.

She headed for the back door. When she saw that sleeveless white shirt standing in the kitchen, she immediately turned for the front door. She heard people discussing something real loud like they were excited, bragging about a conquest. Her arm was up, covering the torn section of her top that she'd unsuccessfully attempted to tie together. *Just leave the area as quickly as possible and hope that Jon can find me.*

She'd brought Kessy into it, yet she hadn't found her. *I brought attention to myself and brought Kessy into it! And then I left without her, because I just couldn't stay.* It had seemed brilliant, and then everything had gone horribly fucking wrong. Thinking about how she'd brought Kessy into her mess made her feel worse.

The feeling compounded as she remembered that girl's last words before she had gotten out of the room. The one whose sprayed blue jeans caught her attention during the second she opened her eyes. She'd recognized her from the previous night. Thinking about it now, it somehow felt like it put more attention on Kessy as well. Like somehow that girl knew why she was there and, given the accusing tone of her voice, was going to do something about it. The girl in the room had said, "What the fuck is going on?" *Did she know I was there for Kessy? Did she see what happened? She knows where we're staying. In the cabin! She asked, but maybe she doesn't know for sure.*

She wanted to turn back around and say something to that girl. *If only I were that Brave.*

Chapter 10

The sound of stones shifting behind her made her freeze. Squeezing her arms over her chest, Cristy felt like someone was trying to catch up to her. She imagined that Chris or the girl locked in the room had run after her to finish what they'd started. She thought seriously of screaming her lungs out until Jon called out to her.

"Cristy . . ."

He sounded out of breath and in as much pain as she was. Without a word, he got to her side, and they both slowly began making their way back, staring straight ahead. They didn't say a word to each other the rest of the way back.

Night had fallen. The cool air drifted over her, touching the dried sweat on her chest. Cristy hoped that no one would be up so the state of her top would go unnoticed.

***

As their cabin became visible through the trees, they saw a light on in the kitchen. Returning without Kessy was clearly going to require an explanation.

Jon had nothing to report other than a vague belief that Kessy might have been made to down a shot while she was there. He also would have to explain what had happened to Trevor. *Fairly sure the guy's still unconscious on the floor in that attic.* It all made the day feel like a complete waste.

They adjusted their pace to make their return quiet. Jon remembered the small pile of photos still squeezed in his right hand. He still wanted to study them, more so now that he'd stolen them in the midst of the onslaught on Trevor. Maybe he could salvage their trip with something from the photos.

Getting closer to the door, the only sound was their shuffling feet. *Maybe the others didn't wait up.* But then he noticed the smell of cigarettes resting in the air, more pungent as they approached the screen door. A haze rested in the kitchen.

Jon thought that Tracy might be up but had stopped going outside to smoke. Tracy, being a decent judge of character, might understand what Trevor might have done.

Jon pulled the door open for Cristy. The light from the kitchen made the trails of blood on his hands appear much worse. He noticed the back of Cristy's top. It appeared stretched at the side, as though it had been pulled around her.

The cigarette smoke felt palpable in the room. He squinted as she disappeared into the den. Both Tracy and Dan sat at the table, several empty bottles pushed to its center.

Tracy sat with one leg crossed over the other and an arm resting on the back of his chair. His other arm rested on the table, fingers touching a partially drunk bottle. An ashtray sat beside the bottle.

Dan sat on the other side of the table, nearly facing Jon. He sat back in his chair, a foot propped up on the next chair, knee in the air, staring into space.

Tracy gently pushed the bottle around with his fingers. Feeling the need to cough, Jon's closed fist flew up to cover his nose, over his mouth. He stifled it to hear what Tracy had to say.

"Did she say when she was coming back?"

His fist still at his face, he closed his eyes from the smoke. The words "I didn't find her" were obvious, but he didn't know how to explain everything else that had happened while they were there. He was too exhausted.

He had no idea what the photos still squeezed in his hand were of. *I cut my finger open stealing these fucking things from the same room where Trevor was called out and beaten unconscious. There's gotta be something there!* Completely ignoring Tracy's question, he brought the photos up to his chest, in view of the guys.

Chapter 11

Flipping through the photos until he found the one that he'd cut his finger on, Jon studied it in the light, the cigarette smoke stinging his eyes. What he saw was an image of someone lying on the floor, back to the camera, as though she'd stumbled or been pushed.

He saw the legs of people standing. Jeans, tennis shoes, and boots were shaded in the darkness. They stood around this person on the floor while others appeared ready to launch themselves over the table, their fingers at its edge to see this person in the center of the photo. The bottom of the person's shirt was filthy, like it had been dragged through dirt. Jon held it closer, trying to see its color.

"What is that?" Tracy asked as Jon tried to remember what Kessy had been wearing when they were running around in the fog. Dan had gone on about her pink hoodie, but it was hard to be sure. He thought he remembered her in a light pink hoodie, but this was darker, almost red to his eyes, and filthy, but the quality of the photo was terrible. His eyes circled around the image, taking in the jeans and boots that faced the camera.

They're surrounding this person.

"Jon, what is that?"

It reminded him of Trevor laid out on the floor with guys surrounding him, but he couldn't tell who it was or if the person had been beaten unconscious, as Trevor had. Maybe if he kept staring at it, he would see something else through the haze of the smoke that stung his eyes.

Tracy shifted in his seat and then got up when Jon didn't answer. Tracy studied the image, leaning into it. Then he snatched it from Jon.

"Where did you find this?"

"The attic of that cabin."

"Did this happen while you were there?"

"No, these were on the couch where Trevor was." He was too exhausted to tell the story, and the smoke was stifling. Tracy's hand gripped his shirt.

"Did you see Kessy up there? Was she in the attic?"

"No, not that I saw. It was as dark as that photo."

"What was going on?"

"Trevor got called out for looking for her. They asked him if he'd found her. Then they pulled him off the couch next to me and filmed themselves beating him unconscious." These words just fell off his lips.

"What?"

"Trevor. It happened in the same room I found these."

Dan got to his feet as sounds from down in the den distracted Jon's attention from the photo. He couldn't wrap his head around the situation. He pulled against Tracy's grip on him, and slowly he let go.

Chapter 12

Following Cristy's lead down the stairs and into the stuffy den air where the sting in his eyes lessened, he propped a knee on to the couch before crumbling over it, closing his eyes to try and disconnect from the experience in the attic.

Jon sank into the cushions, feeling the dried sweat on his forehead grind into the fabric as he lay facedown. His legs still throbbed. As exhausted as he was, he found himself sitting back up. Gripping the fabric on his thighs, then cupping it above his shoes until he saw broken skin, he'd bled into his jeans.

He leaned back and dragged his fingers through his oily hair, resisting an urge to push his fists into his eyes and gnash his teeth, as the sight reminded him of Trevor on the floor of that attic. The thought of the guy regaining consciousness then picking himself up and making his way back meant there would be more to the story.

Jon sat there listening to the chatter in the kitchen, of Josh asking questions that there were no answers for. He'd seen the photo; the lack of explanation had been enough to torture him.

"Is that my sister? That looks like her hoodie! What did she do? Why are they surrounding her? It's like they ganged up on her. Was she beaten to the floor by a fuckin' crowd of people?"

Tracy's voice broke into Josh's questioning. "Her hood is up and she's facing away from the camera. We don't know what was going on, Josh. The people around her are witnesses; they know something.

"It's more likely that someone had an issue with her for some reason and got into a fight with her. My guess is Kessy didn't put up any kind of fight, and that's why she's on the floor."

"I think they fed her drinks, she got up to leave, fell, and someone took a picture," Dan offered.

"If that were the case, Jon might have seen her."

"Tracy, do you want to believe that Kessy's in some kind of danger up there?" Dan countered

"I'm going off the way they treated us the first time we went up there and what Jon said about Trevor being beaten up and a photo of what might be Kessy surrounded in that cabin.

"It doesn't strike me like what you described. It doesn't seem as though she stumbled after a few too many; it's more like she was shoved from behind to fall over. If she were drunk, the person might have made more of an effort to get her closed eyes in the picture. You can't see her face. What you can see is what I think is some guy's boot stepping on her hand!"

"It does look like that guy's boot is stomping on her." Josh spoke quietly. "I think what Tracy's saying makes more sense."

"Then you should go up after your sister," Dan said.

"I wanna know what Trevor has to say, though."

"Then wait for Trevor!" Dan's responses were snappy. "Josh, what I'm saying is yes, that photo is unsettling, but don't get ahead of yourself. For all we know Trevor might have seen the whole thing and he can tell you what really happened! Just don't get ahead of yourself thinking they were ganging up on her."

"Dan, I think he got your point!" Tracy barked at him, then it was quiet for a moment. "I never got my apology, which means they think nothing of treating a complete stranger like that."

"Ask Trevor when he gets back if he got an 'apology,'" Dan said, mocking him. "I'd be willing to bet that both you and Trevor deserved the way you were treated by those guys."

"Did Jon say that Trevor put up a fight?" Josh asked.

"That doesn't matter," Tracy retorted.

"From what he said, Trevor got called out and—" Dan started.

Tracy cut him off "Yeah, I know where you're goin' with that!"

"Jon said they filmed it! And a photo was taken of Kessy. What do you bet Trevor was there when this photo was taken?" Dan suggested.

"You said that!" Tracy barked, cutting him off.

"You don't think she'd put up a fight?" Josh asked.

"You didn't check the bedrooms. From the sounds of it, neither did Jon, so I'm goin' off that photo, Josh. Surrounded like that, she would be scared. If I was her with that kind of crowd, I would just want it to be over as soon as possible so I could get out of there."

The pacing continued. Jon debated going up to the kitchen, but he had nothing to add; or rather he only had an account of what happened to Trevor to add. And that would only escalate the speculation.

Forcing his hands into the cushions, he slowly raised himself to his feet, still feeling the impact that the table had made in his shins. He made his way up the stairs and wanted to say something to Josh but had no clue what to say.

Jon made it to the wall by the side of the staircase before his legs gave out and he slid down to the floor. Josh joined him at the other side of the staircase.

He's not ready to ask me what or why. All I know is what I was a part of . . . fuck! Josh is trying to figure out how to react to this after seeing such a thing, and so am I!

Jon was going to have to give Josh something. He almost wanted to lie to him, but he couldn't do it.

"I found the pictures on a couch. In the attic. Of that cabin." Glancing at Josh for any reaction, he continued, "I don't know why any of them were taken, but, as I told Tracy, I found them in the attic where I found Trevor . . ."

Josh turned his head.

"I don't know why what happened to Trevor . . . happened, but it happened in the same place I found those photos. Trevor was pulled off the couch from beside me. If I think about it harder, I'll remember what was said, but he was beaten unconscious and it was filmed."

"By who?" Tracy asked the question without a hint of surprise.

Part of him did not want to answer. "I think it was the same group that threw the bottle."

"You said they filmed it?" said Dan from the table behind Jon. *That's the wrong fucking point.* He had to steer the attention back to the photo somehow.

"Yeah, they pulled Trevor off the couch."

"Why?"

Jon's head dropped to his chest and he closed his eyes. *I . . . don't . . . know.*

Tracy's attention stayed on Jon as he answered Dan, "Ask Trevor when he gets back."

Dan said, "You're so intent on putting Kessy in danger, if it tells us what was going on up there, it will probably tell us what happened to Kessy."

The room was quiet. Jon still sat with his head on his chest. *Fucking way to go, Jon. You told him Trevor was beaten unconscious and now he wants to know all about it . . . like it's gonna explain that photo!*

"Did you watch them film it?" Dan demanded.

"No!" he snapped back. "They pulled him off the couch next to me. The guy shoved a table out of the way to do it." Jon pulled up the fabric on his right leg to reveal the red-and-black mark on his shin.

"They shoved a table into you?" Tracy paused. "I believe it. Then you wouldn't be able to get involved."

"What had you done to have that happen?" came an accusing tone from Dan.

"I went searching for the cameraman, Cory, with the idea that he might have filmed Kessy at some point."

"So you got in his face?" Dan said matter of factly.

"Yes and no. I was down in the den, and Cory showed up with a few guys, showing off some footage. I tried to get a peek at it, but that wasn't gonna happen. So I tried to listen in. I thought the footage might have involved Kess—"

"Sorry. What made you think Kessy was on film?" Tracy spoke quickly.

"He was filming women doing shots the moment we got there. It made sense to me . . . a lot of peer pressure."

"You were trying to listen in?" Tracy put him back on track.

"Yeah, something about it reminded me of what happened to you guys. When Cory noticed me, he was surprised at first. When the guys with him noticed me, it was, 'What the fuck is your problem?' I had shot my mouth off just before that, to one of the girls. I told her I was after Cory. So when they asked what my problem was, she spoke up and reminded everyone that I'd said that."

"The guy with the camera," Dan said.

"Yeah."

"How long after—"

"Minutes."

"Sounds like you put yourself into the same position as Trevor. It's interesting that they only hit you with a table. You got off easy."

Tracy waved his hand. "We don't know what happened to Trevor. The fact that they filmed it might say more about this Cory guy than anything Trevor could get himself into. But if you feel the need, Dan, ask him when he gets back."

Josh turned to Jon. "What was the reaction of the guys who saw the footage?"

"They . . ." His irritation level dropped. ". . . they asked for it to be replayed several times. They didn't seem to know what it was."

"Could you hear anything?"

"Some kind of commotion. Loud. People yelling. I remember I thought it might have been the reaction to the bottle being thrown at Tracy."

Dan turned to Tracy. "Was someone filming that?"

Tracy shook his head.

"OK. What was said before they pulled Trevor off the couch?" Dan asked rather pointedly. "Did they film what was said?"

"I think they did, but they didn't say much." At that moment, he remembered what Cory and his friends had accused Trevor of. Trevor had apparently sworn "to God" and had gotten into someone's face. "He apparently got into someone's face."

"OK," Dan said, sounding content.

Josh stared at the photo in his hands. "Can we please talk about the photo of my sister now?"

Tracy took a deep breath, crossed his arms, and asked Jon, "You found it on the couch with all the rest, correct?"

"Yeah."

"Were there others with her anywhere else?"

"Not that I noticed."

"She's surrounded in that photo. Did a lot of people see what happened to Trevor?"

"It was dark, but I don't think so."

"When did it happen?" Dan asked as though Jon knew and just wasn't saying.

When he didn't respond, Tracy did. "There is no time on the photo. I checked."

"How about that other photo? The one of that table has a bag of something on it. If that happened at the same time, Kessy might have Been part of it." Dan suggested.

Dan spoke of a photo Jon hadn't seen, *a bag of something?*

"Don't assume that!" Tracy's statement of shock charged the room.

The quiet was uncomfortable.

"Jon," Dan said calmly. Jon didn't take his eyes off Josh. "Where was Cristy during all of this?"

"She was searching the upstairs! I left her in the kitchen when I went after the guy with the camera. When I left the den, after I made an impression on Cory, she was gone!" he said, clenching his fists. "I assumed she went after Kessy!"

Dan turned to Tracy and asked, "Are these questions that shouldn't be asked?"

"No," Tracy said calmly, trying to ease the tension. "Jon just witnessed one of our guys getting beat up, and Josh discovered a photo that suggests that the same might have happened to his sister. So you're gonna have to approach this with a bit of that in mind, as you're the only one who hasn't been adversely affected by that cabin. Everyone is processing things a bit differently than before."

It felt like Dan was still approaching this like he had Kessy's twenty-first birthday. That time it had been Kessy's choice to leave and her choice to use.

Trevor would be questioned relentlessly when he got back. The thought that Trevor could have done something about it but didn't brought a sinking feeling into the room.

Chapter 13

Anticipation lay like a ragged blanket on the room. Josh fixated on the photo. Jon had nothing more to say to lift the feeling of dread.

Those guys had some reason to go at Trevor. It couldn't have been the same for Kessy.

Past the flash of light over Kessy in the image, the people surrounding her cast a great deal of mystery, made it difficult to understand. Jon leaned toward Josh, trying to see the photo again.

Staring at the filthy pink hoodie, he tried to envision what might have been going on, but his mind was too tired to process a scenario. As much as he tried, closing his eyes to put himself back in the room, his head began to drift. It was still dark out, but he did feel as though he'd lost track of time, wondering if he'd nodded off on the couch. When Dan asked him a question, he realized he was nodding at that moment as he opened his eyes and saw him staring at him.

"Jon, did Trevor say anything to you?"

Unable to remember at that moment, he only wanted to close his eyes again. He felt all their eyes on him as he stared into space long enough for Dan to realize this and speak again as he asked Tracy.

"What time is it?"

"I don't know, two or three, probably later, I think the sun will be up soon. I don't think Trevor will wait for the sunrise. After being knocked out, soon as he comes to, he'll be out of there."

"You think Kessy was knocked out?" Josh spoke quietly again. His words lingered in the air, in silence.

***

Jon's eyes opened again as he heard a dragging sound, what sounded like sandpaper being scraped outside. He pinched the crown of his nose as he saw Tracy and Dan move over to the door. He waited for some indication from them.

"They roughed him up," Tracy said.

"You can see him in the dark?"

"Head dropped, feet dragging. I think he's going to the lake." Jon glanced at Josh, who was still staring at the photo. Tracy turned and, striding over to Josh with his arm out, he plucked the photo from Josh's hand and returned to the door.

Trevor is gonna go jump in the lake? Shit, I'd do the same if I had . . . The thought trailed off as he saw the expression on Tracy's face as he held the photo. He wasn't going to let Trevor relax.

He's gonna shove the photo in his face as soon as he walks up. Jon closed his eyes, feeling like he was in the attic all over again.

The screen door opened. Tracy stepped outside, and the door hissed closed. Jon wondered, *did Trevor know it was me on the couch next to him?*

Tracy spoke softly from outside. "Hey."

"Hey," answered Trevor.

Jon put his hand on the floor and leaned their direction, hoping to hear something. Josh's hands hadn't moved from when he had held the photo. He was waiting in suspense to hear something.

After a moment Dan turned to Josh, giving him a slight nod. Josh slowly pushed to his feet and made his way over. Jon forced himself to his feet and slowly over to the door behind Josh.

"Go," Dan spoke quietly. "Ask him if he saw your sister."

Josh pushed the door open. The desire to see what Tracy described got him as far as the door. But he couldn't see Trevor; it was too dark out. The urge to flick the switch on the wall, to turn the bug light on outside, was shared by Dan as he reached reached for it. Trevor turned away from the light. His wavy, dyed black hair was a mess and his soft blue shirt was filthy, but Tracy and Josh stood in the way of his face.

Tracy spoke quietly. "You and me both, man. You saw that guy throw a bottle at me and got jealous."

Trevor laughed for a second, before he was quiet again, embarrassed. As Trevor shifted his stance, keeping his face out of the light, it brought the side of his head into view.

"What happened to your ear?"

Tracy asked this, and Trevor just stared back at him.

Tracy gestured to the side of Trevor's head. "Your piercing is gone and you got blood on your earlobe."

It took Jon a second after hearing this to connect it; then his heart sank. *Trevor has hollow plug earrings in both ears.*

"He didn't know."

Jon glanced at Dan, who spoke quietly.

"He's checking now. . .touching his ear. If it is gone, he didn't know and he's realizing it now."

They watched Trevor stare down at his fingers.

"He's embarrassed," Dan said. "You said he was knocked out. That's when it came out."

"You lost it at some point while you were up there."

Tracy offering a basic understanding, leaving out Jon's story.

"Listen. Jon headed up after we got back. He found this photo in that cabin." Tracy held the photo for him. "We think it might be Kessy."

It was an awkward transition. The reason for Trevor's missing earring became the elephant in the discussion while they waited for his reaction to the photo. He seemed to glance at it for only a second before feeling distracted.

As Trevor's hand returned to his ear, Jon worried that Tracy would place him in the attic with Trevor in order to focus him.

Dan spoke under his breath, "If you go out there and tell Trevor where you found the photo, it might make him focus and stop thinking about his ear."

Jon glanced at Dan, then shook his head.

"That's not gonna. . . help."

It took Jon a moment to find the word as the thought of doing what Dan suggested made him nervous. It felt confrontational. Telling Trevor exactly where he'd found the photo would only serve to remind the both of them of the moment just before Trevor was pulled off the couch.

"Did you see my sister up there?" Josh finally asked.

The question seemed to grab Trevor, but he acknowledged Tracy, not Josh. Then he studied the photo once more, fidgeting less this time. Both Jon and Dan leaned into the screen.

"That looks about right."

"Did you see it happen?" Tracy asked this, trying to maintain composure.

Trevor's eyes began darting again as he answered, "No."

"Why does it look right?" An uncomfortable moment of silence ensued while everyone waited for the linchpin of his story.

"You were up in that cabin when it happened," Josh said. It was more a statement than a question. He was waiting for the story, but Trevor still only glanced at the photo again.

"I heard it."

"What'd you hear?"

He turned to the forest, as though searching the clearing for his answer.

"Don't lie," Tracy said.

Jon shook his head; he knew Trevor was embarrassed after learning that his earring was missing. *He's gonna fucking lie! That photo is just like—*

"Trevor, Jon was there when you were attacked. That's where he found this photo. We're trying to figure out if what happened to you happened to Kessy."

Trevor, shaking his head, turned and staggered away. Hurriedly, Tracy's hand grabbed his shoulder, stopping him in his tracks, forcing him back into the conversation.

Trevor snapped. He swung, landing a punch on Tracy's cheek. Tracy staggered for a moment before putting his hand on Trevor's shoulder.

"Stop!" Tracy didn't yell, although he spoke with anger. He gripped Trevor's shirt and yanked it up near his ear, the sleeve of it stretching under his armpit.

Now we're not gonna get a FUCKIN' THING from him! Tracy maintained his grip on Trevor's shirt and tried to get his attention on the photo yet again.

You're gonna PULL an answer from him? It's the attic all over again! Tracy's approach was quickly going off the rails.

Jon reached for the door. He'd only pushed it open a few inches when Dan's hand grabbed the back of his shirt and pulled him back a step. The screen door banged shut softly.

At the sound, Tracy let go of Trevor's shirt and handed the photo back to Josh. Jon wasn't sure what he was trying to do. As Trevor stumbled away from Tracy and toward the path, Dan let up on his grip on the back of Jon's shirt. Josh followed after Trevor.

"What did Trevor say to Tracy?" Cristy said from behind Dan and Jon, still standing at the door. She was wearing a hoodie, her arms crossed.

"Jon found a photo of Kessy in the attic of that cabin. She's lying on the floor, facing away from the camera. Surrounded."

"Facing away? How do you know—" she asked, confusion in her voice.

"Pink hoodie."

She thought about this. "Someone took a picture of her?"

"Someone took a photo of the moment with a Polaroid camera. It's a bit old school, I know, but someone up there must own the camera or something. Anyway, she was pushed and someone took a photo of it, probably to shove in her back pocket. That way Kessy could find it."

"She's in a fetal position in the photo. Someone put her on the floor!" Jon cut in, irritated.

"Where is it?" Cristy asked, unaffected by Jon's comment.

"Josh has it. He and Tracy are trying to find out what was going on. Trevor was up there. He said the image 'looked about right' when Tracy asked him."

"He said it *looked* right?" she asked, emphasizing the word.

Dan stared out the screen door. "I think he was in the room when it happened."

"He said he *heard* it," Jon said, stressing the word. "I think Trevor and Tracy were going off the rails trying to find out what was going on in the photo. I hope he's clarifying for Josh now."

Dan shook his head.

"What?" Cristy reacted to him.

"The guy is raw." Dan asserted "He just learned he's missing an earring. After what Jon described, I don't think they're gonna learn anything from Trevor. His face is bruised. He's got a decent cut above his eye. The guy is still in pain." "He tried to get away after he said he'd heard it, and Tracy stopped him. Tracy should have let him go."

"You wanted to get after Trevor yourself earlier. Now you sound like you want to give Trevor a break. Seeing him change Your mind?" Cristy asked.

"No, his comment did. Seeing that photo of Kessy didn't bother me until he said that. And the fact that you said they filmed what they did. My understanding of what's going on in that other cabin is better now."

"What is your understanding of that other cabin?" Cristy asked.

"They threw a bottle at Tracy. They took a photo of Kessy after putting her on the ground. They filmed what they did of Trevor. And you said they possibly filmed Kessy? Was that why you followed Trevor to the attic?"

"I was there before him, but yeah."

Dan continued, "Yeah. They're running a fight club in that cabin. One of those guys probably owns that cabin, and the guy doing the filming must be working for him."

Jon closed his eyes. "Why do you think they all came out after Tracy took that bottle?"

"Because the guys were screaming and people wanted to know why. They were just reacting," Cristy answered logically.

Dan remained quiet, his gaze on the others outside.

"You really think the same thing happened to Kessy?" Cristy asked.

"She was surrounded in that photo, like they'd set it up."

Jon's eyes grew with shock, desperate to dissuade this notion. "I'm glad Josh didn't hear that!" *It's too fucking horrible to think of Kessy being subjected to that.* He shook his head. "Trevor was not surrounded like that!"

"You said they filmed it."

"Yeah."

"Maybe they'll post something online. And that photo was probably meant for Kessy's back pocket." Dan turned to the counter beside him, picking up the rest of the stack, inspecting the photos closer. "From the looks of it, someone tried to cut them up. Through the middle of the image . . . like someone threw a switchblade into the stack. Maybe someone had their picture taken and reacted by slicing up the stack."

"They might have got her on the floor with a swi—" started Jon.

"That feels like a whole lot of *malice* for the people in that cabin to have, Dan. A *club* goin' on up there that anyone who crosses their path is subject to?"

"Two things," Cristy interrupted, staring out the screen as she spoke. "Number one. If they post it online, they'll get caught and go to jail. I don't think they're that stupid. Number two. Trevor's back; Kessy's not. If you think they both had the same experience, why isn't Kessy back here after her assault?"

Dan didn't respond as he stepped out the door and slowly over to Tracy. They seemed to say only a few words to each other before turning to study Trevor, staring into the woods, waiting for him to say more. Jon glanced at Cristy and then closed his eyes. Putting Kessy into a scenario as Cristy described was a vicious image. He opened his eyes.

"Trevor's not gonna say a thing with them standing there watching him. He's not making eye contact with Josh," Jon quietly observed.

"You were in the room when it happened?"

He closed his eyes as he nodded his head, irritated again.

You saw *me, Cristy . . .*

"He is not gonna say a fucking thing until Tracy and Dan stop starin' at him!" He felt a bit embarrassed, having raised his voice to such a degree. He rushed back over to the table, wanting to get out of view of the guys.

"They heard you."

Jon's head whipped back to her as he sat down. "What?"

She nodded in the direction of the others and then joined him at the table. "They heard you."

The sound of footsteps on the gravel outside confirmed it; Tracy and Dan were easing off by leaving the area.

***

While Trevor did his best to avoid eye contact; Josh took in the sight of him. In addition to the blood on his earlobe, his hair was a mess and cheek red with rug burn. As the sunrise brought first light Josh noticed the specks that dusted the back his soft blue shirt from being on his back, it was evident Trevor had been shoved into the floor.

Trevor explained his story. "I was standing in the living room. There was a raucous crowd in the attic that pulled the attention of everyone who heard it."

"What does that mean? A 'raw-kus' crowd?"

"They were yelling and screaming a lot toward the end."

That's what he's basing this on? This is gonna be bullshit, Josh thought.

Trevor described how people in the living room and kitchen had turned to the staircase. He described how the attention shifted across the room out of curiosity. From the impression Josh got, Trevor had not gone up the steps, but why he hadn't was not explained.

Trevor said several times, "It made sense to me" and, "Along with the attic commotion, the photo 'looked about right.'" It was as though he had only observed events from afar and hadn't gotten involved.

"Did you try to go up?" Josh forced the words out, afraid of Trevor's answer.

"I couldn't get up the stairs."

Josh felt his eyes well up. He wanted more. He wanted Trevor to keep talking. *You didn't get involved? You don't know what happened to Kessy? You don't know what was happening, but you say it 'looked about right'?* His hands shook as his fingers mashed into the photo.

At this point you should be divulging every fucking thing you can think of! Instead, you're fuckin' standing there, staring off into the forest! I just want a fucking response!

Josh glanced at Trevor's bloody earlobe before he candidly told him what Jon had said Trevor had experienced.

Trevor had slight disdain in his eye, as he listened. It was not something Josh could understand. Trevor's arms began to shake and his jaw clenched as Josh went on. In an attempt to cover his shaking, he reached for his ear. In his anger he pinched the skin until a crimson trail dripped down his hand.

Josh realized he was getting to him. *This might work. Get him back to that place where he's forced to describe what the fuck happened to him!*

Neither knew nor cared what the other was experiencing. Their voices rose and they lashed out at each other with everything they'd been holding back.

Josh described how Trevor had been beaten unconscious.

Trevor pointed out how Kessy's beating might have been taped as well. And how, if it was by the same three guys, they would likely have taken turns with her.

Josh declared how Trevor had been a coward—how he'd sat through both Kessy's and his own assault and done nothing to prevent either, and how he likely deserved it.

Trevor reminded Josh how Kessy was not in that room anymore. He said she had been taken somewhere else and was now being forced to recover with the hell still going on around her. He told him that when the guys who approached him had asked if he'd found his girl, they knew where she was.

Spent, with nothing more to say, an odd sense of calm settled in Josh as he saw a trail of blood travel past Trevor's eye and down his cheek.

Josh imagined Trevor sitting on the couch, witnessing it all. He still believed that Trevor could say more, but it was clearly not going to happen. Josh slowly turned away, feeling he had achieved as much as he could.

The words "three guys" and "taking turns" turned over in Josh's mind, and he felt as though he'd lost in some way.

Trevor had flirted with Kessy at her twenty-first birthday but did not have the concern for her now that Josh thought he would.

Trevor and Jon had both said there was a possibility that Kessy had been filmed. What else could cause such a reaction from such a large group? A terrible image manifested, one he could get rid of only if he were able to open his skull. His pace increased.

Chapter 14

Cory crouched across from Matt by the side of the cabin. Sarah had singled him out as he'd emerged Sunday morning with a drink instead of the caffeine the rest of them had. Sarah, Laura, Chris, and Matt tipped back soda cans to wake up.

She'd asked, "You're getting started already? How are you gonna hold your camera straight?"

Cory ignored her question. He appeared disheveled, as though he'd rolled off a couch only moments ago. His short, oily red hair was scrambled in unnatural directions. On his short body he was still wearing the same faded green shirt with the outline of a pot leaf. The fact that he hadn't yet changed his clothes also made quite an impression when he dragged himself out, carrying a beer.

"You don't have the camera with you! You done showin' off?"

"It's not mine!"

"What?"

"The camera—it's not mine!"

"So less shit is gonna happen when you're around? Is that what you're saying?"

The camera was not his, but that wasn't the point. *The point was, things might not get so out of hand around him without the camera.* He felt a little guilty.

Sarah had seen footage in the den with Cory and the guys last night. "So you're drinking . . . yeah, do that instead."

It was only his first drink, but he stopped. Later, when he was told he should keep drinking so he'd be too drunk to film every goddamn thing that happened, his retort was the same. "It's not my camera!"

Laura asked, "Whose is it?"

He motioned to Matt. "It's his."

"It's my uncle's," Matt confirmed and then turned to Cory and said, "Cory, get yourself a cup of coffee if you don't want soda."

Sarah asked Cory, "You really think Matt's uncle wants you using his camera for that stuff?"

"I didn't film over any of his uncle's footage. His uncle still has a collection of old *Playboys* in a box in that attic along with the cameras and shit he used to film with! He isn't gonna care!"

"You beat a guy with a beer bottle the first night. That's not exactly *Playboy* material. You think that shit would go over with him too?" Sarah asked.

Laura's confusion was evident. "What?"

Matt closed his eyes, pulling his free hand through his short, sandy hair. *Great! Now, he's gonna talk about that shit yet again.*

Cory shook his head. "I didn't film that! I wish I had, though. That story has been so twisted. Everyone's saying I got bitch-slapped, and that's bullshit!" He paused to point out his face. "I woulda had a red mark on my face. I didn't. Three fuckin' people saw what happened, and everyone else started making shit up the second everyone started yellin'!"

"What happened?" Laura asked again.

"These guys were at the door and were asking about something. I can't remember what, but the guy shoved me because I was laughing at something he said! I laughed, and he got right in my face and shoved me. So I threw my bottle at him! It was kinda funny actually, but the guy was bleeding all down the front of his shirt when they left. People saw that and had to know what happened. I didn't say, and shit got made up!"

"I'd slap you too if you were laughing in my face," Sarah responded.

"You were tellin' people what happened after they were gone! You wouldn't let it go because everyone was still screamin' about it!" Matt countered.

"That was right before that guy got in your face," Chris added.

Cory shook his head. "That was something else." Searching the gravel as he spoke, he said, "I can't remember all of what happened, but the guy fucking shoved me because I was laughing! He's a fuckin' hothead!"

Matt shook his head before sipping from his can, as Cory's head dropped, sulking after his words. The girls waited for further comment from him, but he ignored them as he tipped his bottle back.

"Take it easy, Cory. Get yourself a cup of coffee," Matt told him again.

***

"Yeah. And go throw your bottle at that guy's face again!" Sarah added. As the girls went around the corner, Laura asked, "Is he still here? The guy he threw a bottle at? I still don't get what happened."

"I heard everything. Everyone heard it! He was celebrating what he did to the guy." Laura listened as Sarah explained what she'd heard. As she motioned to the path that this guy he'd thrown the bottle at had used, they noticed a guy making his way toward them.

He appeared to be staring at something in his hands. He appeared to be crying and began to walk faster when he saw them looking at him. Something about him gave them pause.

***

Matt and Cory heard the beginning of Sarah's fragmented story. Cory stood up, bottle in hand. Matt, glancing at the approaching guy, shifted with his soda over to the corner to head him off, thinking that he was going to follow after the girls. Instead, Cory continued just a few steps behind Matt.

***

When Matt's arm flew up, Cory thought he was going to toss his soda at him. Cory raised his bottle in defense when the sight of a guy running at them made him tense up. His right hand clenched his bottle as the rest of his body followed suit, bracing, bracing for impact.

Matt caught the guy by the throat, flipping him like a clothesline. It threw the guy's legs into Cory's arm and spun Matt to the ground. Cory's arm had lowered slightly but was still raised, and the guy's legs slammed into his elbow, spraying the remainder of his bottle and throwing them both into the dirt.

"FUUUUCK! GAAAAAD! FUUUCK!" Cory dealt with the pain for a few seconds and then began yelling as his eyes teared up.

Matt held his upper arm where their attacker had hit, his soda gone.

***

Chris raised his own can to his head while his free hand gripped his hair. He had witnessed it, but he still had no fucking clue what had just happened. Cory yelled in pain on his knees. Matt slowly opened his eyes but remained on his knees. The attacker, who seemed to appear out of nowhere, rolled over in the dirt, like the wind had been knocked out of him.

The girls came back around the corner. "Who is that?"

"That was scary!"

Chris couldn't tell who the attacker was. Cory's embarrassment and pain shifted over to a biting anger.

"I know that fucker! He was at that scene at the door Friday night!" exclaimed Cory.

"Well, he just tried to ambush you! Looks like he succeeded!" Sarah gloated.

"Matt clotheslined the fucking guy! He was gunning for Cory; he didn't even notice Matt when he put him down!" Chris argued.

Cory staggered to his feet, speaking through his teeth, "Yeah that . . ." He paused with the pain. "SHIT . . . was self-defense!"

Matt leaned over, his head down as he still gripped his arm in pain. His shirt was shoved halfway up his back from the impact. He didn't say a word or even acknowledge what was happening beyond dealing with his pain.

Laura went past the two of them, reaching to the ground. "He was carrying this!" She held something in the air as Cory stood over the guy, still holding his arm. Chris walked over slowly, still uneasy of the whole thing.

"It's a photo!" She held it up as though he could see it from where he was. He hardly glanced at it before staring at the attacker.

"You know him?"

Laura showed Cory the photo, but he only gave it a heartbeat of attention before glaring back down at the guy. Undeterred, she brought it over to Matt, who was still curled to the ground in pain. The girls both waited for him, hoping he would give it attention. He ignored them as well.

***

Slowly Matt straightened back up, still clearly in pain. His face was red as he held his arm. Sweat ran down his forehead, pulsating with the blood in his veins. His eyes opened partially and quickly closed again. Taking a deep breath through his nose, he could hear Cory talking to Chris behind him.

"That's what I'm saying! It's the same fucking guy coming at me again! This shit is self-defense!"

Matt heard the sound of shuffling as they picked up the guy.

"What are you gonna do?" Sarah asked, but her question was ignored. She yelled at Chris, "Chris, he's bleeding on your arm!"

Matt felt the sweat dripping off his forehead. At the risk of it running in his eyes, he opened them to see what the guys were doing. He got a strobe-like view of Chris carrying the guy by his chest, but it seemed like he was being carried by his throat.

When the pain in his nerves was no longer hammering, Matt finally opened his eyes enough to stare down at the photo still being pushed into his face.

"Do you know what that is?" Laura asked.

People's legs? At first glance at the photo's edge, all he could process was jeans and shoes.

"He had this Polaroid photo with him. Someone on a floor somewhere, wearing a pink hoodie. People around . . . That's really creepy!"

Sarah began questioning Matt, "Is that Cassie? Matt, is that Cassie, is that your sister?"

"What did Cass do?" Laura asked this question. Matt opened his eyes and tried to process what was being said and asked of him. He responded to none of their questions, only taking in the image being pushed in his face. *A Polaroid photo?* Its white border offset a dark square image in the center. He recognized the film stock type.

That's the same film stock from my uncle's camera! He studied it. Its top right corner was sliced off.

"Who has a Polaroid camera these da—" someone asked.

"My uncle." He closed his eyes at the pain when he tried to reach out and take the photo. He'd hardly moved an inch when he had to clench his eyes closed again. The ache eased up after a few seconds, and he opened his eyes again. He searched past her as best he could to where the guy had been on the ground.

Who the hell was that? He studied the photo. *Why did he have a photo tha—It's just like my uncle's!*

"Your uncle has one? Was this taken here? Who was that guy?"

"I don't know, but you put him down!" Laura was excited by the events.

He took a deep breath. "I. Know!" He was not proud of it, and discovering the photo that the guy was carrying felt too familiar for comfort. His anger-based pain compounded by the caffeine churned in his stomach.

He went for another glance at the photo, but Laura's hand had dropped to her side. He leaned forward slightly to get a better view. "Where did they take him?"

"I don't know." She saw him leaning and offered the photo to him. Slowly he brought his left hand up to take it from her. Bringing the photo close to his face, he studied it. He hoped to identify something that would kill the possibility that it was from his uncle's camera, which, as far as he knew, was still in the attic.

It was a horribly taken photo. There wasn't a single face that he could see, only the legs of people standing around someone kneeling in a dark room. He studied the carpet, searching for anything that felt foreign to prove it wasn't taken in their cabin. He hung his head. *Fucker stole my uncle's camera! Whoever the fuck he is! He stole my uncle's camera!* Now he had to know who the hell the guy was.

He pushed to his feet, feeling the stretch in his legs.

"What did Cory say?"

"He said what he was doing was self-defense."

What the fuck does that mean?

"Before that, he said something about—"

"He recognized the guy!"

"He knows him?"

"Yeah, I think from the door scene Friday night or something."

Matt shook his head. *What the fuck is going on?*

"What are they gonna do to that guy?" Laura asked.

When Matt didn't answer, she followed the direction Cory and Chris had taken the guy.

Matt knew he was going to have to follow after them to see what Cory had decided constituted "self-defense." He finally stared at the center of the photo, what the flash had captured. Through the wrinkle, he saw the person in pink wasn't kneeling, they were facedown on the floor.

***

"Grey hoodie! Blue jeans! Curly hair! Five foot eight!"

A guy from the other side of the cabin yelled these descriptors at someone. Matt crept toward the front. He clenched his throbbing arm and wondered, *What the fuck is going on now?*

He debated going around the corner with the photo in hand for a second until he realized that he heard more than just the one guy. He listened to them shuffling over the gravel to the front. Laura glanced at him, her eyes wide. She was clearly wondering what Matt was going to do.

The yelling continued. "You hit him?"

That voice sounds familiar! Squeezing the photo, he had to find out what was going on. He got to the front of the cabin. First peeking around the corner, he stepped lightly over the gravel toward the door and heard the same familiar voice, inside this time.

"I'm LOOKING for the GUY who CLOTHESLINED my BUDDY!" Matt stopped in his tracks. *Fuck!* He waited to hear him again before moving another step.

Now it's on me for putting the guy down, for preventing the full-on collision with Cory! But Cory had to defend himself from the guy lyin' in the dirt! Cory and Chris dragged the guy inside. This is not my fault!

I could wait until the guy finds his buddy. Matt was scared, unnerved by the guy's presence inside. He was still in considerable pain, but he had that photo which he believed was taken with his uncle's camera. *I have to at least find out who took it, what's goin' on.*

Then the guy screamed again, "I'm LOOKIN'! For the GUY! Who HIT! My BUDDY!"

It was early. Everyone in the cabin who had found a place to sleep during the first hours of the morning was now being woken up by his verbal gunshots. *Cory and Chris heard that!* He knew they had. It was dead silent in the cabin, and he was slamming the whole place with his presence.

Matt froze. The sound of that guy's voice and his own role in this continued to throb through his arm and churn in his stomach.

Someone yelled something in the living room. He couldn't quite make it out, but it sounded like "then." With multiple strides thundering down the staircase, he knew this was going to end in the den.

He stepped inside where a group already stood at the top of the stairs that led down into the den. He pushed past them, moving down far enough to see the back of the guy commanding the room with a gesture of his hand.

"WHO! HIT! My BUDDY?"

Matt froze, gripping the handrail with his right hand. Feeling the sweat in his left hand, he held the photo, mashing it under his fingers. The sheer ferocity of the guy made him cower. He stared at the back of the guy's head as he waited for someone to step forward.

That's the same guy Cory threw a bottle at . . . and the guys that were with him, it's the same group!

Within seconds the guys found who they thought they were after. They remembered from the front door incident, and that was enough. People in the room cleared the couches and backed away. Chris appeared pale, trying to remain unnoticed. Then the whole fucking group of guys who had barged into their cabin noticed him. *After Cory recognized him, Chris grabbed the guy by his neck, and he'd bled all down his arm, that's what Laura was talking about.*

"What the fuck?" one of the guys screamed. Before Chris could decide to get involved, he was shoved from behind.

Matt's teeth gritted and the sweat beaded down his forehead as he pulled his arm, still clenching the photo up to his chest. "*NNNNGGGH!*" No one noticed him yelling as the screaming in the room increased tenfold.

"Tracy!"

A different guy yelled, one with a thin face wearing a grey oil-stained shirt, pointing at Chris. Matt stared in shock at the one who was doing all the yelling, glaring at Chris.

"What the fuck is that? You clotheslined my buddy?"

Guy's name is Tracy?

Chris did his best to avoid eye contact with Tracy.

He was right in Chris's face. All Matt thought of for an instant was that this guy was outraged about the guy Chris had pulled off the couch in the attic.

"LOOK AT ME! You CLOTHESLINED MY BUDDY?"

Fuck, Tracy's gonna hit Chris! He said clothesline and that was me, but he's gonna hit Chris for it. The girls told him what happened but not who's responsible.

"Where's your camera, you fuck?"

A guy wearing a black hoodie beside him yelled at Cory just as he punched and shoved, then went for his throat. Matt did a double take on the guy's black hoodie. What appeared to be points of a white star on the upper back of his hoodie, caught his eye.

Is that a pentagram?

It reminded him in that instant of the guy in the attic the previous night—the one he'd seen wander in and sit on the couch, the same one with the goat's head on his chest who Cory made a comment on when he saw him there. Matt hadn't seen the guy's face in the attic either, as he'd wilted just as his buddy had, but the thought that the goat's head was on the other side of that pentagram on his black hoodie, seemed to fit.

Are all these guys from the same cabin?

The question was pushed away as he cringed again in pain before shoving into the room himself. He felt the sweat run over the hairs on his beard and the panic grow in his chest. *What the fuck did Chris do with him?* His eyes darted around the room, expecting to see a body on the floor. Then he saw people with their camera phones aimed at the floor. The sight was infuriating, but instead of stopping it, he shoved his way closer to the guy who was searching for him, Tracy.

"I clotheslined your buddy!" He hadn't yelled loud enough. "I! Clotheslined! Your buddy!" His gravelly voice with the pain in his arm caused his words to garble together.

He couldn't hear himself over the clamor. He couldn't draw enough air to yell harder. He clenched on the shoulders nearest him and pulled tighter into the circle.

"I! CLOTHESLINED! YOUR BUDDY!"

Feeling his throat burn, he shoved his throbbing arm into the guy who was beating Chris's face bloody.

"ENOOOOUFFF! ENOOOOOUFFF!" he screamed at Chris's attacker as he shoved the guy off.

The guy stared at Matt in shock. The guy in the black hoodie who'd hit Cory outside was on the floor, but the swinging stopped.

Matt's throat was on fire as he told him again. His words pushed through the saliva in his mouth. "I! Clotheslined! Your buddy!"

The guy's eyes widened. *This guy is thoroughly fucking shocked at my stopping the fight to confess!*

His head spun and his emotions fogged his mind. His arm throbbed beyond control. Having just screamed his lungs out to break up a fight, Matt waited for the guy to swing at him.

Surprisingly, the guy didn't lay a hand on him, even when he held the photo out. He didn't know why he did it.

Even though he knew nothing about the photo, it felt like his property now. All he could say was that he knew the film that was used, that it was from his uncle's camera.

Though he'd heard the name *Tracy*, Matt wanted to hear from the guy. had to know for his own understanding. His throat burned as he asked, "What's your name?"

"Tracy. You clotheslined my buddy, Josh. That image is why he came up here the way he did. That's a photo of his sister. Why did you take it?"

Feeling the sweat slide down his face, he didn't know how to respond. *It's from my uncle's camera, so that makes it mine?* Matt breathed in the stuffiness of the room, the smell of sweat as he informed Tracy of this. "That's a photo from my uncle's camera."

"You're saying your uncle took it?"

"No. I don't know who took it. I only recognize the stock." Responding as his affected arm trembled; he didn't know the story surrounding the photo and as a result had no idea what else to say to the guy. Matt wasn't sure he was understood, as his voice sounded as though he'd chain-smoked a carton of cigarettes after he'd screamed.

"Do you recognize the person in this photo?" Tracy asked. He leaned in to hear Matt's answer as he held the photo out. It was a horrible photo without one face in it. "Do you recognize them?"

Matt stared at the image, at the legs of those surrounding someone who was on the floor. There was not one person he felt was even remotely identifiable.

Matt shook his head "Who?"

"She's in this cabin," Tracy informed him.

As Tracy said this, Matt glanced at the girls' butt. "Who is?" Matt asked.

Tracy's tone grew impatient like Matt wasn't listening "I told you, the sister of the guy you threw into the dirt! The girl lying facedown at the bottom; *you* took her picture."

Matt shook his head again as Tracy accused him for a second time of taking the photo, he sounded convinced of it and it only created a feeling of resentment in him. *He thinks I took this photo because I recognize the stock!* Tracy was clearly focused on the girl in pink but hadn't said her name. Was he avoiding saying this girl's name?

When an awkward energy blanketed their stunted conversation and Chris slowly staggered to his feet, Matt decided he was done listening. He walked away.

Chris, Cory, and Matt slowly made their way out. Matt's whole body felt exhausted. He heard what sounded like the same guy that yelled at Cory, that black pentagram hoodie moving up the stairs and into the living room. They went around the corner, back to the area where this had all started. Chris stumbled against the side of the cabin to a seated position, but Matt stood, listening to that black pentagram hoodie lose control as he left.

Chapter 15

Jon was finally able to open his eyes, but only for a fraction of a second. Catching a strobe-like glimpse of the people, he was reminded of the photo of Kessy.

He'd started a fight, acting on what what he'd felt since witnessing Cory's filming in the kitchen the evening before. Cory had shoved his sweaty fingers into Jon's eyes, screaming, and had futilely gone for his throat. In a final effort, Jon had gone for Cory's face. Unfortunately, he'd only managed to scrape Cory's face with his nails when his fingers pushed sweat into Jon's eyes, forcing him to retreat. Tending to his eyes, he fell to the floor, feeling the sweat on his face coating his fingers, as he was kicked repeatedly. Someone screamed for the fight to stop.

He heard Tracy's voice and was desperate to hear the words he was saying and to know who he was speaking to, but as he pulled his shirt up to run it over his eyes, he couldn't concentrate and missed all of it. Pressing the fabric into his eyes, he tried to alleviate the sting with shaking hands. Unable to see and unsure of what was going on, he felt desperate.

I fuckin' missed. What happened to Josh? Where the fuck is Kessy?

The shaking spread through his arms as he continued to mash the fabric into his eyes until the skin felt raw.

This fucking stings! It's only getting worse! I gotta get up!

Wasting precious seconds on the floor, he continued to bear down on his eyes until they ached. He was determined to pull the sting out with the fabric, if it meant being able to search for Kessy.

The room was quiet. He could feel the soft thuds on the floor as people around him made their way out of the area. He'd turned to his side, bumping into the wall behind him. The fear that someone would approach him as Cory had was strong because he couldn't keep his eyes open. He flinched when a hand squeezed his bicep. But, rather than continuing the attack, the hand pulled him to his feet.

"Stand. Up." It was Dan's voice, and he still sounded out of breath.

He had a far easier time keeping his eyes open once he was standing. Tracy carried Josh in his arms up the stairs; he and Dan followed.

We're leaving? Cory had left his camera on the floor. *They're moving too fast! They're not gonna stop and look for Kessy?*

He felt as though those left in the room were waiting for them to leave.

This is the time to have the photo! Where the hell is the photo? Jon desperately tried to remember who had the photo. *Dammit! Tracy gave the photo back to Josh! This is the way it's gonna happen? We've got the chance to find Kessy, and the guys are just gonna walk away?*

They were carrying her brother out of this place, and Kessy was still somewhere in it. Jon couldn't believe they were going to leave her there again.

She's lying on the floor somewhere, terrified of all the screaming! Wishing someone would open the door and find her! And we're gonna fuckin' walk away?

His eyes throbbed. His fists clenched, bracing the rest of his body.

"KESSY LANE!"

Yelling her name made his body tremble. It was dead silent. *I gotta go again! She might hear me now!*

He braced himself toward the top of the staircase, shoving his hands against its walls. Feeling the muscles in his stomach quiver, he faced the stairs, sliding his hands off the wall and into fists.

"KESS-SYYY! LAAAANE!"

That fuckin' buuurns! He hunched over, feeling the sweat stream off his forehead and down his face. His breaths came in labored gulps. His eyes welled, and tears streamed down his cheeks.

He strained to hear her calling him. He heard nothing.

I have . . . to keep . . . GOING!

He reached the front door. His body ached as he faced the few left in the room. He clenched his shaking fists before his face. His knees buckled beneath him.

Dragging her name out as he exhaled, he felt light-headed. "KESS-SSSYYYYY! LAAAAAANE!"

Sweat dripped off his face and ran through his eyes, forcing them to close when he needed them to be open. He pulled his shirt to his face.

Kessy! Where! The fuck! Are you?

He wanted to continue his search; it was the perfect time to search the rooms of this cabin, with no one to resist. But his knees buckled again, and it became painful to remain standing.

Those in the living room had run outside, but he was forced to stop screaming. His body couldn't do it anymore.

I have to go . . . I can't keep . . .

A few of the guys at the back door mocked him, screaming in at him.

"HA-AAY!"

He turned away to avoid collapsing in front of them. As he made his way through the clearing, he felt light-headed and his throat throbbed. It felt as though he may have torn something in his throat, screaming as he had.

He hadn't left the property yet but was already regretting his decision to flee, despite the feeling of frailty throughout his body. The hecklers made their way after him. They sounded about twenty feet behind him when they screamed after him.

"HA-AAAAY! HA-AAAAAY!"

I shoulda searched the cabin. I coulda found her . . . somehow.

If he had made his way back up the steps to that attic where he'd found the photo, he would have found Kessy. He wanted to believe that this could have been possible. But nothing had happened when he'd screamed through that cabin. These thoughts twisting in his mind were accented by the yelling he continued to hear, still mocking him in the distance.

Chapter 16

The path was a blur as Jon made his way back. His eyes drifted as the ache in his throat persisted. Sweat beaded off every inch of him, but he was too finished to even wipe it away from his eyes.

"What did you say to him? What did you tell him?" Tracy was yelling at someone.

"What happened to Kessy?"

He's probably ripping into Trevor. I can't go back into the cabin with Tracy like that.

Jon couldn't stand hearing any more of it. A part of him was deeply embarrassed by what he'd done, at losing control as he had. Now to hear Tracy continue on Trevor was almost like torture. It was the last thing he wanted to hear.

As weak as his legs were, he kept going. He went down to the lake to lie in the water, where his eyes and throat could cool off.

***

Tracy and Dan told Cristy that Jon had lost it in that other cabin. She saw him out the window, heading toward the lake. *Somebody will have to go down to the lake and ask Jon if they want to know.* She crossed her arms as she turned and listened to them try and explain what had happened.

Out of the lot of them, Jon was the only one who had shown outright concern for Kessy. And he did it in a way that could be heard clearly from outside.

He'd screamed her name repeatedly, and it seemed to trash Tracy's whole approach to finding Kessy. While Tracy had found the camera's owner, it still paled in comparison to what Jon had done.

So the question of "What was happening in that photo?" had turned into, "What happened after Jon finished screaming in that cabin?"

"Did Kessy hear him?" Cristy asked Tracy.

Shaking his head, he said, "I don't know what happened."

"Everyone heard him. What he did was so awkward and uncomfortable, and he just kept doing it," Dan added.

The three of them stood in the kitchen. Tracy leaned against the counter, arms crossed, while Dan sat in a chair across from Cristy, having grabbed the rest of the Polaroids off the counter. "He just kept going."

"The guy fuckin' let loose! He screamed for Kessy through that whole fuckin' cabin, like he wanted to rip it in half."

While Tracy wanted to know what happened after Jon called for Kessy, he didn't seem to have any desire to go down to the lake to find Jon and ask him about it.

Cristy asked hesitantly, "Should we go ask him what happened?"

When neither answered, she glanced out the window again. *If I didn't know any better, I would believe that they're intimidated by him. Tracy asked a good question, but it doesn't seem as though he'll ask Jon; it's as if he's too unsure of him. And as much as Dan said about that other cabin in the moments before Josh disappeared, he appears thoroughly affected by what was going on. It seems all either of them can do is think about how it felt to hear him scream like that.*

Cristy felt bad for both Josh and Jon. They had both gone to that other cabin, thinking of that image of Kessy, and reacted violently. *Now neither wants anything to do with the rest of us.*

Scraped and bleeding, Josh had shoved her away when she offered to help. Now he was on the couch in the den, alone. And she'd seen Jon making his way to the lake.

Eventually, she left the room. *They aren't going to get any further, sitting here in the kitchen.*

As Cristy stepped outside, heading for the lake, she had a weird feeling of comfort. She believed that Tracy and Dan were finally on the same page.

When she got in sight of the lake, she saw Jon's shirt and shoes at the edge of the shore. Then she saw Jon, lying in the rocks and sand while the water lapped gently over his feet. She took off her shoes, leaving them by his, and joined him. It wasn't until she kneeled in the sand next to him that she realized she had no idea what to say.

Several minutes passed before he spoke, his voice strained. "I stole the tape out of his camera."

Chapter 17

Cory was the only one in the kitchen when he got there. After the screaming stopped inside, an uncomfortable silence hung in the air. No one was keen to start talking after what had happened. The intensity of that guy's screams had been too distressing and painful to talk about yet.

Cory leaned over the sink and blasted the cold water out of the faucet. The rush of the water making its way through the pipes and splashing into the stainless steel sink was the only noise he heard. His hands still shook from the adrenaline of what had happened, making it difficult to hold the water. He tried to splash away the lingering feeling of the scrape of that guy's nails over his face, but he couldn't cup it fast enough. Instead, he only emphasized the marks on his face as he slid his wet fingers over them.

He paused as the water flowed out of his cupped hands and between his fingers. He felt sure he recognized the guy who had screamed at him, but it would take calming down for him to remember.

Where the fuck do I know that guy from?

When he heard people behind him, shuffling back into the kitchen, he splashed water over his face again. He heard Sarah's voice, telling someone what had happened.

Making shit up again.

He remembered that was what she'd done earlier. She'd also gotten on his case for showing off in the den.

Goat head guy! That same fucking goat head guy was waiting for me in the den!

Cory felt a surge of status with the realization that both guys—the one who Matt had put down and goat head guy from the den—had been searching for him. He didn't know why, but it had an interesting energy that invigorated him past the embarrassment of being knocked off his feet. A snide smile pulled his face, as the thought grew brighter in his mind.

There's got to be a reason these guys are coming after me . . . an explanation for what the hell is going on! He was waiting for me that first time. And then the fucker went for my throat the second time!

"Yeah, he was going for Cory, but Matt apparently put the guy down." He heard the middle of their conversation as he turned the faucet off.

He heard the guy whom Sarah was bringing up to speed ask, "Why was he going for Cory?"

"I don't know." She paused as though thinking, and then seeing Cory listening to them, she said, "Cory! What did you do to that guy to make him attack you?"

Realizing they were discussing exactly the same conclusion he'd arrived at, he felt his surge of energy validated with her question. Not knowing why, he didn't want to comment yet, but his silence left them to continue to discuss the guy's screaming.

"You were gonna try and do something else to him, but you froze in the kitchen!" Sarah pushed, trying to draw him into her conversation.

He leaned back into the counter, mesmerized by the water flowing into the drain. Embarrassment crept back in as the scrapes on his face began to sting.

"What happened?" someone with her asked.

"Cory was holding a bottle right where he's standing now when that guy started screaming! He froze, probably praying he wouldn't find him again!"

"Is that true?"

Without thinking, Cory turned toward them and they saw his face.

"Oh, wow! That guy really got you!"

Their gawking at his face as he reached for the nearest bottle was infuriating. Grabbing a bottle of Old English that was half-empty and warm, he took it anyway. Keeping his head down as he pushed past the people, he headed outside where he hoped to escape their attention.

He took a drink from the bottle. He knew they would still talk about his reaction to that guy screaming. Everyone had been affected by that guy's screaming, but the attention was going to stay on him until he was out of sight. At least out of the kitchen he wouldn't have to listen to it.

He figured the guys might regroup at the back of the cabin, but he didn't want to be around any of them, so he sat down at the side of the cabin facing the path, his arms resting over his knees. As the water on his face cooled in the afternoon air, the sting the nails left on his face became piercing. He tipped the bottle back for another drink.

***

A well-placed punch to Chris's nose and the flow of blood that had followed prevented him from having the cigarette he normally would have. Instead, the adrenaline having worn off, he now sulked against the side of the cabin.

Matt stood nearby. The ash trail of the cigarette burning between his fingers slowly grew between his infrequent drags. He squeezed his right bicep with his left hand. He didn't know what to do to get rid of the feeling of impact in his arm. The more the nerves twisted, the more he was forced to think about how it had gotten that way.

It was still grinding on Matt's nerves that he didn't know what the fuck was going on, and he couldn't convince himself to dismiss the whole thing. The hope that he would find out was dashed when he lost composure. It felt like hell to scream as he had to stop the fight. His arm still throbbed but the ache in his throat and the lightheadedness had slowly lifted. Now he tried to remember that Polaroid photo that had caused the mornings' melee.

Someone used my uncle's camera. I told Tracy that, but he still thinks I took it. I don't know what the fuck was going on, but he didn't believe me.

He closed his eyes so he wouldn't have to see Chris's bleeding face. The thought that as soon as the fucker stopped bleeding, he wouldn't care about what happened, got under his skin.

He didn't see it. And he doesn't give a shit. Who the hell was that on the floor?

Why the hell it mattered, he'd never found out. Or if the guy named Tracy had said it, he hadn't been listening.

Chris leaned away from the cabin, pulled his shirt off, and wiped his face with it. He muttered something from behind the shirt before dropping it in his lap. The hair on his chest was slightly stained from the blood on his shirt and was starting to bruise from being punched and shoved.

He held an unlit cigarette in his hand, and Matt could sense the request from Chris approaching. He didn't so much as open his eyes, only held a cigarette out, and said, "Light this."

I'm in no mood to appease you, fucker.

Pulling his lighter from his pocket, Matt dropped it in the dirt by Chris. Chris didn't move, just kept holding out his cigarette as though he expected Matt to light it. Finally after some time, he slowly reached for the lighter himself.

Chris tried to make a tiny flame. The intermittent scraping sound went on for a full minute. Matt expected Chris to ask him for help again, as though he'd been made incapable by what had happened in the den. Then it finally grew quiet again. Either Chris had gotten a light or he had given up.

"What did that guy show you?"

Chapter 18

Cristy paused at Jon's words that he'd taken a tape from that cabin.

He still believed Kessy might have been filmed. She could hear it in his voice. He knew that Trevor had been filmed. She needed to know what was on the tape.

Was someone filming what you guys just did? She wanted to ask but was too scared. It was possible that Jon's screaming had been caught on tape. *Had the guy filmed Jon yelling for Kessy?*

She imagined Jon beating Cory until he dropped the camera, or even fell to the floor, so he could take the tape. This image made her want to have nothing to do with the tape. If Jon had been screaming like the guys said he was, and his voice suggested he had, she didn't want to know what was on the tape.

She glanced at him as he slowly sat up. The idea that Jon had clashed with Cory as he was yelling for Kessy was deeply unsettling. She didn't want the visual of the story that began with Josh being beaten bloody and ended with Jon throwing an explosion of fists to stop himself from being filmed and to take the tape.

He started several times, "The guy filmed Trevor . . ."

I don't want to hear this! Cristy shook her head as he tried to continue. *I so don't want to hear this!*

"What?" Jon asked when he noticed her reaction.

She sat silently, moving her feet through the lake water.

"Tracy tell you what happened?"

She nodded, glancing at him as he stared out into the water. "You sound like you're in pain." It was the first thing she'd said since she'd waded out to where he was. They sat silently for some time.

She waited for him to get up and then followed, moving back to the shore for their shoes. He put his shoes on, then picked up his shirt, revealing the tape on the rocks underneath.

Dan and Tracy were standing outside the cabin, by the edge of the path. Tracy was smoking a cigarette and glancing in their direction as Dan, whose back was to them, appeared to be explaining something to him. The way he gestured with his arms in front of himself reminded her of his shocked reaction to Tracy's actions when they'd first encountered that cabin, and it worried her.

"I get it; I understand your approach. I just think putting the guy on the defense by tellin' him he took it might not be as effective as you think." Dan said.

"It gets in his head. It puts the question into his—" Tracy started.

Dan cut him off. "Jon's approach was more. . . it had an impact."

What Jon did got into their heads? That's obvious. Dan hasn't gotten past his shock. Jon won't even mention the tape if Dan gets on his case. I hope Tracy does the talking.

They would have to see what was on the tape; she knew they would. Jon's sentiment was that Kessy *might* be on it but Trevor *probably* was. Neither was something she wanted to see.

Dan turned, their slow treading over the gravel drawing his attention. Tracy and Dan both peered at Jon with uncertainty, unsure what he would do next. She and Jon stopped a few feet from them.

Jon covered the tape with his shirt. He was clearly waiting to reveal his possession of it to the others.

They stared at each other for what felt like forever. Dan and Tracy seemed to notice the redness in Jon's eyes. Finally, Tracy took a slow drag off his cigarette, and then clarified. "As far as the Polaroid goes, you heard the guy say it was his camera."

Jon shook his head.

"You were on the floor, rubbin' your eyes out with your shirt when he said that," Dan said.

Tracy fixed his attention on the ground between them, embarrassed. "If I remember right, he said the film stock belonged to his uncle's camera." He paused, waiting for a response from Jon.

Cristy turned to him. *He doesn't care . . . yet.*

"Which accounts for the photo being a slightly older style, a unique style."

"I asked him—"

"You accused him," Dan countered.

"—if he had taken the photo himself," Tracy continued. "He didn't say a word after that, but he seemed real confused. I tried to explain who was in the photo, but I don't think he knows what the hell is going on.

"If nothing else, it gave him something to think about. Someone using his uncle's stuff to take that kind of photo . . ."

Tracy paused between drags of his cigarette, waiting for something from Jon. He still seemed uneasy with Jon, like he was trying to avoid asking him about what had happened, or possibly hoping Jon might bring it up himself.

It was getting seriously uncomfortable, but about the wrong thing. The tension should have been around Kessy. One question repeated in Cristy's mind: *Was anybody else concerned for Kessy?*

She desperately wanted one of them to ask him about it. Then, before she realized it, the words quietly found their way off her lips. "Did anybody else look for Kessy?"

Tracy took another drag from his cigarette. Dan responded, "Only Jon."

He sounded almost accusatory. There was another uncomfortable moment of quiet, and she involuntarily glanced at Jon. Noticing a redness around his eyes, she knew where Dan was going, and it hurt to hear.

"You fuckin' snapped, Jon! You went totally unhinged through that whole cabin! You went toe-to-toe with the same guy who threw the bottle at Tracy! That took some serious . . ." Dan's remarks faded as he became aware of the grimace on Jon's face.

Eyes closed, Jon dropped his head.

"What happened after you stopped?" Tracy finally asked.

***

Nothing, Jon thought as he shook his head.

It made him feel frail and inadequate, as he stood before his friends whom he felt might have been disappointed at what he'd done. He'd known they would eventually ask about it, but his head felt as though it had been on fire and he'd only just put it out. Now they wanted to know about *that* moment, the one when he'd failed Kessy, after he'd drained his energy and stood desperately waiting to hear from Kessy before having to walk away. Presenting the tape to them felt like a good way to avoid having to answer the question, until he presented it.

When Jon shifted his shirt, Dan noticed immediately and said, "You stole the tape out of his camera."

His words brought about an unexpected feeling of embarrassment. It sounded so petty when he said it that way. With a sinking feeling, his head dropped as he lifted the tape for someone to take.

Tracy pulled it out of his hand and asked the question Jon desperately wanted to hear. "You OK?"

He felt his eyes well as he closed them. He was exhausted and in pain.

Dan spoke with a bit of urgency in his voice, "I didn't make those comments about you going unhinged because I thought you were wrong to do it, Jon! It was just that what you did was real intense. It shocked the hell out of both of us that you went that far to find Kessy. Ask Cristy, we weren't able to function when we were trying to talk about it in the kitchen."

Tracy's voice was calm when he added, "I didn't try to find Kessy when we got there. I went looking for the guy who hit Josh. But finding Kessy off a dark and terrible photo that was taken somewhere in that cabin . . . The more I think about what you did, I think it was probably a necessary step toward the people whose faces are outta frame.

"Any indication of a person . . . any . . . the possibility of a person being treated that way, then to have a photo taken so that the moment is not allowed to pass . . . And for a guy to travel through that same place, screaming for someone the way you did . . . repeatedly . . . I think it had an effect on everyone that heard you.

"It isn't difficult to connect the two, if you ask me. A guy who does what you did is either screaming at someone or screaming for someone. Either way, it's completely unforgettable, in the same way that the events surrounding that photo are."

***

Cristy attempted to decipher what Tracy was trying to say. *He thinks the people standing around Kessy in the photo would see what happened as unique because it was a Polaroid. They were in the room when the photo was taken. Then they witnessed the fight and heard Jon scream through the cabin. So they might connect the two.*

Cristy hadn't thought about it that way. Tracy was trying to make Jon feel better. It felt like a bit of a stretch, but it was good of him to say.

***

Jon knew what Tracy was trying to say. *He's treading real light around Kessy because he doesn't know how to talk to me after how*

I carried myself leaving that cabin. Tracy would know now that his heavy-handed approach toward Trevor had been a mistake and he was avoiding another conflict.

A weight lifted off his shoulders. "They filmed Trevor in that same room."

"Which room?" Tracy asked.

"Where I found the photo of Kessy."

Chapter 19

"A Polaroid photo."

"Of what?"

"People . . . from the waist down. And someone layin' on the floor. Same one you saw. Laura thought it was of Cass."

"Was it?"

"You can't see anyone's face. You saw it. What'd you think of it?"

Matt asked him this, expecting to hear more about the photo from Chris. Believing that he or Cory was responsible for taking it, because Josh was gunning for Cory the moment before Matt clotheslined him and Chris dragged him inside.

"The guy you clotheslined, you know him?"

Matt shook his head. "The one you dragged inside? His name, Josh."

Chris continued, "Josh, he was with that group of guys at the door Friday night. That whole group of guys; the bigger guy who was searching the area last time was yelling for you this time. That same wailing guy was in the attic Saturday night with the goat on his chest. You remember Cory pointing him out?"

Matt took a drag off his cigarette.

"I know you remember that guy in the blue Blink shirt that stayed then confronted us in the living room!"

"What's your point, Chris?"

"Report them."

"What? Why?"

"Because they're renting Ron's cabin down the path, using the space to get strung out and they're lashing out at anyone they can find. No one is that aggressive all the time! That's like three people at least that have come up looking for a fight.

"Blue blink shirt guy with dyed black hair, he was definitely strung out. Sweating like crazy, possessed look in his eyes, kept swearing to God when he was confronting us. That's actually four guys: Josh, Goat Head, blue Blink shirt and the bigger guy with the weights on his shirt, that was looking for you!"

Matt shook his head, speaking under his breath, "You're embarrassed you got jumped."

"What?"

Matt spoke up, "So you think they're strung out and bored and over the course of their stay, have decided to confront their neighbors?"

"Matt, like I said, no one is that aggressive all the time. For a group of guys to come the way they have—

"Yeah, yeah, you said that! Chris, the first time they came up here and banged on our door, Tracy said . . . He was under the impression that their friend had gotten turned around in the fog and was in the area. I didn't believe him. I wondered why they weren't yelling through the fog, trying to find their friend at that moment. Then they got fired up at nothing, started shoving, then just walked away."

"You don't think they were strung out when they—" Chris started.

"This time the guy had a photo! A Polaroid that could have been . . . it looked familiar."

"Where was it taken . . . what's it got to do with Josh coming up here after Cory?" Matt didn't say anything for some time, and Chris continued, "Wait, Sarah said Cassie was in it; what happened to her?"

Matt shook his head, they'd discussed his sister, Cassie already. He didn't think it was her in the photo.

"Wait! A Polaroid photo. Doesn't your uncle have a camera like that?"

"Yeah. I told Tracy that but he was under the impression I took the picture because I recognized the film."

"Did you take it?"

Matt shook his head. "No, I think someone used my uncle's camera. I don't know when it was taken or what happened and I don't think Tracy has the first clue about it either. He was trying to put me on the offensive by accusing me of taking it. I think he wanted me to correct him. He kept asking me if I recognized the girl but her face isn't visible and he never said her name or told the first thing about her. They're real upset over a photo of a girl who could have tripped or fallen in a drunken stupor. All that's clear was a pink hoodie and the girl's butt."

"Sounds like a photo Cory would take. Matt you weren't in the room yet when goat head guy was yelling at him, something about his camera. Same guy Cory pointed out in the attic."

Matt shook his head. He'd seen the guy Chris was referring to. He remembered seeing what looked like a pentagram on the back of his hoodie. It had made Matt wary of him before he'd started screaming. "That doesn't make sense to either, he jumped Cory over a picture. . ."

"Matt what all did Tracy tell you about it?" Chris pressed him.

"I don't remember him saying anything about it!" Matt shot back.

"Seriously, ask Cory then! The guy with the goat head on his—" Chris started.

"You said that!" Matt cut him off. His free hand went up to pinch the crown of his nose, covering his face after raising his voice.

An awkward silence set in. Chris had nothing more to say and was repeating himself, angry and embarrassed he'd been beat up. Chris leaned his head back against the cabin, glancing in the direction of the path, taking a drag off his cigarette. He spoke quietly, "Do you think they're staying in Ron's cabin down the path? These guys probably talked to him to rent that cabin. Do they know that you're—"

"Ron never tells me about who he rents to. If they did speak with him, I kinda doubt he went into detail—"

"They'd know why he owns both!"

"We could go down and ask them," Matt offered.

Chris's head shot up, and his voice quivered as he spoke, "S-Seriously? You wanna go down there and find out what their deal is after what they just did?"

Matt shook his head, moving his hand from his nose, gesturing for emphasis. "It doesn't matter! If those guys *know* that, they obviously don't care. I'm more curious about what goat head guy was screaming for when he left the cabin just now."

"That guy was *wailing* just now! He left that way because he went at Cory again and he ended up on the floor. That's enough to upset any guy!"

Matt shook his head. "It didn't sound like he was screaming as a result of fighting Cory just now." He took another drag. "That same guy didn't say a word when he was in the attic, but just now he was fuckin' screaming for something like he was going to create a fuckin' sinkhole in the middle of the cabin. He—"

"That's what happens." Chris cut him off. "That's how some guys react when they're put down like that! He lost then started wailing."

"Really? That guy with the Blink shirt in the attic didn't make a fuckin' sound when you went after *him*!" he said, embarrassed that he'd raised his voice again.

"We both went after him because he got in our faces! He had it comin' and he knew it. Fuckin' kid came back inside after you gave him two options."

That's beside the goddamn point! Matt couldn't smoke fast enough.

Chris took a drag off his cigarette as he glanced at Matt then tapped the end of it. "But you were fuckin' screaming like a psycho when you broke up the fight . . . I've never seen you get that unhinged!"

A smirk came to Chris's face after saying this, glancing up at Matt.

"Couldn't stand to see me take the blame for that one, huh?"

Matt's face turned red. He had lost it. It was the first time in years that he could remember losing control like that. But Chris thought it was because he couldn't let him take the blame for what he'd done.

That's not why I did it.

Matt pinched his nose again as he spoke. "That guy; the one who was wailing just now, I remember Cory pointing out the goat on his chest in the attic last night." Matt gestured with his cigarette to make his point. "But he wasn't after screaming Cory's name just now. It sounded more like Cassie."

"You think he knows Cassie?"

Matt took another drag. "I don't know."

Chris's tone took a condescending turn. "He yelled at *Cory* for taking that photo. The guy has been using your uncle's video camera."

As Matt dragged his cigarette to its filter, he tried to remember what the hell was in that photo.

Someone on the floor, surrounded. If Cory's been up in the attic takin' pictures of shit with my uncle's camera to start more fights, I'm gonna feed 'em the fuckin' thing!

Believing he'd taken the picture, he needed to find Cory and let him talk about what he'd done, as he'd done with Chris.

Matt knew Cory would remark on how Matt screamed to break up the fight which he'd caused, just as Cory would comment on the guy wailing, after he'd put him on the floor as he left the cabin. Cory would probably be proud of the clothesline that Matt had executed, protecting him from the guy with the Polaroid.

That was exactly where Matt wanted him to be, gloating, so that he would talk with pride about what Matt had done. That way when Matt brought it up, he would Enjoy telling the story, and then maybe, he could finally find out what the hell was going on with his uncle's stuff.

***

Cory sat against the side of the cabin that faced the path, still feeling a heavy anxiety lingering in his chest. His arm still ached, making it difficult to pinch the cigarette between his fingers.

That guy who was yelling at Matt for clotheslining his buddy was the same guy who was at the front door on Friday. The guy I threw my bottle at came back. And he brought that other guy, the one with the angry goat on his chest. That angry goat came back too.

Cory was rattled by the way that angry goat guy who'd been waiting for him in the basement Saturday night, then yelled at him Sunday morning before they fought, had left the cabin screaming. He'd encountered him twice now. He tried to remember what had been going on during their first encounter.

I still had the video camera with me; I was showing Brian and Peter the footage because they kept askin' about what happened at the front door. I showed them something else and angry goat started eavesdropping.

He was sure the angry goat guy had made some comment to him when he'd noticed him eavesdropping, but he couldn't remember what.

Twice! He's approached me twice now! The first time he was waiting for me; Sarah called him out for it and he chickened out. The second time he was comin' for the attack! He fuckin' let loose through the cabin! Still don't know what his deal was.

Cory shook his head at the memory of it. *Why?*

Three different people that didn't belong in this cabin had a problem with him, two with violent behavior. After all the screaming and fists that had been thrown, he'd felt a certain thrill in putting him on the floor. The thought shocked and left him rather speechless.

What the hell did he say in the den?

He felt that if he could remember that detail, it would eliminate the mystery around the guy and make him feel less confrontational. It would make him feel like someone he could deal with again, if he returned.

I don't even know the guy, and he's got a fuckin' problem with me! This is high school bullshit.

Cory shook his head in disgust. He was thoroughly wrapped in these thoughts when the sound of dragging sandpaper over the gravel gradually broke into his single-mindedness.

"Your cigarette's out."

Cas-sie! He flicked the cigarette as he made the connection. *Fucker never found you!*

"You came through after he left," he muttered under his breath.

He hadn't wanted to acknowledge her but realized he just had.

"I heard that guy screaming at you in the den. Sounds like you've been filming some people who don't want to be filmed."

She sounded like she knew something he didn't, and he tried to gauge the validity of it.

Had that been the reason the guy came at me? What was in that footage that got his attention? He wanted to view the footage again.

"You're all red, Cory. He must have grabbed your face when you tried slappin' him!"

There's her manipulated version of the story I was waiting to hear.

"What'd you do to him?" She was baiting him.

"I didn't do shit to him! He's just a fuckin' bully! Ask Sarah!" he snapped at her.

"I did! She said he was waiting for you in the den 'cause you filmed something!"

"He's a fuckin' hothead! He was here lookin' for a fight!"

"Like you're fuckin' blameless with your throwing of bottles and your video camera? What the fuck happened?"

His teeth gnashed and fists clenched. He truly wanted to silence this woman, but her question caused his aggression to waver. He had created such an impassioned hatred toward himself this morning, all from what amounted to a failed understanding. He couldn't let it go. With Cassie questioning him, he wanted to remember what he'd said in the den that had grabbed the guy's attention.

He saw the footage! He saw the goddamn footage! The play-back was loud from the footage. Something in it got him! Brian and Peter wanted me to play it again!

"You're tryin' to make something up! I can see it in your face!"

His blood boiled with the thought that she was standing there, staring at him. He staggered to his feet and she backed up, as though she thought he was going to shove her for speaking to him. He was doing his best to ignore her, and in doing so, he accidentally kicked the bottle at his feet and sent it whipping across the gravel. She braced for his strike. Instead, he made his way inside.

Where did I have the camera last?

He made his way toward the front door of the cabin. Matt slowly made his way toward him. He appeared as pissed off as Cory felt at that moment.

He's still pissed off about the fight. Probably wondering the same thing Cass is.

Matt was expecting him to explain why he'd had to clothes-line that guy for him.

Yanking the screen door open, he made his way back down to the den where he'd left the camera. The couches had filled up again, and he got several stares as he searched the room. He had to ignore them and do his damndest to recall the last time he'd had the camera.

Soon as I find the thing, Matt's gonna follow down after me and take it!

This thought made him search as rapidly as the remaining amount of energy he had would allow. He searched around the couches and under the coffee table. When he found the camera overturned in the corner, he knew that wasn't where he'd left it.

Someone threw it in the corner!

Irritated, he opened the screen to inspect its tiny display to search for cracks. There were none.

Fucking work.

The power returned, but the flashing "no tape" icon sent a surge of fear through his heart. If he couldn't find the footage, he had nothing. He heard the fall of footsteps on the staircase behind him.

If I leave the den with this and run into Matt, he's gonna take it right the fuck off me!

He stood, staring at the camera in his hands, feeling the surge of fear spread through his chest as he tried to decide what to do next. Whoever had followed downstairs after him wasn't Cass or Matt.

I switched the tapes! But I thought I left one in here!

Believing that the rest of those tapes were in the attic, he headed back up the stairs. Clutching the camera with his right hand, he pulled himself up by the handrail with his left. He felt the burn in his legs as he skipped steps trying to get there before Matt. He expected to see Matt or Cass waiting for him in the living room, but they weren't there. He reached the main floor and kept going. He reached out for the attic stairs handrail and pulled himself up. He skipped steps again until his muscles ached and beading sweat forming on his legs and forehead slid down his face and had to be wiped away, forcing him to slow down.

He heard a girl's voice from the living room behind him say, "He just went up to the attic with it. Just now!"

Someone's pointed Matt in my direction. He took the steps two at a time.

The air smelled stale in the tiny room, but it was empty, which would make finding the tape far easier. His eyes caught a mess of Polaroid photos on the couch.

Laura showed me a photo that guy had.

He found the old cardboard box that had the vintage *Playboys* in it at the end of the couch.

The camera was by that box.

He quickly scanned inside for the small black box. The fear continued to radiate through his chest until he turned to the coffee table where he saw the tape.

Did I set that there?

He remembered when he was in the attic using the camera last and wondered if he'd replaced the tape then to capture what had happened.

A lot's happened up here.

His hand shook with excitement, getting the tape into the slot. He pushed play. The sound of the footsteps echoed up the stairs as he knelt by the table, waiting for the footage to start.

He turned up the volume on an image he didn't recognize. But, as he was the only one that he knew of using the camera, it had to be his. Yelling and screaming garbled through the tiny speaker. He desperately hoped for some indication of what was going on, something that would remind him what had happened. Then the yelling got louder.

"STOP! STOP! Let her up! LET HER UP!"

His eyes frantically searched the screen. *Holy shit! What was going on here?*

The playback grew louder for just a moment before it cut away. *What was that?*

He maneuvered the buttons to replay what he'd seen; it seemed intense. If Cassie didn't follow him up, he would track her down and present this, but first he had to remember what he'd filmed.

Chapter 20

Cassie stopped by the front door as Matt did, just as Cory disappeared inside.

He listened to the screen door hiss to a close, turned to his sister Cassie's green eyes and curly dark blonde hair. "What's goin' on? What's Cory doin'?"

"Getting the camera." "Why? Did he use—"

"He filmed something. I asked him why that guy in the den was so angry with him."

"Did he use the Polaroid camera?"

"The girls ask you about that Polaroid?" Cassie asked him.

He stared back at her, a touch of shock in his voice. "Did Cory use our Uncle Ron's camera?"

"He's not gonna care."

"He wouldn't, but I do! That guy in the den had a Polaroid photo. The stock is the same as—"

"Uncle Ron's camera has been used to the point that it's been reloaded, Matt!"

"OK, yeah, the girls did ask me about that Polaroid. They thought it was a photo of you on the floor!"

"It's not."

"I kinda figured as much, but—"

"I took it," Cassie admitted.

A slew of questions crashed into each other through his mind, his mouth ready to go as he glanced toward the path; he glanced at a cigarette pack outlining her front pocket. "Come have a smoke with me."

Your voice sounds more smoked than normal! You sure you want more?"

"Yeah, I know. Let's have another."

Pinching cigarettes between their fingers, Matt paced over to the edge of the clearing, followed by Cassie. His arm still throbbed, causing his mind to steam with questions, ready to be upset with his sister.

Is she the reason this shit has gotten so outta hand? 'Cause she roughed up the girl in that photo?

Both lit up, glancing at each other, the path, and back to the cabin while Cassie waited for him to broach the subject with her after losing his temper so vividly. He'd broken up a fight that had boiled down to that photo Tracy accused him of taking. Now finding out that his sister had something to do with it, he was only sure that she wasn't in the photo herself.

He studied the cigarette pinched between his fingers. His arm still throbbed gently, and the sweat on his arm gleamed in the sun as he brought it to his lips.

He took a drag, then finally asked, "When was it taken?"

"Friday night."

Matt thought about this, "Friday night. So the first night they banged on our door."

Cassie nodded.

"What was going on? I'm assuming it was in the den?"

"No, in the attic. She was up there laying on the couch in a fetal position long before they showed up. She stood out to me because she looked out of place in her pink hoodie around our crew."

"Wait a minute." Matt interrupted "I was in the attic last night, and I saw the remains of some bad habits on the coffee table."

The sight of lighters, foil, and glass now sat in his memory along with the image Cassie described of a girl lying fetal on the couch. Matt drew his conclusion, and it created a sense of reckless behavior.

"If she used, I don't need details." He said.

"She did, and you do," Cassie said quietly. "You wanna know what her story is because it will help explain her friend's behavior this weekend. I know you've wondered if they're staying in Ron's rental down the path."

They glanced at each other. Cassie was right; he had wondered that. "Did you watch her do something?" Matt asked this as Cassie's eyes grew. "That's enough for me. I don't need to hear those details."

"Like what exactly led to that photo?"

"I saw what was on the coffee table, Cass. If her getting high was some part of you taking that Polaroid." He shook his head. "That aspect of her story doesn't—"

"Pink wasn't gonna have sex with anyone as payment for what she took if that's what you're thinking." Cassie interrupted him. "She got up from the couch and ran into Chris. He talked to her about her bad habits. Pink told him she was ready to do something else, but he didn't hear her. She only said it once and refused to repeat it!"

Matt raised his hand as she barked this at him, "I believe you!"

"What I'm trying to tell you is that Pink had a plan after she got what she wanted!"

"Yeah, I got that!" He shot back.

Listening to Cassie tell the story that led to that photo with such force was tough. Though hearing Chris was involved and interacted with the girl made this drug-fueled encounter feel less isolated.

"How did she get in?"

Cassie shook her head, "She was in the attic for awhile before I found her."

"Do you know her?"

Cassie took another drag as she shook her head, glancing back at the cabin, "I was gonna wait until she came down then have a little chat with her. Explain to her what she did because chances are she wouldn't remember what happened."

Matt turned to her, "Wait, you said that picture happened on Friday night! You're not still waiting for her to come down?"

Cassie rolled her eyes, then glared at Matt. "I've been keeping tabs on pink hoodie bitch all weekend! She started in the attic, her mental state and what she said and did are the details you don't want to hear."

"Alright! After all of that. After the photo, what'd you do with her?"

"We got her out of the room because Cory was lurking with that fucking video camera. She was in one of the bedrooms with another girl from Ron's rental who was also a wreck. I think the wrecked girl was after the same thing pink was after. She was upset because some guy got aggressive with her when he tried to collect payment, she left after I called her on it. Pink was still fetal at that point. That was Saturday night!"

Matt took a deep breath, pinching the crown of his nose as he heard this.

"She tried to leave as well," Cassie said.

"Pink hoodie girl did? What does that mean, she tried to leave?" Matt tried to clarify.

"Yeah, earlier in the day, before her wrecked girlfriend was in the cabin. Pink hoodie left the room but stopped at the screen door. Chris talked to her, but again she didn't say a word because she was still coming down."

"Still?"

"Ask Chris; she looked like hell." Cassie's head turned back to the cabin. "She washed out her hazel lenses in the sink! I just remembered that." A smirk pulled Cassie's lips as her eyes grew. "She wants guys to tell her she has pretty eyes. But Chris said her eyes looked sunken, like black holes on her face."

Matt thought about it. "So she left the room you put her in and stood by the screen door. Chris spoke to her but again got nothing, so he sent her back. It sounds more like she was sleep-walking." They looked at each other. "It's creepy with you're describing."

"Yeah. You know what Pink did just now? This morning when you were screaming at her friends in the den."

He stared at her.

"She was at the top of the stairs, and I was halfway down them. She described me after someone told her not to get involved in the commotion. No mention of her friends. She described me."

"What do you mean she described you?"

"Green eyes, fair skin and curly hair." She watched his expression twist, the amount of detail was creeping him out. Along with the image of her sleepwalking, he might have finally heard enough about pink hoodies behavior. "Matt think of her behavior as mirroring her friends."

He thought about this "So when she finally spoke she described you." He took another drag "You've had an impact on her this weekend. You seem to care about where she is and what she's doing far more than her friends do."

He could feel Cassie staring at him after saying this. The sentiment she'd 'cared' felt awkward. As though he didn't understand the violent nature of the person that she was trying to describe to him. But while the behavior of the girl did sound odd, the drug fueled violent reaction that Cassie suggested of her that mirrored her friends, Matt couldn't figure out.

Cassie had that girl fetal on the floor on Friday night before she could become aggressive like her friends while on drugs. Apparently, pink hoodie girl was still coming down on Saturday and in no shape to leave. During this she connected with Cassie, spending enough time alone with her to remember her features. All of this amounted to her having developed enough anger toward Cassie to retaliate days later for the way she treated her in the attic?

"What are you thinking?" Cassie asked.

"From what you've described, Pink hoodie girl was strung out on Friday, then she came down and pursued you this morning. You said you kept tabs on her, and it sounds like she doesn't need to be high to fixate on you."

She took a drag "Our renters have spent the whole weekend being aggressive and violent with the same people that the guy they rented from suggested they visit and ask for help from."

Hearing Cassie refer to them as their renters made him realize just how personally she was taking this girl's behavior. For her, it was a family affair. He didn't understand pink hoodies behavior. He wasn't sure Cassie did either. But after she suggested it, the question nagged at him. Had these renters heard from their Uncle when they spoke that his niece and nephew were in the cabin up the path?

Matt, couldn't remember if Tracy mentioned staying in the rental the first time they knocked on their door. He had a clear memory of when he and Chris were confronted by a guy wearing a blue Blink 182 shirt. He remembered interrupting his sweaty, teeth clenched tirade to ask him if his group was staying in the cabin down the path. The question had stopped him in his tracks but yielded no answer. It left Matt thoroughly confused but created a feeling of fear for the exact reasons Cassie described.

"This has never happened with renters before," Matt said. "Usually they make their way up the path at some point just to say hi and have a drink with us. But eventually, the question of cabins layout comes up, why it's so different. Then the awkward conversation of—"

Cassie cut him off. "I'd say Ron doesn't mention why anymore. He used to boast that he owns both. Uncle Ron gives anyone who will listen to him an earful about owning both. He goes on and on about building them the way he wanted. It's only when he explains the layout when people who know anything about cabins ask."

She took a drag then continued, "'Independent film' sounds cool, but then that smirk comes to his face when he talks about filming and mentions the 'women.' Then the outdoorsy guys listening realize that the guy they're listening to brag is a bit of a deviant. They put it together and find out what his industry was in the seventies that not only got him both cabins but continued until we started using his cabin."

"That's likely how he rented it out this weekend. He didn't mention that!" Matt declared. "He likes the reaction until it means him not getting paid for a weekend rental. He'd leave that out and the layout that's so fucked up compared to other cabins."

"They aren't regulars. They probably don't know the difference between the two cabin's layouts," Cassie said. "I wonder if Uncle Ron hit them up for more when he found that out, 'cause he usually asks."

They stood quietly for a moment; both taking drags off their cigarettes thinking this through.

Chris turned to her" You said you got her out of the attic *because* Cory was lurking with the camera? You think he was coming up to film her like he's been doing with girls in the kitchen?"

"I have no idea. But if that was Cory's goal, he might know Pink. Or just the way he's been behaving with Ron's camera if he found her outside and she told him what she was after. He might have gone to the bother of bringing her to that attic only to be interrupted by her friends banging on the door."

"They mentioned a pink hoodie before they started swinging and he didn't say a word. He laughed in their face!" Matt asserted.

"That's what Cory was after just now! Ron's video camera." Cassie declared "I asked him why that guy was screaming at him and he got upset. He might have gotten something on film that was enough for someone to scream at him like that. Cory is the type to enjoy that kind of attention!"

"Yeah, he is. If he filmed something that caused that kind of reaction, he'd be proud of it. He'd present the footage like an achievement."

Chapter 21

Following behind Jon as the screen door hissed to a close in front of her, Cristy paused. Jon, shirt still in hand, glanced to his left, toward the table, before heading down to the den. She knew they were going straight to the VCR, where they would find a way to view the tape. She wanted no part of it.

Stepping in, she saw Trevor sitting at the table with his back to the sink. He sat hunched over. He didn't appear to have responded to any of them. She heard the guys shoving the tape into the VCR.

They've got a tape from that cabin. They're gonna watch it. The words sat on the tip of her tongue, but she didn't know how to say it. Her arms covered her chest.

Trevor hardly moved. They both listened intently, waiting for something to happen.

Does he already . . . know? Did he see the tape?

She wanted to believe that he knew what was going on. But on the off chance that he did not, she wanted to say something. At the same time, she wanted some indication or warning from the den of what she should do.

The chair next to Trevor would put her back facing the den; the chair across from him would give her a chance to peek at what she heard. She decided to sit across from him and wait.

They've got the tape from that cabin. They're gonna watch it.

She had no goddamn clue how to say those words. She saw the bruising on his face and felt a bit heartbroken for what he'd gone through, regardless of the reason.

I gotta imagine there's a reason this happened.

Somehow, this felt easier to ask. Giving him the chance to say what he hadn't been given the chance to say might serve to relax them both. She knew that as soon as she tried to open up a discussion, they'd hear that fucking tape.

They wanna see what happened to Trevor after he didn't tell them a thing about Kessy. They probably blame him for what happened with Josh, too. They wanna see it happen, like it's gonna make them feel better.

She wanted to start talking with him, to create a distraction, before things downstairs captured their attention and they ended up listening to it from a staircase away.

"What happened?" She spoke as softly as she could. The question made her nervous, as she thought it might be met with silence.

But he answered quickly, though vaguely, "I fucked up . . . I was rash."

This felt like a dismissive response, like he was treating her like one of the guys or didn't think she was being sincere and wanted to hear it.

"Were you checking the rooms for Kessy?"

She wanted to imagine that whatever happened to him had something to do with Kessy, on some level. But as he stared down at the table and the playback began in the den, she doubted she would get an answer.

The noise from the den was fairly indiscernible, as voices became muffled through the hush.

He has to know what's going on.

She could not bring herself to bring it up at this point. It felt too obvious, as though saying it would only serve as a reminder of what had happened. She knew he didn't need that.

***

Trevor rested his elbows on the table, and he pushed his fingers through his scalp. He had been waiting to hear some kind of concern for what had happened so he could try to describe what it had been like. He could not bring himself to speak about what had happened to him in that attic.

That was why they had to see what was on the tape, because he'd given them nothing when they'd demanded understanding. His comment on the photo sealed their desire to view that footage. The only question was how they'd gotten it from Cory.

"I was rash when I thought . . . some guys I thought might have . . ."

He had no idea how to explain the experience or where to begin. He remembered standing at the bottom of the staircase, peering up toward the attic at a commotion that was rivaled only by the reaction to Tracy's bleeding. His memory was fogged. His desire to explain something to Cristy, who seemed open to hearing his side, made him want to remember it and to hear her thoughts on it.

"What was going on?"

She hasn't seen the photo.

He found himself leaning on this thought. It made trying to recount easier.

"I was in that cabin, right after you guys left. I was in the living room. I don't know why; I was just there."

"You were there for Kessy."

Shaking his head, he said, "Not at first. Everyone was feeding off the energy of that guy throwing a bottle at Tracy. I thought someone might recognize me from the front door, but no one did; they were all too busy talking about what Cory did.

"I was standing in the living room of that cabin waiting for something to happen. I don't know what it was. Something about our encounter with those guys . . . how they reacted, made me want to know what was going on. I found out the guy at the door, Matt, his uncle owns that cabin; it's like a reunion with friends and frat guys the way they were drinking up there. So many people, they all seemed to know each other. If Kessy was around them the way I think she was, she could have easily missed what

Tracy did. All that energy, that commotion, was already inside and continued up to the attic."

***

Is he trying to say that he thought Kessy was up there?
"Did you go up?"

Trevor shook his head. It was quiet for a moment. The noise from the den became background noise to their conversation. She wondered for a moment how it would sound when the footage they were both anticipating started.

"I tried to get up the stairs, but there were a lot of people on the staircase."

"When did you become rash?"

"Someone was screaming something in the attic . . . I thought . . ."

His answer scared her as much as the possibility of Jon and his tape. Still, she asked, "What were they screaming?"

He hung his head. His gaze was fixed on the table and his voice was a bit muffled as he spoke. "It sounded like what was being screamed was, 'Let her up.'"

He was quiet. Cristy tried to remember how the photo had been described. The photo was now with Tracy downstairs and she wasn't going to go down and get it, especially with Trevor saying this to her and not the guys.

"Let *her* up?"

He nodded.

"Did you think it was Kessy?"

He nodded again.

"Is that why they went at you?"

Nodding, he said, "Yeah, I went at them hard, and they responded."

"Who did?"

"The same guys we encountered at the front door on Friday night."

Cristy was quiet for a moment before she said, "What do you think they did to her?"

"That's what I was turning over and over in my head until I saw the photo that Tracy had. It doesn't have a single face in the image, but there's someone lying on the floor at the bottom of the image. She's wearing a pink hoodie, like the one Kessy was wearing Friday night."

She stared at him, not blinking, as he described the image to her.

He'd spent a lot of time thinking about what happened in the attic. That photo was probably really close to what he'd envisioned.

Cristy had to ask, "Why didn't you go up to the attic when you heard the commotion, if you thought it was Kessy?"

"By the time I heard those words, whatever had happened was over. People were stampeding back down the stairs. I couldn't get up there.

"I wasn't sure what was going on, and it was that fact that drove me off the rails. I assumed the worst based off the sound of the reaction and the word 'her.' The fact that something *had* happened drove every decision I made after that."

"Who did you confront about it?"

"The same guys who were at the front door. Not the one who threw the bottle; he got there later. The two guys next to him. I saw one of them who had been in the attic on the stairs, he made his way into the living room and stood next to the other. I didn't even know their names; I still don't, but I went and confronted them about what had gone on in the attic."

"How long af—"

"Minutes . . . fucking minutes after. I didn't go up the stairs; I went after the one fucker I recognized. He was red faced and sweaty when he was on the stairs on his way down to the living room. So I approached him and did my absolute best to threaten him.

"Speaking through my teeth, and fuckin' shaking uncontrollably, I don't even remember what I said to him. I was off the fucking rails because I thought Kessy was up in that attic and had been the center of that hell that I'd heard. I just didn't know, but after that, it was game on! That demand was the fuckin' linchpin for everything I did, and they fuckin' took me down for it!"

He stared at the table, breathing heavily, clenching his fists by his temples. She waited a moment for him to calm down before she asked the only question that mattered.

"Did you ever see Kessy?"

"No. And that's what Tracy and Dan and Josh fuckin' hated when I got back after all this happened! I said that the photo Tracy showed me 'looked about right.' It proved what I'd heard and made me think that—"

"Why didn't you go up to the attic?" She felt like he still hadn't answered this question. His clenched fists shook over his temples for several seconds.

Were you too scared? She stopped herself from saying these words. It didn't feel like they would help when she wanted him to tell her more. She was running out of questions.

He closed his eyes, opened his fists, and ran them over his scalp, but he didn't answer.

He could have gone up afterward. Even if people were stampeding down, he could have gone up.

"These aren't things that are easy to think about. You reacted from your gut, with little forethought, it sounds like," she offered.

"It's hard to remember because there's a feeling of insanity gripping it. It's like I literally can't tell if all these things I remember actually happened. After seeing that photo, it all felt confirmed, and my reaction was regret. I fucking regret it."

Cristy's heart sank at his last comment. The parallels between their experiences were too many for comfort, and it pulled her attention back to what she'd tried to do in that cabin. It felt as though she'd had a somewhat similar outcome.

The sound of yelling voices forcing their way through the TV speakers crept up the stairs, straining the old set. It was hard to listen to.

We have been so affected by that cabin at this point; I wonder what they think of us?

Chapter 22

The playback began, and a hush filled the room. Jon sat on the couch, his jeans still wet, staring down at the carpet. He didn't acknowledge Josh, who sat next to him. They'd had a mutual experience in that cabin, and it was hard to get past.

Listening to the hush broken only by the cameraman's feet grazing over the gravel as he made his way over the clearing of that other cabin, they both stared at the TV. Jon thought back over the encounter between Josh and Trevor. He wanted to ask about it.

He said the photo looked about right. That pushed him right to the edge and he threw himself off.

I wonder if he heard me . . .

***

Josh had been fighting the urge to cry since he'd lain down on the Couch. His whole body ached after having the wind knocked out of him knocked out of him and it was exhausting just to sit up on the couch. But it was Trevor's words that constricted around his heart, sinking in. He had the feeling that Trevor had witnessed the effects of Kessy's treatment, as Josh had Trevor's. He'd already pushed the guys away, not wanting to well up in front of them. But a hush filled the room, drawing him out of these distraught feelings and forcing him to pay attention to what the guys were doing. They'd messed with the TV after they'd appeared with a purpose on the stairs, and now, as he gave his attention to the screen, he saw what appeared to be video camera footage.

***

The yelling and screaming on the TV, with the volume at high, was painful to listen to.

"We're probably back at our cabin by now," Dan said confidently. "When did you start screaming her name? What time was that?"

It took Jon a moment to realize Dan was talking to him. He was hardly paying attention to the footage and had to think about Dan's words. He didn't want to answer.

You know the answer . . . you were there.

Jon stared at the screen as the yelling and screaming became more frequent and the people in the video ran around the cabin in the fog. It brought him back to Friday night when Josh, Cristy, and himself, with Trevor somewhere nearby, searched for Kessy as Dan and Tracy called into the forest at the other side of the cabin. He remembered thinking that their approach would not work in the fog, and so he'd begun screaming.

That was just a precursor to what I did in the cabin. The exact same thing.

His mind was still back at that scene in the clearing. He remembered standing at the edge of the forest, screaming. Even though the fog was thick and he wanted his voice to carry, he was thinking at the time, *I'm going too far.* But when he yelled in that cabin, what now felt like ages ago, the gripping thought had been, *I can't yell hard enough!*

"Jon." Dan had turned from the TV and was waiting for an answer.

Jon raised his arms up, resting his elbows on his knees. His hands covering his mouth, he stared at the screen. He didn't say a word.

Please fuck off . . .

Tracy turned away from the TV and stared into space as he spoke, "You were on the other side of the cabin when Jon was yelling for Kessy. We both were."

The screaming in the distance continued, as the cameraman's pace over the gravel slowed down, appearing to lie in wait by the side of that cabin. Then the image dropped, and it seemed like the camera had been placed on the ground. Its operator came into the frame and knelt by the corner.

Jon leaned in. *Why did he put the camera down?*

He sounded like he was talking to someone.

Who's he talking to?

Dan turned the volume up to a near-deafening level. They leaned in for the moment this quiet exchange took place. The cameraman maneuvered and then stood. When he moved back across the frame, he had someone with him.

Jon and Josh slid to the edge of the couch, desperate to get a glimpse of the person with him. They looked past the cameraman's dark jeans and shoes to glimpse lighter jeans and shoes. Then all they heard was the sound of the two people's slow pace, walking over the gravel as they left the area.

Chapter 23

The sound of a screen door hissing gently in the background stopped while they stared into the fog. The camera remained outside, and the frame stayed on the ground for some time before Dan paused it, increasing the suspension.

"If he taped anything, I think it'll happen next. When he puts Kessy where he wants her, he'll probably have to remember where he left the camera; he might have run out of tape. And when he turns it back on, it'll be inside, and all that energy is gonna be inside."

He continued, "We got there; that camera wasn't there. Thing is, we were all on our last nerves after Jon screamed into the forest. That's the energy we took into our conversation with those guys, and that's a lot of the reason why—"

"We know, Dan!" Tracy interrupted him. "We almost got into it with those guys, but we left. The fucker probably reveled in the fact that he'd thrown that bottle into my face! So if you're saying that something happened after we left . . . Yeah, I thought of that too! That cabin damn near exploded with excitement.

"Now we're seeing the outside of that same cabin while that same guy makes his way inside with someone! Possibly Kessy! And I'd rather not wait any longer to see if any of the shit that followed made it onto that tape! So please, for the sake of us all, play the fucking tape!"

Dan was quiet as he did what Tracy asked. The fact that Dan had singled out Jon's efforts made him feel like he'd done something wrong, and he was glad Tracy had cut Dan off. The hush of the fog was again punctuated by screams.

Fixated, Jon imagined the guy moving Kessy up the steps to the attic.

Cory is with Kessy. He'll bring her inside, warm her up . . . Then Tracy and them get up there and all hell breaks loose.

Shaking his head briefly at the thought, the screen went black and only the beam of light off the camera cut through the room.

Jon waited for something that would indicate what was going on. His hands shook. He wanted to see Kessy, but he didn't want the events of the photo to happen.

The fucker is filming Kessy or getting ready to film her right now.

Jon thought again about the photo. He had found it with the mashed ends of blunts and pipes and other paraphernalia on that table. He envisioned Kessy being forced into taking part in things before being thrust to the floor.

The camera's light glided over the coffee table again before resting on the couch where two people sat, only their jeans showing. They sat hunched in their seats as though they'd been punched in the gut.

What the hell is going on?

The image panned away to the guy who'd broken up their fight that morning. Tracy leaned forward.

The guy who broke up the fight knew about the photo . . .

A reaction from Tracy would indicate something about the guy or when the photo would take place. The guy on the screen fixated on something on the couch. The frame couldn't pan fast enough for Jon as the camera slowly panned away from him.

What did he see? Was Kessy on the couch?

When the camera panning finally stopped, it rested on the person in the middle of the couch. The image sat at an angle, forcing him to cock his head. The grainy image reminded him of the photo.

Who is that? I can't see the fucking . . .

Tracy, sitting on the other couch much closer to the TV, hung his head. Jon's eyes darted between him and the screen. The person on the couch hunched down even further.

That's not Kessy! Who the fuck is that?

"YOU FIND . . . GIRL, ANN?"

The words, ending the hush, slid through the long, thin speakers on either side of the TV to sounding disjointed in the room. It seemed as though the guy holding the camera had covered part of the microphone.

He recognized the voice and the question felt familiar, but the girl's name didn't fit.

"Jon, you wanna see this again?" Tracy asked over the volume of the footage.

Jon's head tilted a degree and his eyes squinted gently. It took him longer than it should have to put together why Tracy said this. Jon finally understood what he'd seen on the screen. He hung his head as Tracy had. Then, with an uncomfortable desire to slam his fists into the side of his head, he turned away.

I'm there right now! I'm gonna lean in to see this fucking happen to Trevor? Shit!

The onslaught that had left the poor guy bloody and unconscious playing back now forced him to revisit the memory of that assault. Dropping his head as his eyes closed, and gnashing his teeth, Jon's hand found its way to the handrail. His aching legs and exhausted feet barely lifted over the floor, as he tried to get out of the room before he heard any more of those familiar questions. He wanted to scream again, but the words only slammed through his head.

GOD DAMMIT! GAWD DAMMIT! GAAAWD! DAMMIT!

Though it was all internal, Jon's body reacted to the anger. Beads of sweat slid down his face as the ache in his throat was reignited. As he climbed the steps, his eyes were still closed; he didn't lift his foot high enough and stumbled. Gripping the railing tighter, he tripped a second time and finally opened his eyes to find he was a few steps from the top of the stairs. As he got into the kitchen, the first thing he saw was the milky white pitcher that still held a small amount of water.

Water.

His need to distract himself was so desperate that he thought of stopping for a drink, if only for a moment. But he could still clearly hear the noise of the footage, and the idea of stopping to get a drink of water vanished.

Chapter 24

Cristy followed Jon as far as the screen door. Her hands came up to her chest as she saw him through the dirty glass. His hands dragged over his scalp as he paced back and forth through the clearing.

He shouldn't have gone down to see that.

As more conversation made its way up the stairs at full volume, she felt compelled to do the same. As Trevor leaned back in his chair, she said, "You don't have to—"

She hadn't finished her sentence before he was out of his chair and following Jon out to the clearing.

She followed Trevor out the door. "Why is the volume up so high?"

He didn't turn or hesitate as he answered, "So they don't miss anything while they're *searching* for Kessy in the footage!"

"Did you see her?" Cristy asked.

"No," Jon snapped.

"Why did you leave?" she asked.

"Because Tracy told me to!" Jon barked into the clearing.

She shied away for a moment. *That doesn't make sense. What did he see?* "What did Tracy see?"

"Me . . . ," Jon spoke quietly.

As did Trevor, ". . . and me."

They finished in unison. "On the couch."

Even though both Jon and Trevor knew that the assault on Trevor was playing out on that tape in their den, Trevor appeared to be a bit more comfortable, more confident.

Cristy had the feeling that they would finally be able to talk about it, without its presence on film hindering their ability to concentrate on anything else. They both waited for Jon to at least turn and see them standing there.

When Jon did turn, his eyes had coiled, as though viewing the tape had renewed his hatred for the situation. His cheeks were red. He'd been breathing heavily to try and calm himself. His hands rested on his hips, and he locked eyes with Trevor without wavering. He seemed just as angry, but she had no idea why.

Trevor waited for Jon, arms at his sides.

Jon stared at the path for a moment, then back to Trevor.

"What happened to Kessy?"

"I wasn't in the room."

"Where were you?"

"I was in the living room after you guys left. Whatever happened in the attic, I couldn't get up to see it."

"Why not?"

"Because the staircase was full of people wanting to see what was going on."

"What was going on?"

"A lot of screaming! I didn't know if it had anything to do with Kessy until someone yelled, 'Let her up!'"

"Let *her* up?"

"Yeah."

"That's all they said?"

"Yeah. After that I was pushed back as people were stampeding down the stairs. I picked out one of the guys we'd seen at the front door to threaten."

"No shit!" Jon walked over to him, and Cristy hid a smile. "What'd you tell him?"

"Enough to have that footage happen!"

"Did you accuse them of going after Kessy?"

"I don't remember. I was losing it at the time. I was afraid of what might have been going on in the attic, and angry that it could have involved Kessy. Though I couldn't think what the hell she could have done to be in any kind of—"

"Enough to gather an audience."

"I've tried not to think about *that* possibility."

"Her clothes were on in that photo," Cristy injected.

"That was the first thing I noticed," Trevor answered promptly.

"What did you tell Josh about what happened to her?" Jon asked Trevor.

"I still had a lot of scenarios in my mind when he shoved that photo in my face."

"So the worst shit you could think of, basically," Jon said with an accusing tone.

Trevor seemed to lose a bit of his confidence with Jon's accusation.

Cristy wanted to interject. She noticed that the noise from inside was gone. She addressed Jon, "After what happened to him, to have that ignored by everyone and then have a photo of Kessy . . ." She paused to take a breath. "To be expected to comment on it and hope to get a clear-headed answer—"

Jon interrupted her before she could finish. "It was a fucked-up decision to mess with Josh like that after seeing that photo!"

An uncomfortable silence settled on them.

Jon's angry, but not like when he was screaming Kessy's name in the woods. He's in more pain now. After the way he left that cabin, Dan's comments about his being unhinged, and his seeing some of that footage before Tracy told him to leave . . . especially if he saw himself in it . . . it's like he's forced himself to shift into a different state of mind.

She wanted Trevor to tell him something, to push away the energy of blaming Trevor. Then Jon switched gears.

"I saw you in the attic! How the fuck did you miss Kessy? If she was up there as that photo suggests and you were up there too." Jon's eyes grew into a glare with a subtle realization. "Kessy left the room. She had to have gotten out of there, because why the hell would anyone stay? How did you miss that?"

To Cristy, it was a decent question, but it didn't matter. Jon was assuming Kessy got up and left on her own, but that didn't seem right. She didn't know why it didn't sit well with her at first, but as Trevor tried to answer, it struck her.

"I went and threatened the guy and they talked about her being up there," Trevor answered.

"What did they say?"

"They were reacting to me losing my cool, so they . . ."

She could tell he was desperately trying to remember their exact words, like their questions prompted him to remember other parts before the attic. It was pulling her interest, but what Jon said had started a mental process of her own.

I don't think Kessy could just walk away from that!

The words sat on her tongue, but she hesitated making them a part of the conversation.

What the girls experience in that cabin is different!

Jon continued to decipher what Trevor told him. "So they knew you were still there for 'her'. . . Or they knew you were there for Kessy . . . Or more than likely they thought you were using that shit on the table and were reacting to what you'd seen . . . Or they thought you'd seen something in the att—"

"I tried to find Kessy too! And I had about as much luck as Trevor! Only they didn't catch what they did to me on film!" Cristy interrupted Jon. She stared between them, trying to hold back her emotions as she felt her eyes well. "You had gone after Cory and his camera and I'd stayed in the kitchen—"

The sound of feet walking on the wood floor through the kitchen pulled their attention back to the cabin. Josh burst through the screen door and saw them. His glare felt directed at Trevor, like that of Jon's a moment ago.

As Josh stood there, Cristy was afraid that what she had finally begun to talk about would remain unsaid and leave her on edge. As her heart sank, it made her wish she hadn't said a thing. She had the feeling that she wouldn't remember what she'd said to get herself to this place.

"Dan, hang on! We can't talk about it without Josh!" They heard Tracy yelling as he made his way up the steps and into the kitchen. "You gotta come back down. I know you don't want to, but ya gotta come back down!"

"He was on the floor! Just like Kessy was in that photo!" Josh pleaded to Tracy.

"I know! I know! I know!"

"Do you think they did that same thin—"

"I don't know. We can watch and find out! It's real intense, but we gotta do it!"

"JOSH! I recognize what they're doin' in that footage!" Dan shouted from the den.

"Dan! Wait!" Tracy shouted back at him. "Josh. Josh! Breathe, just breathe!"

She had the image of Tracy standing by the staircase as Josh paced around the table, gnashing his teeth and pulling at his hair in response to Dan's words. The thought that Dan understood and could justify it was unsettling. The thought that that was why Josh had left the den, especially if he'd tried to bring Kessy into it, was rough.

It grew quiet and Cristy glanced back to the cabin, straining for more from Tracy. She waited for something that would let her know that Tracy had calmed Josh as much as he could.

Is Jon gonna go back in and found out what's going on?

Dan's voice in the den was loud enough for them to hear, but she was unable to make out the words. She hoped Jon would go back in or that he'd forgotten what she had begun to say about what she'd done to try and find Kessy herself. She didn't want to bring it up again; for her the moment had passed.

She looked down at the grass and gravel. She wanted Jon and Trevor to listen to Dan and forget about her. Instead, she heard Jon take a deep breath before asking just that.

"Cristy," he said softly, and her heart sank. "You said you tried to find Kessy?"

She was quiet, still hoping he wouldn't continue.

"You were in the kitchen," he recalled.

He gave her a place to begin again. It felt insane to be led back into her story by the guy who had left her in that kitchen. She did *not* want to go back through it.

"What did you do?"

He wanted her to tell the story, slight desperation in his voice.

Cristy complied. "They invited me to sit down, and I did, on the condition that I could find my girlfriend first. So with my drink in hand, I was ready to go from room to room." She paused, taking a deep breath. She'd calmed down since beginning this story the first time, having taken a deep breath and wiping her eyes. She felt numb.

"The same table where they were doing shots?"

"The person who invited me to sit at the table followed me."

She paused, remembering that she had given the impression in that kitchen that she'd been drinking the whole time. She'd done this intentionally, but she left that part out; she didn't want to hear about it from Jon.

"What happened?" Jon asked quietly.

"Someone in one of the rooms I was gonna check got involved."

She left it there, not wanting to go any further. It left a nauseous feeling in her stomach, leaving it that way, knowing it begged for more details.

Jon had to know. "Was there a picture?"

Feeling as though she had already mentioned that at some point, she ignored his question.

"They treat girls differently up there. Because you guys . . . ," she trailed off, not quite sure what she was trying to say, but it felt right, or at least honest, so she kept talking. "You guys have gone through that cabin . . . everything you've done so far is just . . . so brutal. That's the only word I can think to describe it. Brutal. Everything you guys have done has affected that cabin. And everything you've done to that cabin has affected the way they approach us. It's almost like you think screaming hard enough is going to get your point across.

"That's completely insane. And it scares me. It probably scares the people in that cabin too. And, it's definitely going to scare Kessy. Listening to the people around her, to some voices she might even recognize . . . she's gonna think she's lost her mind the way you guys sound there."

She was starting to sound like she had an idea of what had happened to Kessy but didn't know how to explain it.

She continued, "You said that Kessy left the attic before Trevor was up there. But I think there was a reason she couldn't! And if you were screaming for her when you left just now, there has to be a reason Kessy couldn't leave."

Chapter 25

"Just start from the beginning, Dan. You were running your mouth and Josh missed a lot of it," Tracy said as he stood next to Josh at the bottom of the steps.

Dan stood at the other side of the room, his attention on the paused TV screen. Josh did his best to ignore it.

I'm gonna have to hear that shit again? How Dan somehow recognized the footage . . .

"I think the UFC guy you were talking about on Saturday, the one you thought owned that cabin that took issue with Cory after he threw that bottle. I think he made a decision as soon as that confrontation happened. How to handle the situation that didn't involve a melee in the clearing, I think that's why he yelled after Cory to stop. Not because he was embarrassed and felt any need to apologize, because he'd made a decision in that moment. He knew how he was going to handle what happened."

Dan continued "Even when you halfway explained the photo before assuming he'd taken it. He said it was his uncle's camera and you used that fact against him, but you really didn't hear it."

"Where are you going with this, Dan?" Tracy interrupted him. "You think he started calculating and the footage we just saw of Trevor and the photo of Kessy in the result? You think UFC guy was ready and willing for conflict but only on his terms?"

"That's the only experience we have with them. That's his understanding.

"I wasn't running my mouth," explained Dan. "That footage that we saw with the two women undressing just after Trevor's footage ended, I think that was filmed in that cabin; it looked similar to the room we're in."

Josh brought his hands up to his face in fists, covering his eyes.

Tracy saw this. "That's not what—"

Dan kept going. "The grainy image and those hairstyles, that was seventies at least. I think this cabin was a filming location, like a low-budget sex den that—"

Josh waved his hands, turning to leave. "I got it! I got it!"

"Agreed!" Tracy declared as he put his arm out to stop Josh. "We know what this cabin was rented for in the past! Says more about its owner, I'd say—"

"I fuckin' got it, Tracy! I don't—" Josh shouted, pulling at his arm.

"I know, I know! Dan, that's not what we need to focus on. You were saying something about Trevor's footage when Josh was upstairs." Tracy pointed at the screen. "We just watched the guy being beaten unconscious and you made a comment about the footage."

Dan stood looking at the blank TV screen. "What I was saying was I've seen situations that were similar to that footage of Trevor." Josh had heard this part before. "There was a fight club off campus where I went to school." Dan pointed to the TV screen. "That's real similar to what happens in those groups." That idea didn't bother him.

"The photo of Kessy looked just like what happened to Trevor," Dan concluded.

Josh wanted to gnash his teeth again, if it weren't for the ache and throb that already shot though his jaw. He mashed his fists into his eyes as they welled up, so they wouldn't see him reacting this way. Listening to Dan speak of this scenario was like getting punched.

"What I was saying when you left was, I think the situation was set up the same way. It was real similar to what happened to Trevor, but it was between Kessy and those people around her."

Josh thought he was going to lose his mind all over again. The fact that Tracy thought this shit was something he needed to hear made him want to scream. It felt like he'd been shown what was going on in that attic with Kessy.

That isn't the fucking case! That didn't happen! Josh's head hung. He had no fucking clue what to say in response to Dan's suggestion that Kessy was involved in a fight club.

"You're making a leap, Dan! A big, fucking, leap!" Tracy responded. "I see where you're goin' with it, but I gotta question, WHY?"

Dan crossed his arms. "When do you think that photo happened?"

"What?"

"That photo of Kessy; when do you think it happened? When was it actually taken?"

Josh glanced at Tracy, who was silent, then to Dan.

"Our first visit to that cabin on Friday night, we got into it with them! It almost came to blows, Tracy! You took a bottle to your face, and they erupted! They were still ready to go as we were leaving! All we heard as we left down that path was those guys screaming about how much you were bleeding and that Cory guy soaking up all that attention!"

Dan took a breath. "If Kessy found her way up to that cabin, and if that footage where he left the camera outside is any indication, I'd say a guy found Kessy outside the cabin, brought her in and up to that attic, and shortly after that, we got there. Now how long from when we got up there did it take for things to get out of hand? The atmosphere we left was exactly what I thought of when I saw that photo."

Josh's head felt light. Dan's thought process could be right. This fight club notion could be possible.

"You think someone beat my sister unconscious?" These were difficult words to speak, and the question barely made its way out.

Dan had no response.

"If this 'club' idea is true, it's something you see Kessy not only taking part in, but sticking around for?" Tracy asked Dan.

Dan pointed to the TV. "I'm just going off what I saw. This is what makes sense to me."

"Think about it this way. If that cabin is the kind of free-for-all atmosphere you're sayin' it is, do you think that's the kind of situation Kessy would be involved in and stick around for?"

"No. I think she would have been pressured into it and probably had no way out."

"That definitely eliminates the volunteering aspect."

Dan shook his head. "You've never been there, Tracy. You've always been the 'winner.' When you're in that situation, you're not worried about sizing the other person up. You've already made your decision and you're operating from that place of confidence. In the situation I'm describing, the person doesn't get to size the other up, it just happens."

Tracy shook his head. "That might be what happened to Trevor. The questions they threw at him definitely sounded like they were from that type of thought process.

"The thing is, everything you described as a 'club' is far more mutual, and more importantly, it's more male. That, to me, is why we didn't see Kessy. You're applying a distinctively male situation—"

"Again, Tracy, you've never been there! You've never seen two chicks fight! It's fucking vicious, and what was going on in that photo was probably just the beginning! Talkin' gender differences is trying to convince yourself and Josh that what went—"

"Kessy is fucking surrounded in that photo!" Tracy cut him off. "Being in a fight with someone you don't know, surrounded by a bunch of fucking strangers where you don't have an out is terrifying! And it does not end with a prolonged stay in that place!

"The camera goes on. Words are said. And your own personal hell unfolds as you're put on the floor because you're outnumbered and scared! But after it's over, you fucking leave. You pick yourself up off the floor, ignore all the people staring at you, and you get the fuck out of there!"

Tracy pointed at the TV and said, "That isn't a club you fucking stay at! When it's over you get the fuck out because you are still fucking outnumbered."

"You think something else is goin' on with Kessy?" Dan asked, almost like a challenge.

"I think it's really terrible to put that notion into this situation."

"You wanna give those guys up there the approval of your understanding because you've been there? Keep it to your fucking self!" Tracy countered.

"Fuck you, Tracy. Don't make this about me! I believe, based on everything I've seen so far and based on how we've clashed with that cabin so far, that as soon as she got up there, someone sized Kessy the fuck up!"

Dan pointed at the TV. "The cameraman probably checked her out as he was leading her into the cabin. Then someone heard the banging on the door, followed by an encounter, which resulted in a shoving match until that fucking bottle was thrown! At that point, everyone was sizing everyone up, and I mean fucking everyone! Whether they would admit it or not, they were fucking ready to go!

"That was the energy we helped create in that place, and that's when that Polaroid happened! Everyone was fired up, and Kessy in her pink hoodie stood out, and you know why?" Dan glared at Tracy as he asked this.

Dan pointed at Tracy as he spoke. "Because a guy at the door with a posse behind him, who never even told us his name, went on about a pink hoodie in the area before he started swinging! You said you pushed his arm away? You better believe that story fucking escalated the second after it happened! You know how much of an impression that makes on a group of guys on their first night at their own cabin? It sets the pace for subsequent encounters, ours and the encounter they had when they found a pink hoodie! They wouldn't have known what to think had you not behaved the way you did. That's why!"

Dan shook his head as he continued to criticize Tracy. "You gave them a problem they didn't understand. And they continued to not understand until you confirmed it with that fucking photo!"

Tracy clenched his fists by his head. "Are you fucking insane? You think someone is that fucked up that they would take the energy from a little scuffle at the front door to deliberately find someone they don't know just so they can beat her into the floor? That's deranged thinking, and having a momentary shoving match to incite that kind of behavior is just an excuse!"

Tracy pointed the direction of the other cabin. "They're not the fucking villains you want to make them out to be! There a bunch of guys in the woods, just like us! The only difference is, one of them had a fucking video camera and is escalating everything in every room he enters!"

"What do you think is goin' on then?" Dan pushed back. "Based on the reaction you got from the guy you showed that photo to, what do *you* think is going on?"

Josh couldn't listen anymore. He'd been grateful at first that Tracy seemed to be pushing back, but then it turned into a verbal fistfight. He slowly made his way back toward the stairs, and their sparing dropped off. The silence that followed was agonizing.

If Kessy heard this . . .

The image of Kessy's face being beaten bloody was fixated in his mind, and he couldn't get rid of it. It made him want to scream at them, but he didn't have the energy. Instead he continued to walk away and hoped that neither followed this time.

Chapter 26

Having Jon ask her what she thought happened to Kessy, after everything she'd told him, then hearing the same brutal tone between Tracy and Dan was unbearable. The sound brought tears to Cristy's eyes, and she had to get away from it. She wandered aimlessly toward the woods at first. Then when Jon called out to her, she turned toward the lake.

"Cristy . . ."

The sound of her feet on the gravel was soon accompanied by the sound of what she assumed were his.

***

Trevor walked over to the edge of the path but with no real reason to follow, he stood there as Jon and Cristy walked away. He'd lost much of the confidence he'd gained getting some of this off his chest. His inability to explain further made him shrink back again. He wanted to remember what the hell he'd been trying to do when he'd been in that cabin. There was a reason, or at least he wanted to believe there was. He did not want to be pulled into Tracy and Dan's verbal sparring.

***

Josh wanted to talk to Jon about that footage and what it meant for Kessy. *He was just here! He was just out here!* He crossed his arms over his chest as his teeth gnashed. Now he truly felt alone.

In his desperation, he headed toward the path, feeling he had no choice but to go at that cabin as he had, again.

He heard the screen door opening behind him followed by a fast, almost sprinting pace over the gravel, until it stopped just behind him.

Tracy spoke quietly. "Josh! I'm sorry, that was fucked up! We went too far again!"

Josh stared at the gravel, a bit embarrassed that Tracy was seeing him this emotional. After everything they'd said in the den, he was not sure Tracy would go with him. When he began moving, Tracy did the same.

Chapter 27

With Tracy at the wheel, their van slowly made its way down the narrow path, driving awkwardly over the uneven ground as a dense fog made its way through the forest. Kessy, sitting in back next to Cristy, hugged herself, mesmerized as the fog engulfed the forest around them.

"That is so cool!"

From the driver's seat, Tracy said, "We know we're on the right path; all that fog is from the lake."

Riding shotgun, Jon said, "It's gonna be impossible to see the cabin with it so close to the lake."

From the middle seat, next to Josh, Trevor suggested, "Run around it until we find a door."

"Yeah!" Kessy said.

"It won't be that bad," Tracy said, and then continued, "Would be fun, though."

***

Cutting through the woods, Kessy wanted to get the jump on Jon and Tracy as they circled the cabin. She made her way through the thickening fog, hoping to sneak up behind them. She climbed through the forest, imagining their reactions as she forged farther and farther. Pausing for a minute, she tried to rub the dryness from the contact lenses in her eyes as she peered into the fog, searching for the shape of the cabin. Not seeing anything, her excitement shifted slightly, and she felt a touch of fear. In the wall of fog, she changed her direction, heading for the clearing. It was so quiet, only her heavy breathing filled the cool air.

Navigating her steps through the branches and avoiding stumbling over rocks, Kessy concentrated on the forest floor that was right in front of her. Believing the clearing was only a short distance from where she was, she pushed ahead. After what felt like enough time, she stumbled out of the forest and onto the path with a wave of relief. Hugging her hoodie around her, she made her way back over the path.

***

As they wiped off the beads of sweat that made trails down their foreheads, they sat on the couches and on the floor, still breathing heavily. They regrouped in the den of the cabin as the fog grew too dense to see through, comparing routes through the fog and around the cabin as they waited for the others.

Sitting on the floor against the couch, Josh's attention alternated from recounting some of his route to Trevor to searching the stairway for Kessy. After several minutes he disengaged from the conversation completely. The others broke off as he stood and peered up the stairs, still breathing heavily. The smiles on their faces slowly fell as the tone in the room shifted. He stood like that for another moment before heading up the stairs, standing in the kitchen for another moment before returning back down enough steps to see Cristy sitting on the floor. He called out to her, "Was Kessy with you?"

***

Kessy paid little attention to the distance she'd traveled on the path, through its narrow track through the forest and around its bends. Following the tire tracks that their van had driven through to get to the cabin, she didn't look up until the path opened into a clearing.

She saw a truck parked in the clearing ahead of her, but didn't see anyone outside. Its fog lights were on, casting a beam of light on a cabin that had the same cedar boards but seemed different. She couldn't remember the size of the one they'd driven up to, but this one felt much bigger. Her eyes glanced back at the truck again and again, forcing her to realize that she'd gone the wrong way.

She rejected the thought of turning back around and heading down the path in favor of waiting at this cabin. She headed for the beam of light to follow it to a front door, but with a click from the truck it vanished.

Aware of every step she took through the clearing, she walked slowly into the darker shadow of the cabin, hoping to follow it to a front door. As she reached the side, the sound of screaming caused her to freeze.

"Hey!" It sounded like it had come from behind her, but she wasn't going to turn.

"What?" A different voice from a different direction replied. Both sounded like guys screaming because they could. She stood, staring at the grey boards, wishing she could blame the shake in her legs and arms on the cold of the fog.

***

Josh emerged with Cristy from the cabin into the fog, confident that she would lead him to where she had left Kessy. They began quietly so as not to embarrass Kessy, as though she needed to be looked after. Despite the fog, Josh still resisted the urge to call out for her for fear that it would be heard by the others inside. He reminded himself that it was unnecessary to call out to his sister, who was still in the immediate area and had only to be located and told that everyone was inside.

Cristy finally stopped. She held her hands together, not quite clasping at her chest, as an expression of dread filled her soft blue eyes as if to say, "I don't know." She grew a bit red in her cheeks as she couldn't think of anywhere else to search.

"Kessy!" It made his heart race just a bit to call out, but it felt like what he should have been doing the entire time. "KESSY!" He called out to her with enough volume that she would hear if she were still in the woods or just on the other side of the cabin.

***

Cristy clasped her hands tighter, beginning to worry at the thought of Kessy being out in the woods alone. "She might have gone back in the cabin after we got out."

***

At their arrival back in the den, everyone stood up. Tracy glanced at Josh, who scanned the room before shaking his head, not sure what to say, but he and Jon remained standing. The sound of feet swishing over the stairs behind him put his heart at ease for a moment, but it was only Dan. As he shared the results of their search, the mood seemed to be a collective and determined, "Let's find her."

Josh got back outside first. He checked the van, thinking she might have climbed inside and fallen asleep. Cristy and Jon followed, leaning into the windows to help him search the cushions as Tracy, Trevor, and Dan circled around either side of the cabin. They called out to her more calmly than Jon had, still believing she was close by. After the van proved to be empty, Josh, Cristy, and Jon stood by it, searching the woods for some sign of movement. Cristy got closer to the edge of the trees. "Kess-yyyy! Where are you?"

Tracy, accompanied by Dan, started at the other side. "Kessy, if you can hear my voice, follow it back to the cabin!"

"Kessy, come back to the cabin!" Dan called into the forest, then began spitting words at Tracy. "Is she serious? If Kessy can't hear us, it means she's still moving and getting herself more lost!"

Tracy glanced at Dan as he shook his head, turning back to the wall of trees and fog. "She's climbing through the forest wearing that pink hoodie, sweating into its thin fabric. As soon as she stops moving she's gonna be shivering in this cool fog."

Tracy shook his head then cupped his hands around his mouth. "Kessy! Follow my voice back to the cabin!"

Cristy, standing close to the cabin overheard this. Though discouraged by Dan's tone she turned to the cabin, and went after one of her own hoodies to wrap Kessy in as soon as they found her.

She pushed open the screen door with a screech, clutching a grey hoodie. Seeing Jon tilting his head away into the fog, Cristy ran over to the edge of the woods and called again, "Kess-yyyy! Where are you?"

Jon turned, shaking his head.

Josh saw him do this. *Why is he shaking his head?* He figured it was annoyance at Kessy for needing to be "looked after" again.

As Cristy made her way around the clearing, calling out every few feet, Tracy called out, "Where did you last see her, Cristy?"

Jon continued to shake his head.

"What?" Josh finally asked him.

"The fog is really dense; it's . . . I don't think their voices are gonna . . ." Jon's voice trailed off as his expression shifted from annoyance in shaking his head to a contained irritation as his cheeks grew red. As Jon went over to the side of the clearing, Josh could guess what he was going to do.

"Kessy! Kes-syyyy!" he nearly screamed into the forest.

They heard the sound of shifting gravel at the other side as Dan shifted from calling into the forest to marching around the cabin. Wide-eyed, he stared at Jon without saying anything.

"Kess-yyyyy!"

He became a little self-conscious as Dan stared at him. Jon said, "It needs to carry!" Then with a deep breath, he began calling out to her again.

Dan shook his head once, cupped his hands around his mouth, and called, "Kessy! Follow my voice back to the cabin!"

Josh grew nervous again, listening to them both. The rest felt more calm and rational, but it didn't seem like their voices were going very far. Jon's way was more frantic but felt like it was getting farther through the fog. He was tempted to charge into the forest and scream out for her as Jon was, but he was too embarrassed to bring himself to do anything.

He told himself neither way was working. Neither had brought Kessy back. They needed to try something different. If he could find some rope, they could carry on as Jon was, only with them each holding an end of the rope and moving through the fog. He spent several minutes searching the cabin.

He could hear Jon shouting his lungs out into the forest outside. It felt like his cousin was beginning to freak out. When he could only find a short section of rope, it felt as though he'd wasted all that time. By the time he got back outside, he saw Dan and Cristy but didn't see Jon.

Noticing, Dan said, "He's checking the lake." Dan turned back to the forest and called again, "Kessy! If you can hear my voice, follow it back to the cabin!"

Josh shook his head as Cristy approached him. Dan was well intentioned, but his voice wasn't carrying through the fog. He asked Cristy, "Where's Jon?"

"Dan told him to check the lake. There's a path behind the cabin down to it. I tried to tell Dan that Kessy and I weren't down there, but Jon took off anyway. He said our voices wouldn't carry down there because the fog is too thick."

Josh called out toward Dan, feeling his voice quiver. "Th-Th-This isn't gonna cut it."

"Kessy! Follow my voice back to the cabin!" Tracy's shout cut between them.

"What do you wanna do?" Cristy asked. When he didn't respond, she continued, "I'll help you do what Jon was doing; that way it'll carry."

"I wanted to find rope, but it's not long enough," said Josh. "This isn't gonna cut it!"

Cristy shook her head at his idea then asked, "Do we have any neighbors up here?"

***

Kessy planned to go around to the front door of this cabin and tell them what happened. The yelling continued. It sounded as though the voices were converging in the forest right in front of her.

"H-AAAY!" She thought the guy was screaming at her so she shoved her back into the boards, trying to avoid his attention. She felt the cold moisture that coated the wooden slats sinking into the back of her hoodie and pulling at the warmth she had left.

"H-AAAAAAY!"

Disoriented, she pulled her arms in to hug her stomach and sank down along the cabin wall. She felt what heat she'd held on to lift right off, causing her to shiver even more.

"Fuck Y-OOOOOU!" Another voice screamed from her left, making her cup her hands over the fabric of her hoodie on her ears. It sounded like it was approaching from every side. She pulled her legs in close to her chest, dragging them over the gravel just enough to feel that she'd hidden her presence against their cabin. Her fear of being found by one of these screaming voices kept her mind off the sting of the moisture saturating her clothes. She couldn't shiver enough to make it go away. It made her aware of the discomfort of her dry contacts even more, and as the screaming cut through the fog again from somewhere in front of her, she fought the urge to scream back at them.

"H-AAAAAAAAY!

"NNNNNN!"

She'd made a sound. She hadn't intended to, hadn't even opened her mouth, but she'd made a sound.

He knows I'm here . . . Someone knows I'm here.

No sooner had the thought gripped her mind with panic than she heard the sound of footsteps. They were kicking the gravel her direction. All she could do was put her head into her knees, hiding her face, and hope she was small enough not to be noticed. Then the kicking stopped by her.

Is he gonna scream now?

Her body tensed as she waited. The anticipation was terrible. If he'd seen her, he was fucking staring down at her right now.

Whether it was fear, panic, or the stinging cold, a shiver ran through her body until a hand appeared on her shoulder. She jumped and tried to squirm away as he finally spoke, "Are you OK?" She knew he could feel her shivering.

"Hey, you're shivering. You should come inside."

She felt his hand squeeze around her arm near her still-hidden face. He wasn't giving her a choice. He pulled her up to her feet as she worried that this guy had been one of the screaming voices she'd heard.

Did he hear my feet?

Her hood was still up. He couldn't see her face, and she didn't want him to. Her aching legs felt ready to fold beneath her, and he almost had to drag her around the corner. Positioning himself at her side, he reached over with one arm and grabbed her arm beneath her armpit, and with his other arm he reached around to hold her shoulders.

"You gotta lift your feet!" he quietly demanded of her. She saw the shine of a flashlight at their feet. She expected him to pause so he could pick it up and light their way but was confused and even more uncertain of him when he pushed her past without acknowledging it.

Moving inside, the warmth of the cabin was only a slight change from what was outside, but at least she was away from all that screaming. They stood just inside the door for a moment. Her arms returned to her waist as she peeked around. It was darker in the cabin than it was outside, and there didn't seem to be another soul there besides them. She had no idea what to do next and was still feeling the heavy sting from the cold water saturating her clothes. She could feel his eyes on her, like he was waiting for her to relax, lower her hood, or maybe say something.

"Did you ride up with Chris?"

This was her chance to explain that she'd gotten herself lost, but the sting dragging down her back was just too constant and far more present in the warmth of the cabin.

"What's your name?"

Still shivering, her mouth opened to answer, but when he leaned over to make eye contact, she shied away.

"I'm Cory. You wanna . . ." He gestured to the room. ". . . sit on one of the couches?"

He waited for an answer. She could hardly control her mouth for the shivers.

"If you're still cold, it might be warmer up in the attic . . ."

She could feel his eyes on her, waiting for her to respond, to say anything. He let go of her, and she began to shiver more.

"You can go up to the attic if you want."

He turned away and she followed him up a flight of stairs. Her legs felt frozen as she pulled them up each step. Reaching the top, she followed him through a doorway into a small attic space. It felt warmer in here, but the cold in her clothing still stung.

He spoke again as he turned and moved past her back toward the stairs. "You can sit . . ." She listened to his footsteps down the staircase until he reached the main floor. A few seconds later she heard the sound of the screen door banging.

She waited by the doorway for a moment longer, wondering if she would hear the sound of the door, signaling his return. When she didn't, Kessy turned to the room. She was the only one there.

She settled on to the couch farthest from the door, arms still wrapped around her and hood still up. She felt the cold of her damp hoodie and jeans press against her skin as she leaned into the cushion. She could still hear the yelling carrying on outside, but it was much quieter here. She closed her eyes, hoping she would stop shivering soon.

***

Kessy's eyes sprang open and her fingers clenched at the sound of feet racing up the staircase. Though her contacts felt dry, her eyes fixed on the attic door. Heavy breathing and laughter traveled up ahead of them. They burst into the room, talking about how thick the fog was getting, before landing on the other couch, which faced the room's sole window. Their conversation quieted in the darkness of the room, and they continued in more hushed tones.

She kept her head lowered, keeping her face from view. She grew anxious as their laughter continued, thinking that these might be the guys who had been screaming downstairs and now they'd landed up here to start something else. She worried about them recognizing her and making her a target because they'd seen her curled up by the side of the cabin and knew she shouldn't be there. She considered leaving then but froze as the traffic on the steps quickly became a steady flow as more people poured into the attic.

Chapter 28

With the number of vehicles who had parked in the clearing, it was hard to keep track of everyone. Cassie peered into the fog, unable to recognize many of them.

Who the fuck are all these people? There were several that were complete strangers. *Chris or Matt can't know 'em all . . .*

The fact that everyone was gently masked in the fog added to her unease. They all just kept screaming and running between the trucks and around the cabin. They kept screaming as they ran into each other and then ran off before people could react.

"Prick!" someone called out from the fog.

Fuck! Someone's gonna end up getting punched in the face for that!

When the sound of rapid footsteps trampling over the gravel somewhere close behind her worked on her nerves, she finally had to get away and go back inside, where the drinking had begun.

Cassie lingered, drink in hand, near the kitchen, as the guys stumbled in, some with huge grins plastered on their faces. She felt disdain for them, as their expressions showed that they'd been the ones running up on people outside.

When she saw Cory with his camera, she left the counter and headed for the attic. There were more people in the attic, but it was significantly quieter. Both couches were full. People were sitting on the floor against the wall with the room's sole window that brought fog-filtered moonlight into the space. She went over and sat beneath the window, observing the people on the couch in front of her—a guy and a girl she didn't recognize—placing a plastic bag with a white substance and what appeared to be a razor blade that they took out of a black bag on the table in front of them. They took out a larger blade, and when it reflected the light it brought a knowing smirk to Cassie's face.

"I wanna see 'em get high then run into those assholes outside!"

With her knees propped up, arms stretched out across them and drink in hand, she was mesmerized by the guy as he carried through the motions with a quiet intensity, pulling the plastic bag open and positioning the mirror before piling on some of its powder. When he picked up the blade, the sound of it clicking over the glass spread to the rest of the room within minutes. He leaned back, letting the girl next to him take over. It was intriguing for Cassie just to see the things the guy had set up for her.

Cassie took a drink, and a snide smile pulled on her face as she noticed the attention in the room seemed to land on the couple. By the expressions on some faces, uneasy as they glanced to the table, it was clear they'd seen this only in the movies. It gave her as much of a rush to see their reactions as it did to observe the actions carried out like a performance.

The only person in the room whose attention was not captured by this scene was a girl wearing a pink hoodie on the far couch. The pink of her hoodie stood out in the room full of darker colors, as did the way she sat on the couch. Her thin arms were hugged around her waist, and a hood covered her face as she stared into her lap.

This girly-girl doesn't belong here . . . Is she paranoid as hell? What the fuck is she doin'?

Cassie wasn't quite brave enough to call her out for it, but an idea grew as she continued to eyeball that pink hoodie. She imagined this girly-girl being subjected to what was going on in the room, and for a moment, she thought about getting the girl's attention.

"Open the window, Cass," someone leaning against the wall just a few feet from her said. The quiet conversations in the room stopped. From the corner of her eye she saw the pink hoodie stir. Old wood, aged glass, and the creaky handle complained as she turned the handle and opened the window enough for a bit of fresh air. She settled back against the wall, eyeing the pink hoodie again.

She saw it. She knows what's goin' on!

The rush she'd felt earlier coursed through her again. The words "You're missing it!" came to mind as she thought about how to grab the girl's attention and keep it present in the room. She was ready to engage her when a heavy banging on the door downstairs derailed her attention.

She followed downstairs with several others and joined what turned out to be a good number of people from the living room who crowded near the door. Cassie and many others were forced to hear it from the bottom of the stairs where they could only see Matt, Chris, and Cory at the door.

As soon as the door was opened, a cop or park ranger was throwing questions at them. Then she heard another guy's voice speaking quickly and sounding panicked. Cassie couldn't make out all of what he said, but as Cory and Chris reacted, shaking their heads in disgust, she thought he must be threatening to restrain them. Their eyes widened as they leaned away.

Who is it?

"Have you seen her in the area, wearing a pink hoodie?"

When no one answered the question, and an awkward silence ensued, Cassie thought of what she'd seen in the attic and connected them. An article of clothing mentioned, and that girl whom she wanted to notice the drug use going on in the room. *Is a cop looking for her?* The thought of getting her out of the cabin disappeared quickly as the reality set in of how Cassie believed the girl would respond. *They'll notice it as soon as they ask her a question, then she'll snitch!*

Those behind Cassie began pushing down the rest of the steps, wanting to see this panicked cop. She glanced up to the attic door, wondering if that girl would overhear their conversation.

"Have you seen her in the area?"

"Who are you talking about?" Cory asked the cop.

"In this cabin?" Matt asked at the same time.

"Yes! In this area! She's got dark hair—"

Matt responded, "Hey, take it easy—"

"Who the fuck are you talking about?" Cory interrupted Matt, and an awkward silence ensued.

Cassie glanced at Cory, trying to see who he was talking to. *He's already drunk enough to mouth off to a cop?*

Several long seconds dragged out before he was answered with a name Cassie couldn't make out.

"Kessy La—"

Cory hunched over as though the guy had decided to start throwing punches instead of questions. Cassie and the others pushed closer.

What the hell is goin' on?

"Ha ha! What the fuck kinda name is that?" Cory said, barely able to get the words out. When he stood up for air, his eyes were squeezed shut and his face red with laughter as he turned away from the guy at the door. He seemed to be laughing at something only he heard and an uncomfortable moment ensued. Cory's reaction spread to Chris next to him as he covered his mouth to hide a smile.

The laughter continued until Cory appeared to go at the guy outside, his drink out in front of him. When arms appeared on him from outside, Cory sobered up in the space of seconds. He stared at the guy with wide-eyed shock before shoving him back and raising his bottle at the guy. When he pitched it at the guy and a spray of white foam and amber liquid ricocheted back inside, a cringe-worthy moment of disbelief overtook Cassie.

Did he really throw a fucking bottle at that cop?

Cory, Matt, and Chris stepped farther outside, and as they heard the sound of gravel being kicked about, those inside desired to witness just what the hell had escalated so quickly.

"Cory, what'd you do? Cory! What'd you do?"

"He threw his bottle at the guy with the tattoo!"

"Oh shit! Oh shit!"

Cassie heard the people outside reacting too. When she heard the sound of her brother Matt's gravelly voice yelling through the clearing, the group that was still on the stairs behind her began shoving their way down. They shoved Cassie and everyone else out the door. Being shoved made her fume, but she also wanted to get outside to see if Cory had thrown a bottle at the cop's face and if Matt was yelling at Cory for it, so she let the momentum carry her forward. The image of this officer, out-numbered by the dozen or so wanting to see him covered in beer and possibly bleeding, drove everyone on.

The fact that a red-faced Cory was grinning from ear to ear and not being cuffed by the officer confused her.

What the hell happened? Who did he throw his bottle at?

As people began spreading out through the fog, she saw a number of people moving around the clearing, and she began searching the fog for Matt when he yelled again, upset with Cory.

"Cory! Knock it off!" His distinct gravelly voice turned into a growl as he yelled into the fog. Cassie watched him as he walked toward the path after Cory.

"What happened?" she called out to Matt, and a guy out in front of her said, "Cory threw a bottle at some guy!"

"Who?"

"The big guy walkin' toward the path with the rag on his face. The one with the black band tattoo."

She peered again toward the group she'd seen earlier. They were quickly moving out of visibility through the fog. She didn't see any tattoo, but she saw one guy holding what appeared to be a blanket to his face, being followed by several guys.

That's gotta be him. He seems to be holding something to his face. *Is he bleeding? Who is he?*

She saw Chris standing in the clearing, wide eyed, a hand still covering the smile on his face. It disappeared when their eyes met.

"Who was that guy?"

"I don't know . . ."

"Why did Cory throw his bottle at him?"

"He tried to shove him when he started laughing at him."

"Why was he laughing?"

"I don't even remember. It only lasted about ten seconds, but the guy tried to shove Cory for laughing. He's a fuckin' hothead. Did you hear him?"

"Yeah, I did. I thought he was a cop the way he was asking his questions! For a second, I thought Cory threw a bottle at a cop!"

"Yeah, no shit! Talkin' like some wannabe cop!"

"What did he want?"

"I think he was tryin' to find someone."

"Looking for someone? He said something about being in the area a lot. I thought—" Chris started but was cut off as the crowd made its way back inside.

"Cory got him! Fuckin' bleeding all down the front of his shirt!" a guy jogging back to the cabin from the path said.

"Yeah, that was weird, especially in this fog! To emerge from the fog like that and go off on the first people you see after banging on their door! I thought they were making it up at first, the way they were behaving!" someone else added.

"Who is he?" a girl asked the guy who commented on the blood.

"I don't know!"

"God, that's fuckin' creepy! Some guy's just walking down the path—"

"Yeah, Cory got him good. His nose, his whole face just opened up. It was dripping out of his nose, his lip—"

"He was looking for someone? And you thought he made it up?" Cassie asked as she scanned the clearing. "There are a lot of fuckin' people here I don't know!"

"Yeah, the more I think about it, that was real fuckin' creepy!" he said, pushing his fingers through his short hair.

"You sure they're leaving?" Cassie tried again.

"What the fuck did he say to you?"

"He was lookin' for someone in the area—dark hair, pink hoodie . . . That's just fuckin' obscure, the more I think about it."

"And to think they're probably stayin' at that cabin down the path!" one of the guys near them added when he heard their conversation. His statement made the whole situation feel more visceral, and there was a pull in their stomach as though their first few drinks didn't agree with them anymore.

Now that Cassie knew it wasn't a cop, hearing the hoodie reference again, it made her suspicious of their motives. "Did he say why he was banging on the door for a pink hoodie?"

"Shit! Yeah, the cabin just down the path we came up on," Chris answered and then turned to Matt. "Doesn't your uncle own that one?"

"So they'll be back?" Cassie asked, and Chris thought about this for a moment, concern in his eyes. "Why were they looking for a pink hoodie?"

"The person they were here for is wearing a pink hoodie."

"Why was Cory laughing? What did she do?"

"I don't remember, it happened so f—"

"You were laughing at her name!" Matt cut in, growling at him. "It did sound like a made-up name." He pointed at Cassie. "I actually thought he was talking about you for a second before Cory started laughing. I thought he said 'Cassie' and I wondered—"

"I thought that too until Cory started laughing and making fun of it!" Chris added, cutting Matt off.

Cassie glared at Matt, wanting him to finish his thought as Chris continued.

"They were after someone they thought was in the area, I guess. Dark hair. That rules you out, Cass. You're dirty blonde." He thought about it and then said, "And a pink hoodie. That's specific enough. Everyone here has a black hoodie on." He turned around as if to double-check.

Cassie watched him search for a moment, and then watched Matt, who made no attempt to confirm this.

"What were you wondering?" she asked him.

As Matt watched Chris walk closer to the path entrance he shook his head, speaking quietly. "Not a good start."

"Matt, what were you wondering?"

"The way he was behaving, real frantic and shaky like that. He got far too upset with Cory, if he really needed help." Shaking his head again, he said, "I was wondering if they made it up!"

"You think he might have been on something?" she asked.

"I don't know!" Matt growled again.

"Where's their car? Did they say where they were coming from?" asked a young girl by the door.

"Did he get under your skin?"

Matt glared at her, gesturing to the path. "I don't understand what the fuck just happened! The guy started swinging within the first minute of barking questions at us. If they were really trying to find someone, they might have been a bit more civil and a little less . . . I don't know, whatever it was they were."

"You think they made it up?" Cassie asked him this and he shook his head.

The desire to grab his arm and lead him up to the attic was intense; *I wanna see the look on his face!* But their behavior as described by Matt and his demeanor now made her hesitate.

She studied his reaction, his deep breaths, red cheeks, and shaking head; *he's gonna be even more pissed when he realizes she wasn't made up and he'll confront her 'cause that's what her gang did! But he doesn't realize what she's been doin' up there the whole time!*

The thought of that pink hoodie reacting with more volatility than her gang had because she was *caught* while continuing the drug use she'd started in her cabin played in Cassie's mind. *She wouldn't be able to walk away. If she lashes out like her gang did, I wanna be the one she tries to retaliate against! I wanna see that happen!*

As Chris made his way back through the clearing over to Matt, Cassie turned to the front door. Thinking about the person she'd seen in the attic, the one who was curled into herself on the couch, she wondered if the girl was as confrontational as that guy; the thought dropped a knot of fear in her stomach.

Is she still up there? Does she know her gang just tried to jump my brother? How the hell is she gonna respond when I approach her?

Despite the dozen or so people that dotted the clearing, her arms gently trembled as she reached for the screen door. It had been slammed open too far at some point and no longer closed all the way.

She stopped just inside, where the guys had been standing, and looked back at the staircase that was now clear of people. She thought again how that pink hoodie might still be in the attic, partaking in the items on the table by this point. That guy's panicked voice that barked questions at the guys still echoed through her mind, intimidating her even after he'd gone. It didn't help that he'd left bleeding, as though that was the only thing stopping him from still going toe-to-toe with Cory.

As she decided what she wanted to do next, she heard how the story had already begun to spin out of control.

"No, Cory didn't throw the bottle at the guy. Matt did; Cory can't throw that hard."

"Yeah, he can!"

"No, he can't!"

Cassie waited at the door as these guys who were already manipulating the story pushed past her and saw Chris step inside, glancing at them as they made their way out. The thought that Matt was going to get credit for throwing the bottle, like he was protecting his uncle's cabin from those guys, would piss him off. Cassie could see it happening. She didn't want to hear any more of the argument and glanced at Chris to see what he was going to do. He followed her as she went back toward the attic, where she'd been before this mess started.

As she made her way over, she felt Chris following her up the stairs. The faint smell of pot hung in the air at the top by the door, and it began to take her mind off everything that had just happened at the front door.

She took a deep breath and turned toward the small doorway. Some people had returned to the room, although the two on the couch hadn't budged. She went back to where she'd been sitting against the wall under the window. She still felt Chris nearby and was sure he would realize the pink hoodie wasn't made up.

When he settled next to her on the wall, he leaned over to her. "What's goin' on? Do you know her?"

She said nothing, just eyed the person sitting on the couch, her arms still wrapped around her stomach, hood up. He asked again, "What are you doin'?"

Chapter 29

Kessy had finally warmed up, but with the warmth brought a feeling of thorough exhaustion. Her body was drained from the ride up, running around the cabin, moving through the forest, and landing at this cabin. Night had fallen, and she could feel the weight of people on the couch next to her. It was a difficult task to keep her eyes open, much less pull her arms from around her waist. The quiet in the room was uneasy, but not enough to make her wary. The noises she did hear, she didn't quite understand and was unable to put enough energy into listening to them.

Chapter 30

People continued traveling up the staircase, and Chris turned back each time he heard another footstep on the steps. The room was filling up, yet people were sitting on the floor despite the lack of room. The yelling and reactions to what had happened earlier at the front door had shifted inside. As Chris listened to the conversations of those who entered the attic and sat on the floor, the word "blood" seemed to dot most of their discussions.

Chris thought the girl in the pink hoodie would leave at the sound of the crowd. He wanted to lean into Cassie and ask her again if she knew the girl, and this was why she waited, until one of the guys sitting on the couch at the opposite wall spoke up.

"Close the door!"

Chris wanted the girl in the pink hoodie to realize what was going on and leave. But another part of him wanted to engage her.

She didn't move a muscle. She's got no fuckin' clue that her friends did everything they could to start a fight at the front door just a few minutes ago. Either that or she seriously doesn't give a shit! She was up here with this table of drugs long before I got up here . . . probably wasted out of her mind.

The fact that he didn't know how to approach her without anticipating a response like the one they'd gotten at the front door made him hesitate. Cassie had led him up here; he would follow her lead.

***

The possibility that the guy that had barked at Matt had been high and was staying in her uncle's cabin down the path churned the annoyance that had gripped Cassie earlier and turned it into hatred. Feeling as though everyone wanted to fight had made her heart race in defensive anticipation.

Now as she sat against the wall, Cassie needed to figure out this girl in the pink hoodie.

Has she moved? Did she hear the screaming outside? She heard something, I opened the window earlier! She heard something and decided she wanted to stay put!

This guy on the couch across from her seemed as irritated as she was. He opened his eyes just enough to glance at the girl next to him. Cassie asked him, "Did she even move during all that shit at the front door?"

Laura, the girl sitting next to him, answered, "Who?"

"That girl in the pink hoodie!" Cassie spat out as she nodded toward the girl.

"Was she . . . supposed to?"

Cassie's attention was drawn back over to the girl in the pink hoodie as she explained, "Some guys were just at the front door yellin' for someone in a pink hoodie before they started a knock-down, drag-out fight with Cory!"

Several in the room glanced at Cassie with annoyance.

Laura glanced at the window above Cassie. "Yelling? You talkin' about all those people screaming in the clearing?" Then when Cassie glared at her, she added, "You could see them out the window."

"The ones who started that fight at the front door! The guy who started it just left bleeding!"

"What does it have to do with—"

Cassie cut her off, irritated at being forced to repeat herself. "He was goin' on about a pink hoodie before he started swinging!"

Laura shook her head, skeptical.

"I was standing right there." Chris spoke confidently, emboldened at how quickly the mood in the room had shifted.

The sole incandescent light in the corner cast a subtle yellow glow over this girl in the pink hoodie. The mood was tense in a room still on edge from the recent fight. As Laura studied the drugs on the table then glanced over to this pink hoodie, she observed her body language. Her hood up and arms wrapped around herself as though holding on for dear life.

"What's *she* gonna do?" Laura asked quietly. They watched pink for a moment, as though Laura's asking this would prompt a reaction. Laura shook her head gently and, turning to the guy next to her, she whispered something to him.

He replied, "She's been here the whole time."

***

Cassie stood up and navigated her way around the people on the floor and over to the pink hoodie girl.

"Do you want some more?"

Pink hoodie girl didn't react.

Was she ignoring her or too high to even notice? Chris wondered.

Cassie leaned in closer. Then, inches from the hood, she almost yelled, "Do you *want* some more?"

The arms lifted slightly, legs pulled in closer, and the head turned subtly beneath the hood that remained in place. Laura pointed out, "Look! She heard you! She's tryin' to ignore you, but she heard you!"

Chapter 31

Hearing an angry voice in the room woke Kessy. She believed for a few moments that she was back in her cabin when she heard a girl talk about a bloody fight and mention a pink hoodie.

What's Cristy talking about? She heard some of what was said but didn't recognize the girl's voice. *That's not Cristy. Where am I?*

Realizing she didn't know where she was, she tried to lift her head to get a peek at the room. Her eyes stung with dry contact lenses and her whole body ached from an afternoon of travel and an evening of feeling lost; Kessy was exhausted. This scared her, bringing a cold sense of vulnerability to her chest, making her lips purse as she balled trembling fists. She tried to take a deep breath and regretted it immediately, as the smell of sweat and cigarette smoke that coated her eyes made her gag.

Where am I?

She was as desperate to know the answer to this as she was to get out of the room, but uneasy about pulling attention to herself. It felt as though she were in a nightmare; unable to shift her exhausted body, surrounded by strangers and breathing in the reek of cigarettes and other things.

The boards creaked as someone in the room got up. Kessy opened her eyes just enough to see blue jeans brushed gently with yellow light creeping through the room. The jeans navigated around someone else sitting on the floor in front of her and then disappeared past the edge of her hood. She grew nervous wondering why someone would stand behind her like that, and it woke her up completely.

The same girl's voice she'd heard earlier asked a question she didn't understand. She sat motionless.

She isn't asking me. She's asking someone else in the room. She'll get her answer and then she'll go away.

Kessy held her breath, waiting. When the girl spoke again, she was closer to her head. Her body ached and she wanted to disappear. She pulled into herself as best she could and at the same time opened her eyes wider, fixating on her lap.

When the girl spoke again, she accused Kessy of trying to ignore the question. She was certain now that she was the one being questioned and, from the whispers around her, that she had the attention of at least one other person in the room.

Given the feeling of fear crippling her up to that point, she now felt bullied into responding. The thought of being forced to react to this attention made her palms sweat and body ache. Slowly raising her head, she saw the guy who was now leaning over to see her face. She jerked away and immediately dropped her eyes back to her lap. Something about the way he stared at her made her uncomfortable. With the sound of more creaking wood, she felt she had the attention of the entire room. Kessy had no idea what the girl meant by, "Do you want some more?" But she did know that it meant that it was time for her to leave.

Slowly she pulled her arms from around herself. She was barely able to feel her hands, like the blood had drained from them. She slowly pushed herself up and felt the blood rushing back to her legs. She searched for a path out and got an inkling of the number of people sitting on the floor that she was going to have to make her way through just to get out of the room.

She saw A coffee with sketchy items she seen only in movies and dropped back onto the couch with a sudden realization of what the girl must have meant.

More? She thinks I had some of that? This girl thinks I'm already on something!

She began pushing herself off the couch but felt the same lack of feeling in her arms and in her legs. She fell forward as if she'd been drinking for the last hour, colliding with someone on the floor before banging face-first, feeling a pop at the crown of her nose as she fell on the thin carpet on the floor.

"What the fuck!" The girl she'd run into shoved away from her, but otherwise the room was silent. She felt a burn grip her nose from the impact; a thick warm fluid squeezed from her nose and dripped into the carpet. No one seemed too concerned, as they were far too stunned for this to be funny yet.

Kessy pressed her fists into the floor and slowly made her way to her feet, making no attempt to wipe the blood away. Feeling the drip fall from her nose, she set one leg in front of the other.

Bumping into several others as she made her way out of the room, she saw a guy in a white sleeveless shirt step over to the table and realized it was the same guy who had been staring at her earlier. She hoped he wouldn't acknowledge her. But as the blood flowed from her nose, over her lips, and off her chin onto her hoodie, it caught his attention. As she was about to navigate around him, he stepped into her path.

"You OK?"

Her eyes drifted over to the table to avoid his, and the materials on it distracted her from his question. His words made her sick. "That sometimes happens. First time?"

Her lips pursed and her body trembled. She had no idea how to respond. When he asked again, less concerned than before, she heard her brother's voice in her head. *Kessy, walk away!* She knew this was the best response.

She felt a drop of blood run into her mouth as she opened it to speak. "I—I'm gonna leave," she said just above a whisper.

He quickly leaned down to make eye contact and quietly asked, "*What* did you say?"

He reached up and lifted her hood, forcing her to look at him though her eyes stung at that point and it was difficult to focus on anything. He raised his voice. "I didn't hear you! What did you *say*?"

Chapter 32

Chris's voice was loud enough for everyone in the room to hear, and some people stood up, expecting blows. Only then did they notice the girl's bleeding nose staining the front of her pink hoodie. Something wasn't right with her. She must have been having an adverse reaction to her first time using.

"I *didn't* hear you! What did you say?" The sheer level of animosity that had crept into Chris's tone yanked the attention of everyone in the room and a few from the staircase.

Cassie wondered, *Here it is! Will she snap or crumble?*

Chapter 33

Tears streamed down Kessy's cheeks, and the blood dripping from her nose made her light-headed. They weren't going to leave her alone, and they weren't going to let her leave. All she could do was wait for them to stop tormenting her with questions.

"Can you hear me?"

Chapter 34

Chris stared at the girl in the pink hoodie.

"I was right! It was this pink hoodie's first time! Girly girl's fuckin' bleeding from her first time!" Cassie declared.

The fact that pink hoodie was bleeding just like her hot-headed friend, except that this was entirely her own doing, was exciting. After how willing her friends had been to clash with total strangers, the thought of having proof of her behavior was too perfect. It would be a very clear "fuck you" for their troubles.

Matt's uncle's Polaroid was on the table. It was old school and unique and no one had touched it yet. A plan formed in her mind. All Cassie needed to do was get the girl on the floor. It would look like a fight. The guys would go wild for a chick fight and would escalate the story of Cassie and some coked-out chick catfighting in the attic.

Putting her plan into motion made her heart race. She wanted to get over to the table without anyone interrupting her plan.

Chapter 35

Kessy heard a swish of feet over the carpet behind her and the voice of the girl who'd offered her the drugs. "What did she say, Chris?"

"*I'm gonna* . . . something; I didn't catch the rest."

"*Leave*, maybe? But her friends already left without her."

"More like pass out. She's dripping sweat and pissing blood out of her nose. I think it was her first time."

My friends were here? She felt a tug at the back of her hood, finally exposing her to the room.

"Holy shit!"

"She's fuckin' pale as a ghost and bleeding out!"

As the lights from camera phone flashes cut through the room, a hand gripped her shoulder, as though to pull her away from the flashes. But instead of Kessy turning from the lights, she fell off her feet and collided headfirst into someone.

Chapter 36

Cassie yanked the neck of the pink hoodie and the girl fell into her. The sound of her hitting the floor was enough to trigger the yelling. And because it was two girls, people shoved in, and several others leaned over the table for a better view. As Chris stepped on her hand, the girl curled on the floor, and Cassie knew it was the image she wanted. As she stood over the girl, fumbling for the right shot, a brighter light cast over the room brought the circle into view perfectly for what she needed to do.

Chapter 37

Trevor glared up the staircase at those crowding the doorway to see in. With growing anxiety, his hands gripped the handrail near the bottom. His path up was blocked by others whose attention was pulled for the exact same reason.

"I didn't hear you! What did you say?" said an insistent and threatening voice from the attic that revived the uncomfortable energy in his chest he'd experienced at the front door.

I recognize that voice! Why is that fucker in the attic making such a big damn deal about not hearing someone? Is he yelling at . . . ?

His stomach knotted with the possibility.

"What did she say, Chris?" A woman's voice, not as demanding as the guy's, spoke.

Is that Ke—? It could . . . Was she talking back to him?

The thought made him clench his sweaty palms into fists as people excitedly pushed past him. Though he desired to make his own way up, he was keenly aware that Tracy and the others had left already. He'd scanned the immediate area and hadn't found any sign of Kessy.

At this point, the possibility that Kessy was inside somewhere was only as real as his panicked imagination. The blood dripping out of Tracy's face had been very real. If he was found out, he was sure he would get the full assault that Tracy would have received had he stayed. This threat was more powerful than the chance that it was Kessy in the attic being hassled with questions. He turned to make his way out of the cabin.

"Holy shit!"

"She's fuckin' pale and bleeding out!"

He was fairly sure someone had said *she*. He stopped, shaking with anger and fear. He clenched his fist by his mouth. *Oh God, please don't let it be Kessy!*

The sheer volume of yells throughout the rest of the cabin meant he couldn't be sure. He wanted to push farther up the steps and turn back to the rest of the cabin and scream at them to shut the fuck up.

Oh God, if that's Kessy, I'm gonna fuckin' kill that guy for talkin' to her like that!

Hardly taking the time to wipe his sweaty hands on his jeans, he tried to push past the people in front of him, but the first guy he tried to shove out of the way just shoved him back harder. "Dude. Fuck off!"

Trevor waited. He didn't want to waste his anger. He crouched as his arms trembled with adrenaline.

He envisioned himself stepping on people's hands and shoulders until he was forced to crowd surf his way into the room and fall between people to rescue Kessy. As he fantasized for the opportunity, he imagined the sound of the screams that would barrel down from the attic.

A frantic need to act coursed through his body at the sound, and he was shoved again. The sweat that saturated his shirt caused his blue shirt to stick to his chest. As the guy shoved past him, Trevor immediately recognized him from the scene at the front door. He was short like Trevor, but the outline of a pot leaf on his green shirt was unmistakable. "You're the fucker that laughed at her name!"

Trevor yelled, but the guy barely acknowledged him. When the guy turned away, Trevor's glare aimed at a video camera in his hand. People seemed to avoid its light. Trevor was too startled to follow the guy who had pitched a bottle into Tracy's face.

What the fuck is HE gonna do?

The guy held his camera over his head, as he was too short to see between heads or over shoulders in an effort to capture what was happening in the room.

The thought that the screaming in the attic was revolving around Kessy and the sight of that fucker filming it was sickening. Trevor decided he'd had enough. *How long is that piece of shit gonna film?*

"Hey! HAAAY!" He couldn't scream loud enough, and he desperately wanted the guy's attention.

Turning to the first person behind him, he asked, "The guy with the camera! What's his name?"

"Cory, I think."

Turning back, he put his hands back around his mouth and yelled, "C-OOOORRRRY!"

He saw the light falter as he grew light-headed. His yelling caused a shiver to flow through his body and had gathered wide-eyed faces around him, but the filming hadn't stopped. The screaming continued for a moment, and then he heard another guy's voice from the attic.

"Let her up! Let her UUUUP!"

Trevor crouched again, gnashing his teeth again, and his eyes squeezed shut.

Her? Fuck!

When he opened them again and saw that Cory was still filming, he was ready to scream. Then people started pushing their way out of the room. Trevor's eyes flitted to everyone who trampled down the steps.

"What happened?" the girl behind him asked, but they all kept right on moving, staring down at the steps before them. He glanced at each one, hoping for something. There was still chatter from the attic, but he couldn't make it out. Whatever had happened, it felt awkward now that the yelling and screaming had stopped and the witnesses wanted nothing more to do with it.

Then another voice from the attic yelled something else that Trevor couldn't make out, nor would he get a chance to as the number of people leaving the room forced him back down the steps.

What they'd done to Kessy, it was over. After everything that Trevor had imagined, he wanted to run into the guy who had done all the questioning.

As he was forced to the bottom of the steps, the option to get involved was taken away. Forced back toward the living room of this cabin, he wondered at the number of people flowing down after him.

Jeez, how many people were up there?

He waited as they all shuffled down, breathing heavily. Feeling the sweat run down his face, he brushed his palms over his jeans. He waited there, believing that he would know the guy by his voice when he was asked what happened.

As the flow of people slowed, he got a better sense of them. Their faces were pale, as though they'd witnessed an accident.

The temptation to approach one of them was strong, but he took this subtle change as a sign that the guy he was after was just behind them. Trevor stood at the edge of the living room and the hall to the front door of the cabin.

This was the reason he'd separated himself from the guys when the bottle was thrown; why he'd backed off the opposite direction as them; and why, when someone had asked him what had happened, he'd waited, because now he wasn't being associated with them.

Cory knows I'm here, but that's it so far . . .

When he saw the guy who had been laughing at Cory mocking Kessy's name, he studied him.

Sandy blonde hair, sleeveless white senorfrogs shirt . . . built. It's like he's going out of his way to not make eye contact with anyone.

Glaring at him as he lurched through the living room and stopped by another guy about his build wearing a black UFC shirt, he realized who they were.

They're the other two that were at the front door!

Trevor stared at them for some time, deciding how to approach them. The idea of it felt like a lead weight in his stomach, and planning slowly gave way to terrible feelings.

How the fuck am I going to tell this guy that . . . ? No. Describe Kessy . . . No. Just tell him you know who he was questioning. Go from there . . .

When the senor frog guy tried to engage the guy in the UFC shirt, Trevor got closer to hear the response. The UFC guy seemed genuinely pissed off.

"Not how I wanted to start things off, Chris . . ."

This guy fuckin' knows something! The thought sent a surge of fire through him that bolstered his courage. He felt like he could tell them everything—exactly when he'd met them, who Kessy was, and why he was still there. He was ready to tell them how Chris had gone completely wrong berating Kessy with questions.

When Trevor was within feet of them he opened his mouth, but his body began to shake, which strained his ability to articulate, and his words slid out with little or no thought.

They both stared at him, shocked. Trevor's unfiltered and unaware delivery continued until UFC guy with Chris put his arm out. The unexpected gesture seemed like concern until Chris snapped at Trevor.

"What?"

His words cut off abruptly and the situation grew painfully awkward. Trevor was certain that somewhere during his tirade, he'd threatened to kill Chris. No one said another word for what felt like an eternity. They waited on him, but his spew of words had ceased as soon as they questioned him. If he'd made any mention of having been at the front door to begin with, what he'd said next was more than enough cause for alarm.

"You were at the front door earlier? And you're still here? Are you stayin' down the path" The guy who was upset with Chris, was now focused on Trevor. Trevor felt a wave of adrenaline dwindle as beads of sweat trailed down his brow and dripped off his face.

No one said another word, and the silence was painful.

"You want to know what happened in the attic. Either go up there, or leave!" Trevor staggered toward the back door, feeling their eyes boring into him.

He stood outside in view of the path, staring at it for some time. Like the fog still covering the path, the last few minutes were a haze in his mind. The longer he stood there, the more everything he'd experienced in the cabin felt like it had happened so long ago. As his emotions slowly found their way back to normal, though not fully making it there, he felt like a completely different person from the guy who had unleashed himself on those guys.

He was losing steam, but his hatred for how the situation had turned out was still twisting his mind.

Yelling and laughter from the other side of the cabin kept him from leaving. He didn't know what was being said, but he wanted to believe he could still confront someone over what had happened in the attic.

He crept back over the gravel, trying to hear what was being said before he was in sight of anyone. When he peered around the corner, he saw a dozen people or more. Trying to see a familiar face in the fog was difficult, and he slowly crept closer, assuming he would recognize someone.

"He made that guy bleed! Cory made that guy bleed!"

"Did you get it on film?"

"Cory, did you film it?"

Where is he? He might remember me!

Sliding his hands into his pockets, Trevor strolled over, trying to act casual until he saw the guy they called Cory. Trevor believed his presence would alarm Cory after the way he'd screamed at him on the staircase. At least that's what Trevor was hoping for—a chance to make an impact on someone in this cabin.

He scanned every face in the group, not seeing Cory on the edges of the crowd.

Cory has to be somewhere . . . Someone just asked him a question! When he looked in the center of the group, he recognized a guy whose head was down, the one with all the attention, even though he couldn't fully see him.

He's surrounded. The thought held him back. He didn't know how he was going to confront the guy like this.

"Cory, did you get that on film?"

That's gotta be the same fucking camera he filmed . . . He's watching what . . . Kessy!

The thought almost made him launch himself at the guy. Trevor thought about yelling at Cory about whether he'd gotten Kessy on film as he wanted to, or if he'd missed it all because he'd been too late and too fucking short to see anything. Imagining it emboldened him.

Chapter 38

"That guy was at the front door earlier! He didn't leave with his gang. He stayed! Guy was even more frantic than the guy Cory threw his bottle at, swearin' to God like that . . . now I'm positive they were on something! The sight of his buddy bleeding out didn't make him leave," Matt said, shaking his head. He still stood next to Chris, who listened to this. "He *was* part of that group that was here, wasn't he? Are they staying in the cabin down the path?"

Chris nodded. "Maybe."

"That's insane that he stayed. Fuck, now I wanna know what the hell his deal was, don't you?" Matt asked as he glanced at Chris, then to the screen door. "Did he actually leave?"

They both went from the living room to the screen door to check the back clearing. Moving outside, they scanned the faces in the yard.

"I don't see him," Chris said.

"You seem real calm after that."

"Huh?"

Matt gestured inside. "The guy started a fight out front then stayed behind to threaten us."

Chris shook his head. "It's your uncle's cabin. It makes sense that you're concerned about what happens in it."

"And you're not? He was lookin' at you when he was saying most of that shit. That didn't bother you?"

Chris turned to him. "He left, Matt. As soon as we remembered him, he lost his confidence and he couldn't look us in the eye after we called him on it."

"Let's go check the front." Matt quickly went back in. Chris followed.

From a window at the front, they saw him in the clearing, wearing his blue shirt and black jeans. He appeared to maintain the same level of animosity toward the crowd out front that he'd had with them, if not more.

"No shit!" Chris said, sounding shocked.

"Who's he staring at?" Matt said as they both leaned into the window. Then they saw who the guy was glaring at. A crowd was clustered around Cory and his camera.

"Cory threw a bottle at his buddy!"

"Then why the fuck didn't he threaten Cory? Why'd he have to sneak inside and get in our faces if he had a problem with Cory?" Matt said.

Chris peered through the window at the guy. "Because he thinks he can take Cory! He's workin' himself up right now to go do the same fuckin' thing to Cory!"

Matt looked at him. "You gonna stand here while that happens?"

Chris backed away slowly from the window, toward the front screen door. Matt followed as he answered. "If Cory didn't have that crowd around him, it would have happened already!"

Scrutinizing Chris as he pushed quietly out the screen door, his eyes grew as he saw the guy to his left, and Matt shook his head.

NOW you're excited?

Chapter 39

He's a shorter fucker, this guy, Cory!

Trevor had finally gotten a good impression of him. Believing he could take the guy, Trevor began to build his courage to confront him despite the crowd.

"Did you film it?"

"Cory, did you film what happened?"

The guys crowded around Cory to see the footage on the camera in his hands. As they did, he stared down at it with a maniacal grin on his face, proud and loving the attention. His only response was a shake of his head. Trevor himself could hardly remember all of what had happened, and he listened carefully to their accounts.

"That guy was bleeding!"

"You break his nose, Cory?"

Again, he didn't answer, only grinning at the camera in his hands.

"Cory threw a bottle at a guy and he ran home cryin' like a bitch!"

That's not true!

Trevor wanted to throw himself into the discussion, despite the hostility of the people around. He grew excited at the idea of knocking Cory out and leaving, knowing that he wouldn't ever see the guy again.

That's something I could tell the guys back at the cabin.

He clenched his fists and quickly made his way toward Cory. Just as he started to push through the crowd, fingers clenched the back of his shirt by its neck. The front constricted across his throat. He was yanked back with enough force to pull him off his feet.

His hands shot up to his neck and his eyes clenched closed from the brief feeling of being choked by his own shirt. Unable to react fast enough to break his fall, he impacted the gravel like a dropped board, slamming the ground with his whole body. Feeling it from the back of his legs to the back of his head, he lay there for a second, hands shaking as they shot up to cover his head. He turned to his side, trying to cover his face as it burst with sweat. He'd had the wind knocked out of him and was gasping for air. He began churning over the gravel as he tried desperately to pull air back in his lungs, dragging his shoes over the stones, again and again.

"What's going on?"

"Why'd you do that? Chris! Why did you do that?" Two girls voiced concern from Cory's direction.

Trevor felt thankful for the attention. Their hearts were clearly going out to him.

"Chris! Why did you do that?"

"What was that?"

No answer was given. And until his body stopped twisting over the gravel, nothing else happened. He felt all of the physical hate flowing out of his body while his hands continued to cover his face. His hate-fueled readiness to pummel Cory had disappeared completely.

When he finally stopped moving and lay there for a moment, a question was finally aimed at him from one of the girls.

"Are you OK?" and then back to Chris, "Why'd you do that? If you're done doin' whatever you're doin' to him, bring him inside, Chris."

Trevor stopped moving completely at this suggestion.

"I think you hurt him!"

"Chris you're standing there like you're still pissed off at the guy after you put him on the ground! You gonna start kicking him or you gonna bring him inside?"

It was quiet for another moment.

"What'd he do, Chris?"

"You remember what he said inside?"

Trevor vaguely recognized the voice. One or both guys he'd threatened stood over him.

"Why don't you BRING him back inside!" Her voice demanded it.

Feeling the damp and dirt pull off the ground and cling to the back of his shirt, he continued to try and cover his face as someone finally picked him up off the ground. Wrapping an arm around his chest, Chris dragged Trevor inside.

The sweat dripping off his face still, his body felt exhausted and frail as he was carried through the cabin and into a room. As Trevor leaned into what felt like a bed frame, he felt the guy lean over him.

"You got gall staying, bro. Approaching me and Matt like you wanted to get into a fight just now. You're lucky."

"Chris, he's passed out. When he wakes up, maybe he'll finally leave."

Chris leaned closer, getting personal. "Seen your face, bro."

Trevor had no idea how long he was out. He could barely move, and his head ached as he lay there for what felt like an eternity, mashing his fingers over his eyes. This had started when he tried to get up those steps when he thought Kessy might have been in the attic.

I shoulda gone up . . . Fuck, I shoulda gone up.

But his encounters with those guys felt as though they had happened ages ago.

His head still ached when the sound of voices outside the room brought him back to again, still in a daze but able to lift his limbs. As time when on, they grew louder and made the ache feel worse.

"Ohhh! Who's next? Who's next?"

Time to go.

When he finally got to his feet, Chris's comment still sat in his head.

"Seen your face, bro!"

He reached for the knob.

Chapter 40

The moment Cassie's eyes opened, she knew she hadn't slept long. Her eyes stung as her eyelids slid over them and her head ached. She'd returned to the attic at some point before she'd fallen asleep. Searching the room, she studied the mess of bits on the coffee table and immediately remembered that girl from the night before.

Did she leave? The question pushed her up off the floor. The image of her still lying on the floor in the bedroom on the main floor was fixed in her mind. As she made her way down the attic steps, her energy was fueled by her anticipation. She didn't know what she would do if that pink hoodie was still here, but she desperately wanted to know.

The rest of the cabin still seemed to be out cold as she made her way quickly through the den and to that hall. She couldn't reach the door fast enough. She turned the knob and it opened with a creak. She crept in just enough to see a piece of that pink fabric. She stood frozen, staring at it. The girl was right where she had left her.

Seeing someone light a cigarette outside, she closed the door to do the same thing.

Bumming a cigarette and the small talk that followed were momentary distractions, as she found herself glancing back into the cabin, waiting for that pink hoodie to show her face as she staggered down the hall and out of the cabin.

It would be a funny sight. She imagined that she would nod to the guy who gave her the cig for him to see this happen. But it didn't happen, and eventually the guy went back inside and she sat against the side of the cabin.

The sound of someone walking on the gravel made her jump. Her head whipped back and forth, searching for its source. Not seeing anyone, she went around the cabin toward the front. When she didn't find anyone there either, she settled where she thought she would be out of sight, against the side of the cabin. She'd been as sociable as necessary to get a cig, but at that moment, everyone could just fuck off.

After hearing the screech of the screen door a second time and listening to the footsteps on the gravel travel back through the clearing, she pushed slowly back to her feet. She felt the strain in her muscles as she used her left arm against the side of the cabin to steady herself. She wanted to see who had the nerve to go through the cabin like they owned it and just leave. Cassie stood by the back corner of the cabin to see two guys leaving the area, heading toward the path entrance, and one said something to the other. As they left, it made her want to check on that pink hoodie again.

As the morning wore on and the lingering ache in her head from a lack of sleep went away a bit, she found herself returning to that bedroom again and again. Each time she expected that pink hoodie to be gone. Throughout the morning and into the afternoon, she smoked one cigarette after another between checking the room and eyeing it like a hawk from the kitchen.

Even when she remembered the details of what had happened in the attic, one question still persisted. *How fucking long is it gonna take that pink hoodie to come down?*

Then she remembered the amount she'd bled out and what Chris had said about the light being her first time doing drugs. Thinking that her body was probably recuperating after everything she'd done last night, Cassie backed off. *If she's awake, then she probably can't move and wants to die. And if she's still passed out, well, she did lose a lot of blood.*

Cassie decided she wanted to be the first person that pink hoodie had contact with when she sobered up and saw where she still was. She wasn't sure anymore if she wanted her to leave. *I wanna be there when she discovers the photo in her back pocket!*

The idea invigorated Cassie, and suddenly she felt quite willing to wait for the pink hoodie to regain her senses and discover where she was. She'd been asleep for so long she might even think she was in her own cabin, at least until she saw Cassie. And she wanted to see the splash of emotions on her face when she checked her back pocket and saw herself surrounded on the floor in that photo.

The fantasy that played out in her mind slowly turned to paranoia as the morning turned over to afternoon and the pink hoodie girl still hadn't shown signs that Cassie witnessed. She'd forgotten the time that the photo had been taken that morning. And with the amount that she'd bled, she didn't know how much time her body would need to recuperate. And the fact that she would be thoroughly out of it would set her up perfectly. Cassie would have to inform her of the photo, wait while it sunk in, and then get to witness her reaction.

Cassie wanted a reaction. She hadn't gotten one in the attic.

She didn't do a single other thing that day. Ignoring the traffic of others throughout the cabin was not difficult as her mind was still a bit burnt out from the lack of sleep. When evening began to fall and she realized she hadn't checked on her for some time (although she'd still been eyeing the room like a hawk), she decided that it had to happen soon.

She's gotta be awake by now. If not aware, she's awake.

She was tempted to rattle her into wide-eyed shock but decided instead to wait in there with a drink in hand. This would guarantee that she witnessed the discovery of the photo, and it would get her away from the drinking games beginning in the kitchen.

Chapter 41

Kessy's body was in agony. Feeling as though she'd woken during a terrible hangover, she was unable to so much as open her eyes without feeling the dryness of her contacts. Still, wanting to know where she was, she forced them open.

It's so dark. Where am I?

She remembered the attic as she slowly unclenched her hands from over her chest to pull her fingers over her eyes. She felt the dried blood cracking off her lips

What is that? She felt something rough beneath her. *Where am I?*

The room was quiet now, but the thought that she was in the same attic space made her feel like she'd had a nightmare. She opened her eyes enough to see the underside of a bed she was lying at the side of. *I fell out of bed?*

Thinking she had had a nightmare and fell out of the bed and banged her nose was somehow comforting. The door creaked open, and she felt a touch of fear. A guy's voice standing over her spoke quietly.

"You awake?"

Kessy felt a hand slide slowly over her shoulder. As it squeezed, she stirred.

"Hey Pink, you awake?"

Kessy still had no idea where she was and now had a splitting headache that mirrored the ache throughout her body that caused her to pull further into a fetal position.

Feeling her hood being tapped before it was pulled back, Kessy's lips pursed as her hands shifted up to cover her face.

"Yeah, you're awake."

He grabbed Kessy's arm, pulling it away from her face.

"You sober? Looks like you stopped bleeding."

He gripped Kessy's arm, pulling her to an upright position. Kessy finally opened her eyes to see this guy's sandy blonde hair and the the same shirt with frogs on it. They made eye contact briefly before the dryness in her contact lenses forced her gaze to drop to her lap.

"Look at me."

She trembled as his fingers squeezed and she spoke without thinking. "I-I fell out of bed. I had a nightmare." Kessy said this, attempting to explain why she was lying on the floor.

He pulled her arm, causing her to flinch, as he tried to make eye contact with her.

"What'd you say? I didn't hear you, what'd you say?"

As he leaned in still trying to make eye contact, Kessy said it again.

"I fell out of bed. I had a nightmare."

"A nightmare?"

As he questioned her, Kessy didn't know what else to say so she repeated herself. "I had a nightmare!"

"You didn't have a nightmare. Hey, look at me!"

Reluctantly Kessy faced him to see this guy's eyes staring into hers. Kessy stared at his sandy blonde hair and face speckled with dirt from being outside.

"You didn't have a nightmare; you got into a fight and were knocked unconscious in the attic of our cabin Friday night. I'm Chris. We spoke just before it happened. I explained to you why your nose was dripping blood but if you don't remember that, then you're still coming down. You've got blood on your face because you had a bad reaction to using drugs in our attic. Not because you fell out of bed."

Kessy didn't want to hear this; she wanted to lie back down on the floor. She took a deep breath before she continued to describe the only thing she knew for sure at that moment, that she'd had a nightmare. "I was in a small, dark room full of strangers. I don't remember how I got there."

"You *were* in the attic. That dark room full of strangers, that was the attic. You came up the path looking to get a fix and found it in the attic. I think you promised sex in exchange until you had such a bad reaction to your fix."

Kessy turned away, closing her eyes as her lips pursed. It was painful to listen to Chris say this. What he suggested didn't feel true. But he'd sounded so convinced. "A *girl* asked me if I wanted more."

"That was Cassie."

"She asked me if I wanted more and I tried to leave, but a guy stopped me."

"That was me. I stopped you."

Chris leaned forward after saying this, still trying to make eye contact with Kessy.

"You don't have a clue where you are. These interactions you're talking about, they happened in the attic. You got into a fight and were beaten unconscious."

Chris repeated the words "beaten unconscious" while pointing to the fabric and dried blood lines on Kessy's face. Hearing them again made her sink.

Chris watched this, then continued, "Hearing your perspective, hearing you describe it as a nightmare, it sounds like you don't believe any of this actually happened."

He shook his head. "You gotta remember me talking to you. You said you were gonna do something that you wouldn't repeat. You might not even remember, but I think you were too paranoid and trying to threaten your way out."

Chris's words felt familiar and fell right in with the ache that was twisting her mind as Kessy finally muttered under her breath, "You're part of my nightmare."

"You already said that," Chris snapped back "Jesus, you sound like a victim!"

Kessy's eyes began to well as she turned away, lying back down, moving away from his words.

He got up and stood over her.

"Girl, you look like hell. You look like a fucking dead body! You've been out cold for . . . it's past noon and you're still coming down. I came in to help you leave if you didn't come back and pull the same shit again! Jesus, you're out cold again; you're not hearing any of this! You really are a junkie."

After he left, the sound of the slamming door echoed through her mind. It faded after time, and when Kessy stirred again at the sound of yelling outside the cabin, it felt as though ages had passed.

Listening to it was nauseating. But one word sliced through her mind as she opened her eyes and dragged her dry tongue against her teeth: *water.*

Her mouth felt like a desert and her limbs felt frail as she tried to lift them. *Water.* The other aches in her mind and body were gone for need of water. She turned her head and blinked slowly through the sting of her lenses as she tried to keep her eyes open, but her gaze flew around the room like a fly before she closed them again.

Getting out of the room for water meant seeing more of the cabin. Kessy lay there for another moment with this thought in mind, the time it would take and the people she might encounter. But the need for water outweighed any anxiety she felt. She struggled to her feet; her legs trembled like a newborn fawn until she got to a standing position.

Though they still stung, it was easier to keep her eyes open as she slowly moved out of the room and down a short hall. There were people in the living room, figures off to her left as she found the kitchen to her right. Both rooms were separated by a screen door on the far wall ahead of her whose sunlit windowpanes made her blink.

Turning away from it toward the kitchen, going for the sink, she twisted the knob and splashed her eyes in an attempt to alleviate the sting. Instinctively she began tugging at the skin around them to allow her contacts to fall out. After dropping into the basin, they floated into a strainer, and she glanced at their hazel texture as she began using her hands to scoop the water into her mouth.

Kessy listened to the hush of the water moving through the pipes. While it flowed between her fingers she was mesmerized between scoops as it reflected the dim light above her. She felt a presence of someone behind her in the kitchen. He spoke, but she couldn't hear him over the hush of the water and its splash in the stainless steel sink.

She continued to scoop the water until she felt cool inside, then began splashing her face. Feeling the cool water glide over her makeup and the layer of sweat on her forehead and cheeks as she did this, the same voice said the same thing, or at least the same inflection was used. Again Kessy couldn't make it out.

She leaned further into the basin as she alternated between her face and her mouth until her face began to feel as cool as her stomach did. She turned the handle to stop the flow, and then had to reach into the sink. Placing her hands palms down over the metal, she slowly pushed her waist off the counter, ready to get back to an upright position. As she did this, she could feel the person getting closer behind her.

"Drink too much?"

A guy spoke softly, so unlike the guy she'd heard earlier. The word *thirsty* sat in her mind, but Kessy didn't want to speak. She gripped the edge of the sink, ready to push off with enough force to launch her into walking, but the edge was wet with the spray of water and she slipped back into the basin. He came closer and wrapped his hand around her arm, helping her back to a standing position.

"You're shaking. Why don't you sit down?"

She wanted to take this offer, but as she turned toward him and saw a bottle in his free hand at the same time he saw the front of her hoodie, he let go of her. The two of them stood there for a moment, his eyelids peeled back, gawking at her.

"Are you OK?"

It was awkward; he'd stood and stared as she used the water, made a few comments, then offered his help when she struggled. When he finally saw the state of her front, he had no clue what to do.

"You wanna go lie down?"

Kessy didn't want to. A feeling of dehydration still lingered in her and, while she was unsure she had the strength in her legs to flee, she had to try. The thought of getting outside the cabin, in view of Josh and Jon, became an image in her mind as she slowly began moving, but her legs felt ready to buckle if she tried. Still, she put one foot in front of the other as he glanced at the screen door just to her right.

"Where are you goin'?"

She was within a few steps of the door when a cigarette smell wafting through the screen stopped her.

"What are you doin'? Are you gonna answer anything I ask you?"

He spoke louder this time as Kessy kept taking in the smell, distracted by it while the guy grew irritated waiting for a response. It took Kessy a moment to be reminded of the reek of that attic space and the last time she tried to leave, having the back of her hood grabbed at her neck before she fell to the floor and was stepped on.

That smell was pungent when a girl spoke to her and said, "Do you want some more?" She wanted to go out the screen door, fighting the urge to see the person who'd said that to her, and just keep moving.

Kessy's lips pursed at the thought of whether she had the physical ability to do this, while the expectation of being stopped a second time became a stronger possibility the more she took in the smell of that cigarette.

"Hey Pink, are you gonna leave?"

He demanded a response, and the sound of feet shifting over rocks outside was enough for Kessy to be concerned that his addressing her by her clothing had identified her.

While the room had fewer people this time, the guy pestering her, and a few people on the couches in the adjoining living room had begun to take notice. She had the same visceral response as she matched the smell of that cigarette to the reek in the attic.

Is it gonna happen again?

What she would do differently would be to not respond, as the emotion had developed the memory. Her plan to leave and not stop, despite what she'd heard, began to dwell in what courage she had at that moment.

A spent cigarette butt flew across the window on the screen door. Like confirmation of immediate proximity, the thought of confrontation weighed heavily when a hand gripped her shoulder.

She turned to see Chris.

"If you're gonna leave, leave. But if you're still sobering up, go back to that room and do what you gotta do!"

This was what she wanted, but his barking tone and still being able to smell that cigarette kept her standing as he leaned closer to get a look at her as he had when she was on the floor.

"You have black eyes. And they're real bloodshot. You're still coming down. You look better than you did a few hours ago, but you still look like you're fucking out of it, girl! You *clearly* can't take care of yourself! Go back to that room and don't even think of goin' back to the attic."

With these words, he didn't give her a choice, as he gripped her arm and, turning her around, he brought Kessy back to the room at the end of the hall. As he pulled the door closed behind her, the conversation she heard clarified their opinion of her.

"What'd that girl do?" said a voice Kessy didn't know, likely one of the girls who had seen her from the couch.

"She was in the attic!" he proclaimed.

"What does that mean?"

As the screen door pulled with an awful screech, Kessy waited to hear from cigarette girl whom she believed was waiting for her.

She was waiting for me. She flicked her cigarette so I would see it.

"Why are you so upset with her?" couch girl asked again. "What does her being in the attic mean?"

Chris informed her, with the same barking tone he'd used with Kessy.

"It all comes back on her! That girl in the pink hoodie that stood here aimlessly, staring into space. She was in the attic Friday night; I didn't even see her come in. Cassie came and got me and it was actually Saturday morning when I saw her. I didn't know what to make of her at first!"

Why does Chris keep calling her pink? His conviction was staggering; her belief that she'd had a nightmare and this was how she ended up on the floor was torn away.

"She was wearing colored contact lenses."

The same guy who was nagging her as she stood at the sink, spoke up as he made this discovery.

"What?" the same girl from the couch asked.

"Colored lenses." He said this and the hurried sound of shuffling feet rushed over to see this. "She washed them out of her eyes and left them in the sink."

"You know her?" she asked.

"No. What color are those?"

"They're hazel," she said. "She was wearing those and she just left them there? That's kinda weird. Chris, you said her eyes were black?"

It was quiet for a moment. Kessy imagined Chris, who had sent her back to the room, leaning over the counter.

"I tried to make eye contact with her in the attic Friday night and again this morning. I didn't see *that*. They looked like black holes on her face just now."

"That's creepy."

Hearing her dark brown eyes being mistaken for black and described as black holes on her face made Kessy's lips curl as her hands came up to cover them.

The guy spoke again. "She wants hazel eyes. She wants people to tell her she has pretty eyes and not black holes on her face."

"Who is she?"

"She was in the attic Friday night, right after that fight at the front door happened!" He barked at her as though she hadn't listened when he'd said this a moment ago. "Cassie found her wrpped in her pink hoodie and nearly fetal on the couch, basically paranoid as hell." Chris was quiet for a moment, then continued "What she took was only laid out for her because she's pretty. No one tells someone that attractive no."

Kessy lay there, waiting to hear cigarette girl's reaction, whether it was something couch girl could be made to understand or if she would find any fault in his behavior, as she seemed to be the only one with enough to concern to ask what was going on.

"We got here Saturday morning. We didn't see any of that, but we heard something happened just after you guys arrived, but it honestly sounded made up," couch girl said.

"Nope. Ask Matt!"

"So a group wandered up here to start a fight with you guys. One of them was high, and before he started swinging he went on about that girl's pink hoodie?" she clarified. "That sounds—"

"I know how it sounds!" Chris cut her off. "But you just saw me talkin' to her."

"I don't understand. Why is she still here if she's part of the same group that started a fight?" couch girl asked.

"They're staying in that small cabin right down the path!" The voice of that cigarette girl who approached her in the attic declared this. One that she associated with the attic's stuffy reek spoke up finally. It confirmed for Kessy what she'd been anticipating after she breathed in that smell.

"What does that mean?" couch girl asked.

"Did Ron tell you guys he was renting it out this weekend?" Chris asked.

"No, he didn't, and I don't like when he does that, renting it and not telling us," Reek said.

"Who's Ron?" couch girl asked.

"My uncle. He owns this cabin and the one down the path."

"I'm confused. I though you said you were upset with her because she was doing drugs in the attic. But now you're saying that your uncle knows them?"

"No. Uncle Ron rented his cabin to strangers for the weekend." Reek continued, "He brags about owning both cabins, that's when he tells them his niece and nephew are in this cabin; he's using the family angle to make the deal. My issue is that these renters know this and have decided to confront and attack the family."

"He doesn't tell you who he rents to?" couch girl asked.

"He didn't vet them properly. He had no idea what he was getting us into; he just wanted the money."

"So what you're doing to that girl is his fault?"

"These renters lied to my uncle. They misled family and they've been confronting family since our first night up here on Friday. You fucking get it now?"

"What did the renters lie to your uncle about?"

"What they were gonna use his cabin for. Their pink hoodie that's coming off her high in that room, she was looking for *more*. That's when her friends first banged on our door and spoke for less than a minute before starting a fight because they were as paranoid as Pink was; that's the story you heard when you got here."

After Reek's story ended, it was quiet for a moment. Overhearing the cause for her nightmare and Reek's reasons for her behavior toward her, Kessy lay there trying to process this. It just didn't connect. Reek's uncle had spoken to her daddy, and

Kessy hadn't been listening when he explained what had been set up regarding the cabin for the weekend.

"That's kinda scary 'cause I heard people saying they'd be back."

"Who said that?"

Couch girl stated this and Reek asked for clarification. When there was no response, Kessy felt anxiety in her whole body. Couch girl asked one last question. "What are you gonna do with her? The one you sent back to the room?"

"I want her to sober up, then Cassie and I will have a chat with her."

An uneasy silence ensued. Kessy mashed her fists over her eyes as her lips scrunched. She now had learned Reek's name, but they seemed so unconcerned with who she was, only going by a detail of her clothing.

Reek's name is Cassie. She approached me because they both think I was doing drugs in their attic? This is terrible; they expected it!

Chris made her sound like a junkie of a girl who trespassed in this cabin to get her fix, whose friends were even worse than she was.

"Why didn't you just kick her out?"

"What?" Cassie responded.

"When you first found her the way you did in the attic the way you described, why didn't you just kick her out then? Tell her that her friends were just at the door an—"

"Have you ever confronted someone after they've snorted?"

"That's disgusting."

"Have you?" Cassie demanded.

"No."

Cassie began whispering like she knew Kessy would be listening. She pictured her leaning over to this girl for emphasis as she'd done in the attic. Kessy missed most of it but caught one word: violent.

"That's insane. How do you know that?" couch girl spoke up.

"I asked her if she wanted more, and she stood up to me before she ended up on the floor."

"So you did hit her?" couch girl interrupted Cassie.

"When she got up, it was *all* coming back down. Red, white pouring out of her nose, and the rest of her face was turning black and blue."

"That's really disgusting!" She was quiet for a moment. "You're still smirking, Cassie, I think you're—"

"Laura!" Chris cut her off. "That girl in the pink hoodie that you saw standing here as though she were in a trance, gazing out the screen door. Same girl made a comment to me in that attic, she told me she was gonna do something, but when I asked her to speak up, she wouldn't repeat it."

"Maybe you scared her. If the way you approached her now was—"

Couch girl's name is Laura.

"Nothing scares a person when they're in that state of mind. She might have been paranoid as hell, but it didn't show until the end."

Cassie countered and it was quiet for another moment.

"Are you afraid her *gang* will come back?" Laura asked, followed by a heavy silence.

"If they do, they'll think they're indestructible all over again."

It felt as though they were not only expecting the gang to return, but had a plan. The thought of this made Kessy want to scream, trying to understand what was being said of the cabin down the path, while she lay in a fetal position. If Kessy did let loose, the thought of Cassie hearing her and reacting to her as she had in the attic returned. It made Kessy afraid to even think about bringing any attention to herself. The way Cassie sounded convinced of her drug use made Kessy believe Cassie was maintaining the influence that informed her opinion of Kessy.

She knew Chris wouldn't hesitate to put his hands on her to put her in her place, but Cassie sounded more unpredictable. Believing she would be confronted again if she tried to leave the room, Kessy lay there mashing her fists over her eyes until they ached.

She opened them to stare at the underside of the bed she lay by. *Cassie was taking a cigarette break. Chris just sounded upset.*

Cassie held back just now when Chris barked at her, and Kessy began to easily picture her listening to Chris as he explained the "pink hoodie's" behavior and how it deserved this response. Cassie stepped in only when the story that they wove needed a few crude words to make an impact, like the smell Kessy had experienced in the attic.

She didn't get it, feeling as though she'd done something in the attic that was beyond her understanding. But after listening to their opinion of her, it drove her to an edge trying to understand what the fuck it was.

She couldn't stop thinking about the words Cassie had said: *shorting* and *violent*. Their implication created a deeper fear in Kessy.

As the level of chatter and laughter in the cabin increased, the occasional traffic into the room she was in let up. People were willing to explain her state as drunkenness and leave her alone.

As the door creaked open, the thought that Cassie was back to check on her caused her to clench until she heard a voice, the same one who had questioned Chris. Kessy felt her climb onto the bed and stop there for a moment before speaking. Laura asked Kessy the one question no one had when she was on that couch, or when she stood to try to make her way out.

"Did you really *use* in the attic?"

It was the exact question Kessy wanted to hear but was too scared to answer. In fact, she was uneasy about acknowledging this girl in any way. Maybe it was Cassie or just the tone of that heated explanation earlier who made Kessy not want to go against their perception of her.

They'd spoken of another encounter with Josh and the gang and of a "talk" they intended to have with her as soon as she sobered up. The thought of Josh being confronted was terrible, as she didn't know what it meant. Kessy lay quietly, even as Laura went from this question to a more innocent one.

"What's your name?"

When the door opened again, she felt Laura immediately stir from the bed. As the door closed again, whomever it was who had caused Laura to leave didn't say a word. The *shh* sound of fabric sliding down the wall off Kessy's feet, it felt as though the person saw her and was coming down to her level on the floor. Only when the door opened again and they yelled did Kessy realize that Cassie was in the room and wanted her alone.

"Get out!"

Kessy anticipated Cassie's barking words next. She waited for Cassie to make a comment about the attic, but she didn't say anything more, and after several minutes Kessy began to unclench. It slowly became clear that Cassie was waiting for Kessy; she began to imagine a scenario with her where she sat up in the way she had earlier and engaged her in conversation.

She wanted to tell her to tell Chris not to go after her brother. But the fear of being glared at until she stopped speaking and being smirked at as she lay back down kept her fetal with her arms covering her face.

She had a fleeting hope that if Cassie knew her name, she would have a difficult time thinking of her in such violent terms. The thought of sitting up drifted through Kessy's mind over and over. Knowing that Cassie wanted Kessy to herself and that she thought of her as being as violent as her friends seemed kept Kessy from pushing back.

***

Cassie didn't want to hear anything more from the crowd for a while. Half of the people in the cabin believed that her brother Matt threw a bottle at some guy, and the other half believed Chris attacked someone in the attic. Laura and her friends were the only ones who knew what actually happened, and she insisted on questioning until she decided there was fault in Cassie and Chris.

It had gotten under Cassie's skin, the way Laura spoke to her. The incessant questioning had challenged her and created a desire to prove why pink hoodie was acting the way she was.

She worried that pink hoodie girl might try to push this possibility herself, that she had just been scared in the attic, the way that Laura suggested, and that her behavior wasn't induced by the drugs in the room. When Cassie returned to the room to find Kessy back on the floor in a fetal position, she wanted to show Laura, to help confirm her own version of what had happened in the attic.

Cassie wanted some reaction from Kessy, but when she discovered Laura trying to engage her, Cassie spoke to keep others out, never addressing Kessy directly.

The thought of reminding her that her contact lenses were still in the sink and informing Kessy that she knew she couldn't see crossed Cassie's mind. She thought of mentioning Chris's comment about her eyes' hazel color and the black holes. Cassie understood the impression pink wanted people to have of her. She definitely had a desire for attention.

Cassie wanted to mention the Polaroid that she believed was still in Kessy's back pocket. Cassie wanted Kessy to discover it and be repulsed by it. Cassie wanted to see Kessy's natural black eyes and her mouth warping upon seeing the picture.

Believing that because Kessy had just tried to leave, she would try again, and all Cassie had to do was hold back and wait for her to stir. She began fantasizing about the series of actions Kessy would carry out. She wondered how Kessy would react to seeing her waiting, the thought of finally looking each other in the eye. It made her blood rush until a question came to mind.

Is she gonna recognize me? She didn't actually see me in the attic . . . or in the living room! Chris was on her case and she never turned to me. I might have to remind her who I am!

The thought that she might have to remind Kessy who she was, was as curious and thought provoking a notion to Cassie as the photo was. Cassie hoped that Kessy would slowly put it together as they looked at each other.

She hoped she wouldn't have to say a word but could watch as Kessy's face slowly shifted from exhausted to uneasy as she remembered being yanked by the neck of her hoodie.

Cassie sat thinking of this scenario, playing it over in her mind. Despite being inside, she pulled a cigarette from her pocket and lit up. If blowing a cloud of smoke over Kessy stifled her breathing enough to cause her to stir and cough sooner, Cassie didn't mind waiting a few minutes.

Holding the cigarette between her fingers with her arm propped on her knee, she tapped ash on the carpet. Wafting the room with the scent of Virginia Slims, she stared at Kessy for some time, waiting for her to curl, gut first, with the need to cough. But the sound of cheering erupting from the kitchen distracted her, and she had to glance toward it between drags.

The activity in the kitchen strained her attention. As she waited for Kessy to stir and grew irritated at the level of yelling in the kitchen, she had the image of guys surrounding the kitchen table where a few girls sat like wolves around prey. Listening to them demanding for who would be next was quickly becoming a point of ad nauseam for Cassie.

The only thought that kept her going was that the smoke Kessy had surely breathed in might stir her out of this seemingly vegetative state. So Cassie would continue to wait it out.

As the noise died down a bit, Cassie began eavesdropping on a conversation that sounded like Chris's voice. She was unable to make out what he was saying, but it sounded like a drunken girl responded.

Unable to make out her words either, Cassie figured it was a sequence of actions that she was being goaded to perform. These dogs describing the deep-throating style to her and filming her reaction; then it was only a matter of time before she succumbed to the pressure and they would film her taking a shot.

She leaned her head against the wall in anticipation of the cheering to burst out again. When she heard what sounded like stomping feet in the hall, she glanced up at the door. What felt like the impact of a body being shoved into it jarred her from the wall.

"What the . . . ?"

She shook for a moment. The cigarette fell from between her fingers onto the carpet, still producing a trail of smoke. Moving away from the wall, Cassie's eyes grew when she saw the door bowing. As the sounds of the wood popping and cracking filled the room, she glanced at Kessy, then back to the door. What could have been a person being shoved into it scared her, as it was similar to the banging on the door that had led to the fight Friday night.

"What the fuck!"

As Cassie moved to her feet, she accidentally placed her hand on her still lit cigarette. Feeling its ember burn her palm, her teeth gnashed as she stumbled for a moment then stood up. She moved over to the door, balling a fist over the sting of the heat, and slammed her fist into the door.

"Hey! Hey!"

She heard a muffled voice on the other side of the door. What she imagined was a girl with a hand over her mouth being prevented from screaming.

Is it Cory again?

She struck the door again and again. She was angry she'd been startled and had palmed her lit cigarette, and that the drug-addled pink hoodie hadn't moved an inch.

"Hey!"

She yelled again, and then reaching for the knob, she twisted it and the door flew open, banging her arms and forehead as it swung open. She staggered back as a girl with a tank top fell onto the floor in front of her, breasts exposed, hands covering her face.

Expecting to see Cory finding his footing after pushing into the door, Cassie instead caught a glimpse of Chris's blue jeans and frog shirt. He'd turned away the second he could after the door opened. He felt caught. Cassie gripped the door and swung it into this girl's leg, bent over to shove her legs out of the way, then swung it again, slamming it shut.

Cassie stood over this new girl for a moment, wondering what the hell had just happened. She assumed this was the drunken girl she'd heard and that she'd lost the nerve she'd had at the kitchen table when some guy tried to get her into the bedroom.

This should have endeared her to Cassie, but Cassie was still angry. She reached down, grabbing the girl's arm, and pulled her to a corner on the other side of the door before she returned to the other corner to get a better look at her. Her hair and jeans looked familiar. When Cassie spoke to her, she was guessing.

"Are you from the cabin down the path? Were you at our front door last night?"

New girl paused at the question. Cassie expected a verbal response as she dealt with her torn top while trying to cover her face. As she got a glimpse of her as she tried to hold her emotions together, Cassie decided she was right. "I remember you guys leaving!"

When the girl didn't answer, it felt like confirmation. It gave her a rush to know who the people staying in her uncle's other cabin were the same ones that had started the fight.

I wonder if Chris knew that and that's why he approached her?

She tried to cut closer.

"Did you come back to get high like—?"

Cassie cut her own sentence off, remembering new girl had just been in the kitchen.

She did the shot the way the crowd demanded of her and now she's playing the victim because I stopped them. She had a drunken encounter with Chris, crashed against the door, and now she's lost all composure. This one's just sad.

She noticed the pink hoodie curling tighter when she began speaking. Cassie hadn't even thought about it until she had someone to compare her to.

That pink hoodie never shed a tear. Even when Chris was yelling at her, she stood there and took it!

Realizing this made Cassie decide against mentioning the pink hoodie to this broken girl. Cassie glanced back-and-forth between the two, realizing neither knew the other was there.

They both think I'm talking to them!

She wanted to say something that both would be forced to chew on, that their minds would twist trying to make sense of.

"You asked for that shit to happen!"

Cassie felt this cut perfectly between the two as the newest resident of the room gathered herself as quickly as she could before avoiding eye contact and left. She waited for a reaction from Kessy as a smirk twisted her lips.

I remember her from last night. You're both from the same cabin! She's not here for Kessy; I don't know what she's after. I bet that was Chris holding her against the door! I bet he remembered her.

These questions churned in her mind as she turned to Kessy, waiting for some kind of response, but the girl gave her nothing. This was somehow unnerving for Cassie, believing Kessy must have sobered up from her high by now.

She'd heard Chris comment that Kessy appeared better now, so a part of Cassie wanted to go another round with her. She was curious if Kessy was upset that she hadn't been allowed to enjoy herself in their attic. She was curious if Kessy felt anger toward Chris for not allowing her to leave.

Cassie wanted to know what was on her mind at that moment. She wondered if Kessy even remembered what happened in the attic or if it had been lost in the ether of the high.

What she really wanted from her was what she hadn't gotten yet, the reaction to that photo. She'd waited patiently and it hadn't happened the way she wanted it to.

Cassie didn't want to chat. She didn't want to say a fucking word to her. She wanted her to remember their encounter in the attic. And if she didn't, Cassie would remind her how she'd asked, "Do you want some more?"

When Cassie finally stopped staring at Kessy, she stopped to consider the other girl who had just left the room.

That girl left damaged!

She imagined her going back down that path to their cabin and her friends discovering her in this state.

Her gang is gonna think she was attacked!

She wondered if that broken girl could identify Chris and if they remembered him from Friday night. She began anticipating this encounter.

If there's another confrontation, when Kessy leaves and is forced to explain where she's been, that photo is gonna damn her!

Cassie listened as the different activities of the evening took place: shots at the kitchen table, cigarettes lit off the tiki torches outside, and more running through the woods. Cassie kept one eye on the hall and the other on the path entrance.

With every activity that began and eventually ended, she anticipated the unmistakable sight of a group she was eager to see up close. She wondered if the words "attempted rape" had made its way into the other cabin. The more time passed, the more Cassie believed that the girl must have told the others at her cabin what had happened.

As time went on, there was still no sign of them, no shoes on the gravel, no yelling of "Chris" to mark their arrival. Cassie waited for it, but it didn't happen.

She didn't tell 'em what happened. Either she didn't tell 'em or they didn't notice.

Cassie wasn't sure what to do next, still anticipating a confrontation with the people in Ron's rental. She peered back inside to the hall, as though expecting Kessy to try and make her way out again.

The thought that she was still in that room, lying in the same fetal position, encouraged Cassie to confront Kessy about the photo.

As Cassie twisted the cherry off her cigarette, breathing her last drag off it through her nose, she fixated on the hall as she stepped back in.

She had made the decision on some level to engage Kessy.

A friend of hers was here, and she knows I got rid of her.

As she paced back through the cabin, a burst of energy coursed through Cassie at the thought of Kessy finally being of sound mind and body so they could meet eyes and acknowledge each other.

When she got in the room to find Kessy where she'd left her, Cassie stood for a moment. She wanted to get close, stand over her for a second, then put her shoe onto Kessy's arm until she was forced to react. At this point, as she imagined Kessy's arms flailing while her body contorted, Cassie would reach into her back pocket.

This fantasy played through Cassie's mind, similar to her romanticized memory of what she'd done after pulling the trigger on the camera, motivated by the questions that filled the room.

"What happened?" they had said.

Cassie had told them that she'd used. These few words not only created an image in their minds, but made them assume the worst.

Hearing these reactions compelled Cassie to do and say more. But she didn't need to. She only had to listen to the others engage the story and let it escalate on its own. By the time Chris took Kessy out of the attic, she'd gone from stranger to trespasser to enemy.

When it was discovered by a few, including herself, that it was Kessy's friends banging on their door Friday night, she figured Kessy was as unstable as her friends. But having witnessed the damaged girl's emotions hang off her face, it was hard to believe that they were from the same gang. Kessy had a controlled lack of words and a more impressive lack of tears.

Pink and I . . . we're so alike, but she's not giving me a fucking thing, and its pissing me off! Cassie was so ready for Kessy to react to her, but she had to wait.

As night fell and as the wee hours of the morning eventually pulled the majority of the crowd inside to couches and into trucks parked in the clearing to crash, Cassie gradually gave into the same notion.

Pink is gonna be gone as soon as the noise stops!

Cassie considered waiting in that room for just a moment, but her energy trailed off.

I'll hear her leaving from the attic.

She didn't want to admit a feeling of giving up by closing her own eyes, figuring she would be stirred by the sound of footsteps on the gravel soon enough; it was just another version of waiting.

Chapter 42

After the words "get out" cut the silence, Kessy felt fear. As the smell of smoke drifted to her, she realized that Cassie had lit up her cigarette in the room. This gesture was an indication that Cassie wasn't done with her. Kessy tried desperately to stifle the need to cough as she waited for Cassie to say more. The intermittent gusts of smoke felt like a subtle form of abuse and an unmistakable reminder of her presence.

A thump on the door crashed into the tension; Kessy curled tighter. Cassie reacted with anger at what sounded as though someone had been thrown into the door. Her yelling and banging on this side of it continued to startle Kessy; the door opened and the person who was held against it fell on the floor. Cassie's spewing questions and comments were unnerving.

Kessy wasn't sure if the words were intended for her or the person who'd fallen on the floor. Kessy stifled her coughing, inhaling the stench. They'd asked for it, whatever it was, the mystery person left.

Cassie finally left sometime later and the sensation of a vise mashing the sides of Kessy's head set in after she took several deep breaths of smoke. As she coughed, she realized she'd have to shift to breathe the dank cabin air.

Her lips curled and her body shook as the ache grew steadily worse. She tried to curl her legs and as the pain overwhelmed her, she forced her fingers into her eyes until they began to ache more than her head. She did this until they felt raw and she grimaced at the pain. She laid her hands back on the carpet, letting the ache consume her as she waited for Cassie to return.

The noise throughout the cabin slowly went away. When Kessy opened her eyes, it was noticeably darker in the room.

Because her head still ached, she closed them again. She didn't open them again until she heard the sound of voices outside.

***

Feeling the cold in the room, Kessy opened her eyes to see a section of brown wallpaper brought into view by the early morning light. Hoping to hear Josh or Tracy, it took Kessy a moment to remember where she was.

She tried to concentrate on the voices, listening to their words. The voices weren't familiar but ones that brought Kessy back mentally into the cabin. The smell that clouded over her earlier and now marinated in her clothing reminded her of the person who had put it there.

That person's voice wasn't among those that Kessy heard, but remembering where she was and that her brother and his friends weren't there for her—the reason she hadn't left on her own accord—clung to her with a now stale stench.

A man's voice outside, speaking with forced calm, caught her attention. When she also heard a female whose voice sounded more critical, Kessy brought her hands back to her face. Her mouth dropped open as the sound of that critical tone made her cringe. She heard the guy's voice again. "Cory! Get yourself a cup of coffee, if you don't . . ."

"His uncle has a collection of old *Playboys* in the attic!"

That voice.

She thought the guy sounded like the one who'd found her by the side of the cabin.

The conversation escalated, and Kessy pulled her hands to her ears, trying to block the sound, as it made the ache in her head worse. It sounded like the girl was trying to provoke the guy.

"I didn't film that!" he yelled back. And then he continued more thoughtfully, "I wish I had."

"What happened?" a different girl's voice yelled.

What had happened? Being found outside this cabin by the guy who mentioned the *Playboys* was something she'd forgotten about until she heard him.

Still yelling, he continued, "The guy fuckin' shoved me when I laughed! He's a fuckin' hothead!"

Kessy's lips curled with the pain. Her head pounded with listening to talk of fights, and she grinded her face into the carpet. After another moment of back and forth, it was quiet, but only for a second. The voices outside turned to yells and screams.

"Hey!"

Kessy tried to cover her ears as she curled her body away from the noise.

"FUUUUCK! GAAAAAD! FUUUCK!" The guy that had found her outside sounded like he was in a lot of pain.

"That was scary!" a girl's voice said.

They spoke loud enough for her to hear every word.

"Wasn't he at the door on Friday? Chris, was he at the door last night?" The guy that had screamed now sounded almost hysterical, like he was in shock.

"Well he just tried to ambush you! Looks like he succeeded!" the girl said.

"Matt clotheslined the fuckin' guy! He was gunning for Cory; he didn't even notice Matt when he put him down!"

Listening to them carry on was painful, and Kessy was forced to listen to all of it. It sounded as though someone else had been attacked like she had.

"He was carrying this! It's a photo!" the girl's voice was almost lost among the guys' yelling.

"That's what I'm saying! The same fucking guy coming at me again! This shit was self-defense!" Kessy's strength was gone. All she could do was tremble and listen.

"He had this Polaroid photo with him! Someone's on a floor somewhere! Wearing a pink hoodie. People around her. That's really creepy!" the girl said loudly.

Kessy lay there as the words "pink hoodie" twisted in her mind. The same words Cassie had used to describe her. Kessy agonized over what they were going to do with her. The pressure in her head returned.

She was angry with me when she left! She told people about me! How else could they know . . . ?

The thought of how much influence Cassie had was scary.

I should not have called her Reek! Find her . . . apologize. How else could she make it stop?

The chatter that followed the argument continued, but Kessy's mind was enveloped by the need to make it stop. Her body reacted to the feeling. Rolling over, she curled her body to a near-fetal position, desperately wanting these thoughts to go away.

Her fingers trembled as she tried again to force them over her eyelids. She'd raked her fingers over her face so much, the skin was raw. The burn she felt and the pain in her eyes was easier to deal with than the thought that this was her fault.

The sound of a familiar voice yelling outside pulled her out of her head. She opened her eyes, blurry and aching from her efforts. His voice rose above the sound of their stampede over the gravel. "Grey hoodie! Blue jeans! Curly hair! Five foot eight!"

Tracy?

It sounded like Tracy, and the description sounded like her brother's.

Joshie?

He was yelling at someone outside, and she heard a girl's voice answer, but she couldn't make out the words again. The front door screeched open, and the sound of feet vibrated through the cabin floor. A biting anxiety gripped her as she realized that Tracy had just entered the cabin. Her whole body shook as she desperately shoved her hands into the floor, getting herself to a seated position.

Her legs folded beneath her, her hands clenched into fists over her chest. She saw the dried blood that ran down the front of her hoodie. It made her eyes well up and she pursed her lips to keep from crying. It distracted her from what she'd just heard, until Tracy yelled right in the other room. "I'm LOOKING for the GUY who CLOTHESLINED my BUDDY!"

Her whole body tensed up at the sound of his voice. She was instinctively afraid of him, he was so close and sounded so angry. The sound of his feet could be heard throughout the cabin. Tracy had to be drawing tremendous attention to himself.

"I'm LOOKIN! For the GUY! Who HIT! My BUDDY!" He yelled even louder. He was quickly losing his temper. She put her hands over her face, scared he would find her. No one in the cabin responded to him.

Then she realized he wasn't after her.

"I'm looking! For the GUY! Who HIT! My BUDDY!" This time when he screamed, a girl's voice responded. She couldn't make it out, but it was followed by a stampede down a staircase to her right.

Joshie's here? She couldn't get past the possibility that her brother was so close by.

There was a moment of quiet when the guys must have reached the basement. She didn't understand what was happening, but she realized Tracy and possibly more of his friends were now in the basement.

He's here for Joshie. Go after Joshie . . . before Cassie comes back. If I go now, maybe he'll see me before she does.

She was moving her shaking hand toward the bedspread even as the thought crossed her mind. She slowly pushed herself to a standing position despite her aching legs. It felt like they would fold beneath her at any moment, but hope and nerves gripped her, and she pressed on.

She envisioned running into Tracy as she left the room. She imagined his reaction when he saw her pushing past people wearing her bloodstained hoodie, tears streaming down her face, and pale as a ghost from blood loss and exhaustion. He would know that she'd been here the entire time.

Head dropped, Kessy shuffled in a haze. She covered the bloody mess on the front of her hoodie with her hands. Feeling the cold of the metal handle on her fingers, she twisted it. No sooner did she open the door than another voice yelled from the den. "Where's your camera, you fuck?"

That sounds like Jon!

He yelled over and over, and this time, it encouraged her. Kessy made it out of the room and, glancing up, saw the crowd in the hall. It seemed like a dozen people were in front of her, all wanting to see what these guys were going to do. Their eyes were peeled as they aimed their attention like animals down into the basement. She paused, wishing there weren't so many. At the idea of pushing into that crowd, she heard *her* voice again. "Who's down there?"

Kessy searched frantically for the owner of that voice. She caught sight of the girl's curly, dark blonde hair as she slowly drew closer to the staircase. Seeing her again, she was afraid, but she wanted to know who this girl was. She was trying to find the courage to get closer when a guy answered her question, and Kessy slowed. "The same guys that were here before!"

"Who?"

He didn't answer, but as she turned to the stairs Kessy caught a glimpse of her piercing green eyes as she inched forward. Now Kessy was close enough to see the girl's fair skin, freckled face, and small nose. Her heart pounded, afraid the girl would catch the pink of her hoodie from the corner of her eye. She didn't know what the girl would say. If she saw Kessy again, she might not hold back. As more yelling careened up from the den, the girl disappeared down the staircase. This girl appeared to want to see what was happening as much as Kessy did.

She hesitated for a moment but realized she had nothing to gain by following her. Her friends weren't going to be of any help. Tracy wasn't there for her. From what he'd been yelling, he was after Josh. And if her brother was there, he'd gotten himself into something that had nothing to do with her. And while she'd heard Jon yelling, he wasn't yelling for her. No one was here to help her.

She wanted to know who this girl was who had attacked her. She'd approached Kessy in the attic, was in the room with her waiting for her to wake up, and was only upset when someone else from her cabin showed up. It didn't make sense, but this girl was the only one who seemed to care that she was here.

Who is she?

This thought roused her forward, forgetting all about the state of her hoodie and the dried blood still clinging to the fabric. Arms out in front to balance herself, she made her way after the girl. She made it only a few feet before her legs began shaking again. Kessy leaned her shoulder against the wall and slid toward the edge of the stairs. She was only a few feet from the top of the staircase when she ran into a guy who seemed to have the same idea.

She leaned into him, hoping he would move. He glanced back and then turned to stare as he shifted out of the way. She reached out to curl her own fingers around the corner. With the little strength she had left, she slid past him, into view of the stairs. When she caught a glimpse of the girl's curly, dark blonde hair, she felt her heart burn in her chest.

Kessy was within a handful of steps when a hand grabbed her bicep and said, "You don't want to go down there!"

She pulled on the handrail, trying to tug her arm away. He gripped tighter and yelled closer to her ear, "You DON'T . . . WANT . . . to go DOWN THERE!"

She kept pulling, hoping he would let go. He squeezed again, as though trying to put some sense into her. "What are you doing? There's a FIGHT happening down there!"

He pulled her from the stairs, turning her to face him. She spoke so softly, he could hardly hear her. Thinking of the curly, dark blonde hair and fair skin, all that Kessy could explain was a jumbled description of that girl's appearance. "What?"

She dropped her head again.

"What did you say?"

Her eyes welled up as he leaned over to hear her answer. But as he did, he saw her swollen nose and filthy hoodie.

Though he didn't say another word, the question took over his face. *What the hell is wrong with this chick?* It was an ugly expression that replaced his concern, a momentary horrified fascination with this girl covered in blood.

"You're still here?" He recognized her from the attic. "You're pink hoodie. I remember you. You tryin' to get that photo back from Cassie?"

His words brought to mind all the things that had happened to her here. They twisted in her mind and made her want to cry. She'd been thinking that he might have something to say about her condition, but his questions suggested that he'd been in the attic when she'd tried to leave. He knew what happened and, now seeing her again, he wanted to continue where that girl had left off.

The guy, still holding her arm, turned back to her. Glancing once more at the mess on her hoodie and then leaning over to the staircase, he called down, "Cassie!"

It was like he set off a chain reaction as a scream from the den immediately followed his call.

"ENOOOOUFFF!"

Kessy jumped.

"ENOOOOOUFFF!"

All the yelling and talking around her stopped. Only the sound of that guy's gravelly voice, screaming for all to hear, broke the tense silence. "*I* CLOTHESLINED YOUR BUDDY!"

Overcoming her shock, she turned and peered back to the stairs as sounds of a heated discussion erupted from the den.

"You take a picture of his sister, too? Right here. Right here! You took this picture!" Just out of sight, she could make out Tracy's voice downstairs. She faced the den. Between her and him was Cassie. The possibility of Cassie turning around and seeing her made her nerves twist and stomachache. She tried to figure out how to make her way down to the den.

She pulled again to free herself from the guy's grip. With an eye on Cassie's curly hair, she put her foot on the first step. She paused when Tracy's accusing tone, "*You* took this picture," yanked her attention back to the conversation downstairs.

In that moment, while Tracy yelled at someone about a photo, Cassie was right in front of her. Kessy was tired of waiting for something to happen.

Then a pale face appeared at the bottom of the stairs. The pale face, another guy with blood under his nose, and Cory, the one who had found her outside, made their way upstairs. She tried to look behind them for Tracy or Jon. Instead, Cassie was turning around toward her.

Just then, Kessy was pulled back into the hall and pushed back as a stream of people poured out of the staircase. People were still yelling downstairs, but those who'd jammed into the staircase wanted out now. "You're gonna have to BACK the FUCK UP!" she heard Cory yell.

The commotion drew people from the next room wanting to see the results of the fight. She allowed herself to be pushed back away from the stairs and closer to the room she'd been in.

"Cassie!" The guy who gripped her arm and pulled her from the staircase stopped the dark blonde girl.

Cassie. It felt to be in her interest to know the girl's name if they were going to be face to face finally.

Kessy stared at Cassie's face as the guy told her something, she fixed on her piercing green eyes, they made Kessy nervous.

She couldn't hear what he told her, but felt her whole body shaking, readying herself for him to point her direction. When the guys with blood on their faces emerged, Kessy was pushed back farther, and when she got a glimpse back to where the two had been, they were gone.

At the moment when she should have been calling out for Jon or Tracy, she froze in panic. She didn't know what he had said to Cassie and now couldn't see where they'd gone. Greg pointed inside "She just went She clasped her trembling hands over her chest again, wondering when Tracy, Jon, and her brother would draw closer, whether she would be able to see them, and more importantly whether they would see her over the crowd. Taking a deep breath, she pushed back against the crowd toward the stairs and wondered if she had it in her to scream. If she did and one of the guys heard her, she wouldn't be so scared of Cassie.

Instead, she was shoved back. She felt herself shaking, and it grew more difficult to breathe, let alone scream for help. As the crowd grew, she would either be crushed into the wall or would have to stumble back into the room she'd been in. Feeling her eyes welling with frustration, she chose the room. She wondered what they would have done if they could have heard her scream.

Chapter 43

Cassie barely listened to Tom, an acquaintance of hers. She didn't realize he'd seen what she'd done in the attic, as Chris had done most of the retelling of the story to that point. For some reason she felt put on the spot as he gave her credit for taking the photo. She felt panic at the references to the photo. People started shoving.

Shit! I dropped the fucking camera and never got that photo out . . . Could it be the same photo? How the fuck did they get it?

He'd had only a fraction of her attention as he described some girl with a bloody nose who had been pursuing her down the stairs just now. But when he mentioned a "pink hoodie covered in blood," all the blood drained from her face. She glared down the hall for the girl he'd described.

She had just found her when a guy screamed, "CASSIE! HEY!"

It took her a second before she realized it was the guy who'd done most of the yelling in the den. *Chris told Matt, who told this guy!*

As Matt and Chris pushed quickly out, three more followed. She believed they were the same guys who had started the fight at the front door Friday night and now they were back to continue it inside their cabin. Her eyes met the guy carrying his buddy out of the den. She recognized the mark on his nose where he'd taken the bottle.

She glared at him. *YOU were at the door Friday night! YOU left bleeding!*

His cheeks were red and his face dripped sweat as he stared right back at her. When she caught a glimpse of the guy he carried, the sheer amount of blood that trailed over his face caused her to turn for that hall.

That fucking photo! I can't believe I dropped the god-damn camera!

Her eyes grew and arms trembled as she pushed people out of the way to make her way back to the room where she'd left that girl. If the girl heard the comments about the photo, she wouldn't stay quiet.

I must have dropped the goddamn camera on her! She fucking knows about it!

***

"KESS-SYYY! LAAAANE!"

Many of those who had backed up to the bedroom to avoid being crushed in the hallway now stood hoping to see some excitement as the two girls collided onto the bedroom floor. Cassie landed on top. It had seemed accidental at first, but Cassie was already losing her composure. Her red face and pursed lips intensified as the screaming for Kessy Lane continued.

The guy who was screaming reached the top of the stairs, and those standing in the hall or near the doorway didn't notice Cassie as she maneuvered her hands over the other girl's face and mouth. Cassie's actions were frantic and forceful, as though she were afraid of the girl in the pink hoodie. The screams from the hallway paralyzed those who did notice, driving out any inclination to help her from their minds.

In the hallway, the screaming guy emerged hunched over from the staircase. His clenched fists braced against the sides of the doorframe. Sweat dripped off his nose and cheeks. He struggled to breathe after the strain he had put on his voice. As he slowly stepped from the stairs into the living room, the silence between his screams was interrupted only by his labored breathing.

Meanwhile, in the bedroom, the girl in the pink hoodie was desperately trying to escape Cassie's grasp. The sounds of slapping, thudding, and scraping shoes were dulled by the carpet, and her screams were muffled by the full weight of Cassie's body mashing her face into the carpet.

"KESS-SSSYYYYY! LAAAAAANE!" The screaming continued in the living room, and they could hear the strain on his voice. As he did this a third time, Greg, a friend of Matt's who was standing near Cassie and saw the blood squirting from Kessy's nose onto Cassie's hands, took a step and kicked Cassie in her thigh. It had no effect on her.

A moment later the thrashing stopped and the crowd stood frozen, waiting. They stared at the wall or the floor, anywhere except at the guilt in each other's eyes. The silence that followed hung heavy in the room until a voice spoke from the hall.

"Who was that?" A girl in the hall asked this, sounding exhausted. She couldn't see Cassie in the room or hear the sound of Kessy's shoes as she thrashed beneath Cassie, but the others in the room could still feel them through the floor. For them, listening to a guy out there calling her name and witnessing her panic in here as Cassie attacked her was horrifying and nauseating first thing in the morning, most still hung over and unwilling to get involved.

It was the bystander effect for most, the few who weren't still sleeping it off. First standing by while Cassie smothered the girl in the pink hoodie, while a guy tore the cabin apart screaming for her; then after it was over, only one was brave enough to raise concern.

The sound of the screen door screeching open and hissing shut was a welcome interruption. Just as those near the hallway began moving at the sound of the door, several paused for the question put to Cassie by the one guy who took issue with Cassie kicking Kessy.

Greg glared at her as he spoke. "Why'd you do that? What'd she do?"

Cassie stood slowly, staring at the bloody mess on her hands, and was unaffected by the questions being hurled at her.

"Cassie, why'd you do that? What'd she do?"

He demanded an answer, but she gave no indication that he was getting through. Greg's eyes grew in shock at her lack of response, appearing ready to grab her this time to snap her out of her daze and get an answer. As Cassie took a step back, he reached out to do just that when she finally acknowledged him, returning his glare.

His hand didn't reach her, but he still spoke bluntly, "Why?"

She stared at him, and then finally responded. She was out of breath, and as a result he barely heard her.

"She was coming after me . . . she's high."

Greg took in the sight of the girl's lifeless body whose hood now covered her face. Cassie got out as the smell of urine drifted from the bedroom, and the rest of the room swiftly cleared.

Laura asked Greg as he left the room, "What'd she say?"

"Cassie's high! She's fucking delusional. That girl didn't come down the hall after her to deserve that. Cassie just pummeled her!"

He said this and Laura was sure Cassie had heard him. She glanced back at the girl on the floor for a second; no one made any attempt to help her.

They're all scared of Cassie after seeing what she can do when someone screams for her. And that guy screaming in general, no one wants anything to do with this.

Laura and a few others followed him out the back door of the cabin, hoping to find out what had happened. Moving past the kitchen, Laura saw Cassie at the sink washing her hands. Laura waited until they were outside before weighing in.

"That girl's been in that room since—"

"Who is she?" Greg cut her off as he pulled out a cigarette.

"I don't know. I think Cassie knows her. That girl in the pink hoodie was in the attic with her on Friday. I'm beginning to think they both used. Cassie sounded like she was really ready for round 2 with her last night."

Greg pointed inside "She just went one round with her in there! She had blood all down the front of her hoodie before Cassie went after her! You didn't see what she just did!"

"I didn't witness it either time! But I heard Cassie describe how that girl tried to leave and Chris brought her back to the room. They made her sound like a violent person and—"

He interrupted her, "I know. I heard about what happened in the attic. There are about five different versions of what happened, but that pink hoodie girl was beaten bloody then moved to that same room by Cassie. I think it's safe to say that Cassie's the violent one after what she just did to that girl!"

Laura dropped her head, speaking quietly, "You're just as uneasy around her as I am."

"What?"

Turning back to him, she said, "How did Cassie look when she stood up? Was she smirking?"

He tapped the end of his cigarette. "Cassie looked satisfied. She told me she thought that girl was after her. When she was by the staircase, that girl said something but the guy in there stopped her. He told her she didn't want to go down to where that fight was happening. Even if she did say something about going after Cassie, she wasn't capable of doing anything; she wasn't any kind of threat!"

"She might have been! I went in to talk to her after I listened to Cassie; I wasn't in the room five minutes before Cassie burst in and kicked me out. I think there's something going on between those two that's beyond our—"

"You said round 2!" He pointed inside, interrupting her again. "I think she *wanted* to do that! I don't think the girl was after her nor do I believe she was high. I think Cassie enjoyed that!

"and those guys who just screamed their way out have something to do with it! Maybe they know that pink hoodie girl or Cassie does!" He took another drag, pointing again. "But that right there, what Cassie did, fucking smothering her like that into submission. In front of people! If the guys who were screaming and starting fights know who she is and they're staying in the rental, they'll be back real soon."

"That's what Chris said when I was asking Cassie why she was smirking during the conversation! He said those guys—"

Greg's eyes grew wide. "She was smirking because she's a sadist."

"What! A sadist? Seriously?"

A wide-eyed shock covered the face of one of Cassie's friends who shook his head as he cut in to their conversation. A young guy with a faded black shirt and cargo shorts standing a few feet from them was shaking his head as he pulled drags off a cigarette. He didn't make eye contact with Greg as he pushed back on his word choice.

"Cassie never used! That pink hoodie bitch did, and Cassie was forced to react! I saw her follow Cassie down the hall." He glanced at Greg. "How would you have handled that shit? A druggie gunning for you? You think that makes her a sadist? You're an asshole. What the fuck would you have done differently? Believe it or not, what Cassie did just now was brave!"

He took another drag off his cigarette after he said this, glancing at the cabin in the direction of the hall.

After a moment Greg responded, "You didn't see it happen."

Chapter 44

Cory, taken back by the yelling in the playback, examined the small screen for some detail to spark his memory.

When was this? I think I filmed this. What was happening?

He asked himself questions as he saw the footage, the small screen clogged with people moving in the direction of the playback on its way up a staircase. The growing sound of yelling at the top of the stairs gripped his interest.

Where was I going? What are they yelling at?

As the playback began to shake, it became difficult to stay with it.

I was shaking 'cause I was excited. I wanted to see what everyone was yelling at and get it on film!

Cory stayed with it for a moment more before the footage was just too unsettling. Closing the screen, the energy the footage created in him was stifling the embarrassment he'd felt after having his face grabbed and having it pointed out by Cassie. She and Matt had been just behind him when he went in, but apparently hadn't followed.

I want her to see this!

The thought of showing Cassie the footage and having her brother Matt involved brought a mischievous smile to Cory's face as he made his way out of the attic.

She wanted to know what I did.

This was as far as his plan went. His recollection of capturing the footage was part memory and part imagined. But the desire to build on the controlling feeling the footage gave him motivated a decision to present it for them to figure out.

The same emboldened feeling he'd had as he climbed out of the den and yelled at people returned to him now as he made his way out of the attic, clutching the camera.

It didn't take long to find both Cassie and Matt. As he got outside and turned to the clearing, he saw them standing as though they'd been in conversation.

As Cassie saw him, breathing out the smoke from her cigarette, his blood rushed with excitement. *Waitin' for me!*

He made his way through the clearing, kicking stones toward them while stifling a grin, thinking about the footage as they both noticed the camera. He hoped he would be met with little resistance.

He was a few yards away and clutched the camera tighter with his sweaty palm. He had to lift it for her and not let it slip from his hand. Matt flicked his cigarette butt and reached for the camera before Cassie could even react.

Cory said nothing as Matt opened the screen, inspected it for damage, then promptly closed it. Matt stared at him, waiting for Cory to explain himself.

Cory boasted to Cassie, "You wanted to know why that guy was yelling at me in the den!" She took another drag off her cigarette as she sneered at him. "I got footage."

"Of what?" Matt responded quickly.

It was quiet for a moment. Matt glanced at the camera in his hands. "Where did you find this? You dropped it in the den after that guy yelled at you for using it." He thought about it as he wiped the screen with his finger. "We left before they did, and we heard that guy that you put on the floor screaming his way through the cabin."

Growing impatient for an answer, Matt glared at Cory and repeated his question, "Footage of what? What did that guy do that you got on film that pissed him off enough to scream at you in the den?"

Cory named off the elements that grabbed his attention, hoping for a reaction that would take the glare off him and put it on the footage. "I was on my way back to the attic, but a crowd had gathered. I had trouble getting up the stairs because of it.

The crowd was yelling at something, and I did my damndest to get it on film."

"You mean the den," Cassie corrected him. "That guy was yelling at you in the den."

"No, this was . . . before that." He tried to remember when exactly that footage had happened. It was days ago. But it felt as though he could try and weave it into their first encounter with the people from that cabin. "This was when they banged on the door the first time!"

"You didn't have the camera the first time!" Matt retorted. "You were too busy throwing a bottle at—"

"After they left!" Cory said, interrupting. "When I went back up to the attic, just after those guys left."

"That doesn't make sense."

"Everyone was screaming and yelling in the attic the same way they were at the front door. That's what I was making my way up to get on film." Cory powered through with the details he remembered.

A sense of invigoration rocketed through Cory like lightning when Matt's glare turned to Cassie. Hers stayed on Cory for a moment even as Matt turned his attention to the camera, pulling the screen and pushing the buttons.

Cassie glared at Cory while a smile gently pulled his lips and eyes wider. He felt smug, knowing Matt was being pulled into watching the footage that would presumably explain why Cory was being yelled at.

"We were both in the attic, Cory!" Matt closed the screen, staring at the camera. "You said that same guy was messing with you in the den! Same guy who was screaming at you now." Matt shook his head as his eyes grew. "I don't know why I didn't remember that sooner! You've been up to a lot of shit since the moment we got here."

The smile vanished from Cory's face as his gaze drifted. Having to recall further detail from his trek up to the attic began feeling like voyeurism. But he was growing desperate to get

Matt's attention back on the camera. "People were yelling, 'Let her up.'"

"What?" Matt sounded confused as he opened the screen again. As Matt maneuvered the buttons, Cory wasn't sure if this was even accurate, but it felt familiar. Unable to remember if he'd captured those words in the footage, Matt slowly brought the screen closer. When he rewound it further than it needed at first before hitting play, Cory didn't recognize the footage before it. The video was quiet for some time before it cut away to yelling in the distance.

The sound of excited yelling grew louder. None of it was understandable, but the tone was fervent. It carried on for longer than Cory remembered. Matt began adjusting the volume to try and hear the voices in the footage.

"Let her up! Let her up!"

Oh my God! What the fuck?

The sound of yelling crackling through the tiny speakers captured the attention of Cassie, Cory, and Matt as they leaned into the screen. Matt's thumb shifted over the buttons and the yelling stopped. As he held the screen close to his face, Cory realized that he'd shut the screen before seeing what Matt had just seen. He quickly felt as though, with one viewing of the footage, Matt had figured it out.

"You held the camera up!" he said rather matter of factly. "You panned to try and find the action! And you found it a few times!"

Cory immediately wanted to see the footage again. He realized that the first time he'd seen it he'd been too eager to present it to Cassie. Now he had shown it to Matt long before he understood or remembered what all had happened.

"Does it look like the photo you saw?" Cory asked him a bit flippantly.

Matt remained silent as he peered into the display.

At the sound of footsteps on the gravel behind him, Cory turned around to see Chris staring at the camera as he made his way over. "Matt! What are you looking at?"

"Cory decided to locate my uncle's camera on our first night here after he threw a bottle at the guy who hit you this morning. He said he went back to the attic after he threw the bottle."

Chris stood by Cory. "You're talking about that guy who stayed? The one that was hysterical who approached us in the living room? He wasn't with the group this morning, not that I saw at least."

"Before that," Matt said. "We were in the living room talking about what had happened. But I think this footage was from just before our conversation, when that guy approached us."

"What are you trying to find in the footage?" Chris asked him.

"Trying to find out what Cory went *back* for!"

Chapter 45

Matt's eyes slowly traveled up from the screen at Cory, anger and resentment in them, as though he'd figured him out.

"You said yourself you went *back* to the attic. Why'd you go *back*?"

"What are you talking about?" Cory began losing his confidence.

"Cassie said she found pink hoodie girl up there. I was confused by that until you said you went *back* to the attic." He turned off the playback and held it in his hand, "You brought a fucking camera with you when you went back!

Cory felt himself sinking.

"You came out here and presented this camera with so much pride! Saying that the reason you were yelled at in the den this morning was in the footage. I'd say the reason you laughed in their face the first time they knocked on our door and spoke of a pink hoodie is what's in this footage."

Cory began, "What's in the foot—"

"You lied." Matt cut him off as the words slid off his tongue like silk, spoken with sure confidence.

"I didn't get footage of—" Cory tried to back track before Matt cut him off.

"*You liiied!*" He spoke through his teeth, not yelling, but instead drew the words out.

Cory's heart raced again. His confidence had completely vanished. While he continued to make eye contact with Matt, he felt his body shake, intimidated by Matt's anger.

Matt glanced at the camera in his hand, "You lowered the camera."

"Wha—" he started to ask, feeling a weight in his chest as he reached for the camera. He didn't know what the hell Matt meant.

"You were probably disappointed you missed it. Or so you thought . . ." He had everyone's attention now, as well as a bit of their fear.

Though believing Matt was mixing up the encounter in the attic for the one at the front door, Cory was too unsure of himself to respond after he kept cutting him off.

"What made you go back?" asked Matt.

Cory felt his lips quiver.

"Th-the commotion."

Matt's eyes burned into Cory's as he asked again, "What made you go *back to the attic*? What did you want to get on film?"

A long, heavy, and awkward silence ensued. Cory didn't know what Matt wanted him to say. When the words *I found a girl in a pink hoodie outside* spoke through his mind like a recollection, but he was too fucking scared to say them.

I brought her inside to warm up . . . went back for the camera . . . I think I was gonna go back up anyway. But in the photo they had in the den, someone was on the floor, surrounded. Someone fucked her up. Whatever they did, they used Matt's uncle's stuff to get a picture of it. Does he really think I did that?

"You got it!" Matt declared. There was a moment of silence before pushing his point. "The only thing you have filmed with my uncle's camera! And you filmed it every fucking chance you got!" He glanced at the screen. "This footage is complete bullshit; you don't just film this type of thing then turn off the camera. You had a plan, missed your chance and started filming anyway. I want to know what you wanted her to do and what you assured her you had in the attic to persuade her."

"That footage is the detail that you didn't want to know about." Cassie spoke quietly to Matt "Does it remind you of what you did just now in the den?"

Cory didn't know where Matt was going with this and hearing Cassie comment to Matt as she did, led him to believe they both already knew the story Matt was pushing Cory to recall.

"I believe you. But even if this was the result, it still doesn't explain how she got in. I think Cory knows and he's trying to distract from having to explain what he was after with this."

"Matt, what's going on?" Chris asked uneasily.

Matt didn't respond to Chris, his unwavering eyes stayed on Cory.

Chris pleaded, "What did Cory film?"

Finally addressing him, Matt said, "Cassie told me you spoke to the girl in the pink hoodie. The same one that was in the photo. She got what Cory promised her, then she stood up and you spoke with her."

"Cory wasn't there." Chris spoke to correct him.

"You were standing by when that photo was taken."

"Yeah, but Cory wasn't in the room."

"Cory filmed that."

"No he didn't."

Matt and Cassie glanced at each other, he and Chris were going in circles.

"You need to be reminded?" Matt held the camera out to Chris.

Chris was reluctant to take it. When he did, pinching a cigarette between two fingers, Cory's attention followed the camera as Matt's attention stayed on him. He listened to the playback once more, trying to remember more from it. His mind was distracted by the guilt as long as Matt stood nearby.

They listened to the playback again. Cory could feel Matt's eyes on him as he waited to hear it again. He had the feeling that telling Matt that he'd brought a girl up to the attic would somehow confirm his understanding of what Cory was up to.

As the playback grew louder, Cory closed his eyes. He tried to remember more of what he had seen when he had stood at the top of the stairs. The camera had missed a lot that he'd heard. He remembered feeling compelled to climb to the top of the stairs when he heard someone asking, '*I didn't hear you what did you say?*' the repeated question that did not make the playback. Why the hell it didn't get recorded, he didn't know. Then he remembered.

The camera only picked up yelling because that's what was going on in the living room still. And I think my hand was on the fucking mic again, like it was when Chris roughed that guy up. I was holding the camera like a football 'cause I was shaking.

He opened his eyes, now thinking about Chris, remembering that he'd recognized the voice before he'd understood the words.

I wanted to know who he was talking to. That's why I tried to get back up there.

Cory said, "I could hear you all the way down at the bottom of the stairs."

Matt glared at him with crossed arms.

"I wanted to know who you were talking to." Cory stared into space for a moment. "You said, 'I didn't hear you. What did you say?' over and over again. I wanted to know who you were talking to."

"He was talking to the same person you were coming back for!" Cassie informed him "You haven't denied it so it must be accurate."

Chris said, "Yeah I said, it to a girl Cassie found in the attic. I was asking her about her drug use."

Matt and Cassie glanced at each other again.

"What did she tell you?" Matt asked him.

"Nothing. Whatever it was, she wouldn't repeat it. She just stood there with a wicked nose bleed. I think it was her first time using."

"She *knew* what she was doing and she wouldn't let you drag her plan out of her." Cassie asserted.

After hearing that she'd used drugs Cory glanced over to the side of the cabin where he'd found her curled in a ball and shivering. Now learning that she'd had a plan, it was a creepy image.

Matt turned back to Cory, "Cory. Chris and I were standing in the living room and we were approached by a guy in a blue Blink 182 shirt who had been at the front door when you threw the bottle. He behaved almost the same way goat head guy did when he was yelling a you in the den, the same one you pointed out in the attic. Did one of them see you bring her up to the attic? That I think might justify the way they've since they knocked on our door. That would make sense to me."

Listening to Matt devise scenarios was nauseating. Cory was still thinking about her drug use that Chris and Cassie spoke of. The girl he'd encountered didn't strike him as the type, she seemed shy. If it had happened, she might have been forced. With Cassie's aggressive nature and how she spoke of a plan, her grabbing the poor girl by the back of the head more sense to Cory.

"What would make sense to me is if one of those guys saw the way she was treated in the attic. Either of those guys saw something happen. One of them had the photo where she was laying on the floor. The way Cassie knew what she was doing and had a plan and the fact that Chris got nothing out of her. I wonder if Cassie had a hand in her drug use. Hand on the back of head type of thing. If she fell forward it would account for her position in the photo."

Cory glanced at Cassie to see her glaring eyes. It was enough for him to search the gravel by his feet after suggesting this. No one said anything for some time, it felt as though Cory had addressed the elephant in the discussion.

This made for an uneasy silence just as the sound of footsteps making their way over the gravel toward them, pulled their attention. Their heads turned to see the guy Matt had clotheslined a few hours ago along with the guy who followed up after him.

"What's your name, man?" asked Chris.

"Tracy."

Chapter 46

Tracy glanced at the disheveled guy next to him, the one Matt had clotheslined and was writhing in the dirt a few hours ago his short curly hair still dusted, "This is Josh. Right now what you're discussing is his sister!"

The lot of them stared at him.

"Continue!" Tracy demanded.

Fuuuck! Did they hear what I said about her being forced by Cassie? Praying neither heard it so he wouldn't have to repeat it. Cory was still scared of Tracy and couldn't make eye contact with him. He saw the state of the poor guy Matt clotheslined, still disheveled, his gray hoodie and blue jeans still dusted as his hair was. Though he kept his face down, Cory could tell Joshes neck was red, scraped raw from what the group had done to him. Cory couldn't bring himself to even glance in their direction after that.

Chris handed the camera back to Matt, who promptly opened it and began messing with the buttons.

He's gonna show him that footage? Bad idea!

"Said your name is Tracy?" Matt clarified.

"Yeah," Tracy said with one eye on Matt and the other keenly on the camera.

"I'm Matt. This cabin belongs to my uncle."

Matt rewound the tape. Cassie turned avoiding this conversation; she headed swiftly back to the cabin.

As the sound of the playback began, Josh barely acknowledged any of it, terrified of being by Matt again. Cory wondered how Tracy would react to it.

What the fuck is he gonna tell this Tracy guy when the tape ends, and there is nothing to see?

He knew that if he stayed out there that sooner or later, attention would turn to him. Matt would credit him as the cameraman. *They don't know I found her.*

Cory wanted to lie through his teeth, but he'd let it slip that he'd gone *back* to that room. He wanted to get away as Cassie had.

I found your sister. I brought her into the attic, and that was it.

He felt like there was nothing more he could say, but that footage suggested much more. When Chris left, he tried to justify how he could leave too.

Is she still here?

He was uncomfortable but could not bring himself to leave. He felt forced to stay and wait for their reaction to it. He searched for a reason to be pulled inside and away from this.

Then the words started, squeezing out of the tiny speaker.

"Let her up! Let her up!"

Tracy and Josh leaned into the screen to process what they were hearing. Tracy demanded an explanation from Matt.

"What did I just watch?"

Cory was sweating. *Matt has no fucking clue how to answer! He should not have shown them the tape!*

"The photo you showed me . . ." Tracy reached into his back pocket and presented it. "The one you walked away from."

"It was taken in the attic, with my uncle's camera," Matt explained.

"Who took it?" Tracy answered quickly

"My sister Cassie."

"Point her out."

Matt pointed back to the cabin. "Curly blonde hair—"

Tracy turned to the cabin, then peering back at Matt in surprise. "Your sister, the one who walked away when we got here?"

Matt shook his head, "Your girl was *found* in our attic, she was up there doing lines when you were banging on our door. After you had left, she went at my sister and ended up on the floor." Matt pointed at the screen. "That's what that reaction is for."

Tracy crossed his arms, "What do you mean *went at*?"

"Your sister got aggressive after she used. The result of that is what you just saw on the screen."

"You saw this happen? You watched her do your drugs and lash out at your sister?" Tracy asked him.

"It's what we were just talking about! I asked Cassie because I thought it was her in the Polaroid. I'm learning more as I go more about what the guys who rented our Uncles cabin down the path have been doing since they first banged on our door! It sounds as though her efforts to get her fix and lash out are real parallel to the rest of her gang when it comes to confrontation."

Matt glared at Tracy who appeared shocked by this information. He glared back at him, shaking his head as a sense of absurdity quickly overtook Tracy's face. He searched Matt's face for falsity, as though he'd made this up to stop Tracy from confronting him.

Matt waited for a reaction to this information, expecting some weakening of Tracy's approach than a comment. He hoped to hear Tracy say Ron; it would confirm what Cassie said.

When Tracy began searching the gravel and dirt By their feet while trying to make sense of what had Matt said, felt as though this were the moment Cory and Matt were waiting for.

When he faced Matt a confused expression, one that pulled his eyes covered his face.

"We haven't slept since Friday or changed clothes because we saw a photo with his sister face down and surrounded. And we didn't understand why!" Tracy spoke as though searching for words "You said your Uncle owns that cabin? If he saw something like that with your sister in a similar position, how would he have reacted?

Tracy's head turned for a moment after raising his voice, taking a breath, peering at him "I'm pretty sure he would have assumed the fucking worst" gesturing to Josh "just like he did when he saw it! He would be suspicious of everyone in that place and want to know what the fuck was going on!

Tracy leaned into his questions, "Is your Uncle the type to assume rape? Or carry a gun? If it involves family, that doesn't sound unreasonable for a guy that makes smut films. He would protect his interests and his family above all else!"

"What did you tell him when you rented?" Matt demanded

"The father of the young woman on the floor in that pic is the one who spoke to him. Do you think your Uncle will follow up after the weekends over?" He paused and let the question linger.

Matt responded calmly "My Uncle uses the appeal of having family up the path as a way to make the sale on a rental. I guarantee your dad learned that fact, someone in your crew heard it. 'If you guys need anything, my niece and nephew are just up the path' someone heard that pitch; her brother, you, someone." Matt pushed back.

Cory trembled with excitement after Matt said this. It felt like such a good point. How else did they know to come up the path?

Tracy shook his head as he spoke: "Even if Kessy learned names from her dad, that sense of familiarity did not do her any good." He explained to Matt "She made her way up here Friday night after getting turned around in the fog; someone approached her. We saw it happen in the footage on that tape Jon stole a few hours ago!

"Kessy didn't trespass; the person who found her is out of view, they put the camera down to take her inside."

"She didn't say a word!" Cory blurted this out with little thought. Josh broke his preoccupation with the ground as all their eyes grew on Cory, causing him to stagger in his train of thought. Searching for the rest of the story that went with this, their reaction forced him to drag up the memory. "She didn't know anything, I. . ."

His hand trembled as he pulled his fingers over his scalp, as he tried to remember if she had said anything and then what he did with her.

"I brought her inside. . ." He searched for the story, now wanting to shift attention back on to Tracy, "because she was shivering in the cold. I couldn't get a word out of her, she decided on the attic on her own."

"She didn't say a word, but decided on the attic? What did she point?" Tracy questioned his story.

Cory avoided the question as he belted out what he recalled "It wasn't until you banged on our door and berated us that the conversation could continue around the girl! I remember that crystal clear. You were high and talked about having seen a pink hoodie just before you began throwing punches. After you had left, we found out what was going on. There's no reasoning much less conversing with a person when their high and behaving the way you were!"

Tracy glared at Cory after he'd avoided his question, presented himself as suspicious then attempt to throw the blame back to their encounter at the door.

Tracy slowly turned back to Matt, red faced and restraining his tone "Go check your uncle's cabin for the drugs you believed we were supposed to have been high on. There would be *some* evidence of use. Unlike your group, we didn't—"

"It's what your girl was found doing in that attic." Matt cut him off, pointing to the cabin

"You're suggesting Kessy had something with her and used in your attic?" Tracy snapped back.

"My sister found her in a fetal position on the couch! By the time you were banging on our door she was already paranoid and high." Matt said "That's part of the reason that Cassie took it I'd say, ensuring that you're aware of this behavior! Along with the fact that when she got up, she told our friend Chris that she was going to do something she wouldn't repeat."

Tracy shook his head, thumbing to Josh "You're telling me your sister needed proof of his sister on the floor after doing lines and becoming aggressive? That's the justification for the chaos you just showed me? That was *your* sister reacting to *his* sister's behavior."

He continued "That playback is a person doing drugs in an environment like your attic out of habit. That person then behaves violently like shoving a person to the floor for as pithy a reason like an article of clothing and drug induced paranoia. The desire to capture that moment by taking a photo of Kessy surrounded by the crowd I just saw in the video..." Tracy paused a moment, then questioned Matt "Why would your sister treat Kessy that way unless she gets off on it? Unless she was using—"

"You're a fucking asshole Tracy." Matt let the uneasy weight of this insult linger for a moment "You think my sister used? You're not listening, or you just don't want to hear it."

"Why didn't your sister just kick Kessy out when she found her? And by kick her out I don't mean your sisters foot in her back." Tracy demanded this question of Matt, but their mutual hostility was bringing their exchange to a place of stalemate.

Tracy's perspective sounded as though he desperately wanted to blame Cassie for the pink hoodies drug use. But after hearing the playback again, Tracy's take on it forced Cory to think back on the course of events after their confrontation. He forgot about Matt's sister's direct nature for the moment. Could Cassie have used before she confronted that girl? It would in a way, explain the sounds of chaos Tracy described in the playback.

With the quiet, a sweaty awkwardness set in as Tracy glared right through Matt. Cory's anxiety grew, anticipating Matt turning to him and telling him to explain what he'd recorded. If he was the one who brought Kessy inside, then she decided on the attic, was she carrying anything as had been suggested?

Her hands were in the pocket of her pink hoodie. If she had something on her, it was hidden. I left her in the attic. She had time before that commotion happened.

This response began to formulate in his head, one that would leave the implication open. But after the chaotic fight club like scene he'd been so eager to capture on film, it would also thrust question upon him. The way Tracy had jumped down Matt's throat; Cory knew the guy would ask him why he had the camera and what exactly he had intended to get on film?

He didn't have an answer for this that didn't feel skeevy, and as the drug suggestion was solid, Cory was desperately pulling his mind to remember holding the camera at the top of the stairs or create a convincing story within his brief encounter with Kessy to tell this guy.

"What happened was she made her way into our cabin, and this was something she was seen doing."

Cory cringed as Matt tried to push back and Tracy kept going.

"Then she didn't have a choice. Kessy Lane isn't the type to do that sort of thing on her own accord. I believe she was forced by the same girl who just put her on the floor. Her hand on the back of her neck shoving her head into your uncle's table! Is your uncle here? Did he watch this shit happen?"

He heard me! Cory felt the burn in his cheeks as his face turned red knowing he'd been overheard. But it sounded made up coming from him. Cory didn't think Tracy knew the first thing about Cassie; he was only interested in finding someone to blame.

"Tracy, No. You heard us discussing this when you came up just now! I'm telling you what happened by what she was seen doing. I wasn't involved with your girl!"

"Her name is Kessy!" Tracy declared

"I wasn't involved with her! Now, I can explain what she did, but if you're only interested in creating blame, I can let you know that when you started that fight this morning, it led to Kessy approaching Cassie again and her having to defend herself" Matt pointed at the cabin "right in that hallway!

"You shocked everyone out of bed then forced them to defend themselves this morning." gesturing to Josh "Starting with him charging up here, then you started another fight, Kessy continued it, and Cassie finished it. Now your girl was probably still high at the time. If you're so convinced she's not the type, then she likely had an adverse reaction, but she was seen by multiple people, approaching Cass."

"You said Cassie *defended* herself?"

"Kessy made her way into the attic on Friday night, and she was out of her head until Sunday morning. What Cassie told me is that Kessy tried to follow her down the staircase this morning when you were in the den. One of the guys stopped her at the top of the stairs, and Kessy described Cassie to him; hair and eye color. She was warned that a girl in a pink hoodie, who was bleeding down her face, was after her.

"Kessy made no mention of your yelling or fighting; her focus was Cass; she was fixated on her. Cass told me that the guys at the top of the stairs yelled down at her for this girl in her bloody pink hoodie. Only when you guys started to scream—"

"Wait, wait." Tracy shook his head, interrupting him "You're telling me that Kessy wanted some guys to get your sister for her? With her brother and her friends yelling in the den, she asked for help confronting your sister?"

Matt took a moment with this question, before reiterating "The behavior of someone who's under the influence, they're not thinking clearly. It sounds to me like you don't know your friend as well as you thought you did."

It was quiet for a moment as they glared at each other. Josh's head dropped, shaking in response to this, still too unnerved to look Matt in the eye. He spoke softly "What was happening to her that whole time?"

"What'd you say?" Cory asked

"What was—"

Josh started, and Cory cut him off.

"Man, speak up."

"What was happening to her that whole time?" Tracy stepped in, staring down Cory for his attitude before turning back to Matt, "You said Friday night until this morning, what was—"

"Kessy was coming down off her high, would be my guess!" Matt declared "If it was her first time as Cass suggested and she had such an adverse reaction to it if she didn't get another fix then she had to come down. Your girl had to detox."

Josh looked up at Matt red faced, "Did anyone take advantage of her during that time?"

An awkward silence ensued as Matt just stared at him.

Josh spoke up "Something like the type of stuff that was on the tape Jon stole? Like the smut your Uncle made?"

"Did you see your sister in it?" Matt asked with disbelief.

Matt stared at Josh, waiting for an answer until his head dropped again then he went back to Tracy "I was trying to tell you, it was only when you guys disrupted our whole cabin, that your girl was pushed back with everyone else and Cassie was forced to deal with her. Especially after your boy started wailing, forcing everyone to deal with your crew a bit longer."

Tracy shook his head, crossing his arms "So Kessy knew your sister's name. If she asked for help confronting your sister Cass, Kessy learned her name. From the sounds of it, your sister dehumanized her the same way you have by referring to her by a pink hoodie." Matt glanced away, shaking his head. "That makes it easier for you to believe someone's an addict that needed your cabin for a fix."

"You're not hearing me, man!" The gravel was coming through as Matt sounded fed up.

Tracy leaned into his words "What you're saying is your sister thought Jon was searching for her? Is that it?"

"Is that his name?"

"He was screaming *Kessy Lane*! You heard him; your whole cabin heard him! The girl in the pic that your sister took" Tracy's eyes widened with shock and disgust covered his face, "*Cassie* is your sister's name?"

"Yeah. . . I"

Matt's eyes wandered as he thought of the similarities, as the sound of kicked up gravel, spraying through the clearing behind them pulled their attention. The same guy, Jon who screamed his way out as he left a few hours ago, trampling the rocks as he glanced over in Cory's direction several times while the guy with him, who was also in the den, glanced at Tracy but his attention was on the cabin.

Goat head guy is back. Same one I put on the floor who was wailing at Cassie is back. His face is all red from my hittin' him in his eyes. Cory studied him as he passed them, his blue jeans and black shirt a mess of water saturation and dirt; *he went in the lake with his clothes on. All of these guys are wearing the same clothes since they banged on our door Friday night; they've been wearing the same clothes all weekend.*

That same surge of energy ran through Cory as the thought of being eye to eye with him again.

Jon

Tracy turned to Josh. "Go; you got friends inside. Go find Kessy."

Josh turned to them, hesitated for a moment then walked away and in the direction Cassie went. Matt waited until Josh made his way in the front and Jon and the guy with him went in the back door of the cabin before continuing.

"That's unfortunate. His sisters' name is Kessy. I never knew her name, from the sounds of it neither did my sister."

"No one thought to ask this girl what her name is? Before she was attacked or had her face shoved in whatever your friends laid out for her?"

"They were probably still talking about the gang who was banging on the front door, the same ones from this morning who were hassling us the moment they banged on our door; they appeared high and frantic our first night here!

"The only thing we knew is that these guys behaved as though they were high and kept naming a pink hoodie before they started swinging! I thought that was a terrible way to start our weekend off, but when Cassie told me that someone who fit the description was in our attic, I knew something was going on. Your girl in her pink hoodie was in our attic looking for more. I think it was easy to assume the guys staying at the cabin down the path, were a bunch of coked out hotheads and their pink hoodie was the same way. By the time you guys approached us screaming for a fight this morning, it wouldn't have mattered what her name was, our opinion of you is solid!"

Matt was quiet for a moment "This is the conversation you should have had the first time you banged on our door! Instead, you tried to start a fight which forced everyone to make up their mind about your sister. So when Cassie put her on the floor, it seems to me that Cass responded the only way she could!"

"Sounds as though you believe Kessy deserved what your sister did to her?" Tracy retorted, "It sounds as though you weren't at all curious as to what was going on. You laughed in our faces the first time we knocked on your door, Matt!

You made up your minds about us and decided that the girl who fit our description needed to pay? Why the fuck wasn't she kicked out? It sounds to me like your sister Cassie was going after Kessy intentionally!"

"Tracy, I told you! Cassie *found* her in the attic! She was already up there, and was seen doing."

Tracy pointed to the camera still in Matt's hands, "And you just found your Uncles camera to try and film what Cassie did to her!"

"I didn't film this!"

"Who did?"

 Matt pointed at Cory, "He did."

"As I said, I found her by the side of the cabin" Cory stated.

"And as you said, she didn't say a word but chose the attic on her own!" Tracy barked at him.

"I brought her up to the attic to warm up. If she had something on her, she was hiding it. She had time up there before all that happened."

Tracy glared at him, waiting for the rest of the story. After the playback they'd just seen, Cory knew his answer would seem like a malicious lie.

"...and I left her there to do her thing. I wasn't part of what she did ..." He hesitated for a second, then said, "... I just filmed the reaction."

"You just *filmed it*!? Tracy said, glaring.

Tracy let the awkward nature of this statement rest in the air for a second before continuing. Crossing his arms, "You sound like you were concerned for her up until you found her outside." Tracy thought about this for a moment then declared "Then you switched the tapes.

"The guy inside that yelled at you in the den, Jon; he stole the tape out of the camera after you guys left. We saw what you filmed." Tracy turned and pointed to the corner of the cabin. "You left the camera on the rocks over there. Kessy was photographed, and you wanted to film her attack, or you wanted to film her trying what you made available to her." Tracy paused for a moment, letting the awkward feeling this behavior brought up settle in. "Kessy Lane is not the type of girl to get involved in what you brought her to; she wouldn't know how to use what you showed her. She's also not the kind of girl to ignore a friend who sounds as though he is losing his mind trying to find her!"

Cory's head dropped unable to engage Tracy, feeling his whole body shaking as he was accused of introducing Kessy to drugs. It sounded realistic, as though these were the details Cory had left out. Cory glared at the dirt, grass, and gravel at his feet, his ability to explain his leaving her in the room had been crippled. Unable explain why as his memory was fixated on blaming Tracy for their confrontation at the door.

As Tracy turned and walked toward the cabin, Matt began walking a few paces behind him; it didn't feel over as a new voice was heard yelling through the cabin.

"Kessy Lane! We're looking for Kessy Lane! Do you know where she is? She'd been in this cabin since Friday."

"That's Dan" Tracy declared as though introductions were finally in order.

"You guys are back? What is your problem!" A girl's voice yelled back at Dan.

"Her name is Kessy Lane, have you seen her? She's wearing a pink hoodie!"

The sound of Dan finally yelling through the cabin; like a cacophony ricocheting off the walls inside was overtaken by Jon.

"What's your name? What's your name?" You could tell his voice was hoarse, but he just kept going. "WHAT'S your *FUCKING* NAME?" He sounded like he was an identification away from killing someone. "TELL ME! YOUR FUCKING NAAAAME!"

"Her name is Cassie! The same one you were screaming at this morning! Now you found her, are you done screaming?" the same girl that yelled a moment ago.

The sound of shattering glass bottle broke Jon's tirade, as though a bottle was thrown at him this time. It was painful to hear this wailing again. They weren't putting up with it.

"Jon back off! Back off! Josh go." Dan commanded.

"Get away from me! Get the fuck away from me!" another guy's voice demanded.

This new voice was so overwhelmed it had to be Josh.

Cory watched Tracy disappear into the cabin, followed by Matt who turned to him and tossed the camera like he wanted nothing more to do with it. Being accused of getting that girl on drugs was unexpected and made him sick. The thought of getting the camera back made him want to smash it to pieces.

Chapter 47

I wanna hear Cassie explain this to Tracy the way Matt tried to. Cory wondered how Cassie would react to his unrelenting approach.

The idea of these two getting involved made Cory's blood rush. He wanted to do two things: relieve the feeling that Tracy had put in the pit of his stomach by being there when he found Kessy, and he wanted to hear Tracy address that photo with Cassie.

The back screen door was out of view with people so tightly squeezed together wanting to see what was going on; they stood on their toes to witness the scene. Jon's yelling surprised him.

Believing that Jon and Dan had found Kessy and taken her out of the cabin, for a moment he wanted to shove his way through just to see the color of the girl's hoodie. *I'm not gettin' through that.* Then he heard Cassie's voice out back.

Chapter 48

Jon felt as though he'd truly ruptured something inside his throat this time, and his head felt like it was swimming on his shoulders. He felt high, or what he imagined it was like to be high, as he tried to remain standing by a girl who glared at him while Matt avoided him.

He had gotten Cristy's emotional story about the guy they'd seen in the kitchen, and then the moment he and Dan had entered the cabin, the guy had been right there. With her story still twisting his heart, he was quite ready to kick the guy's face in. Then before he knew it, he was screaming at him.

He was pretty sure he was still ten feet from him when he screamed again. This time a bottle was thrown at him. Though it missed and hit the wall, Jon caught the spray of liquid and broken glass on his shirt. A girl he didn't recognize emerged from the room. The girl glared at him, and he noticed the green of her eyes. Jon was answered again by a guy in the hall wearing a faded black shirt and cargo shorts.

"Her name is Cassie Holt! The one you were screaming for this morning, asshole!" He pointed at her as walked past him. "You wanted her, there she is!"

Jon couldn't break eye contact with her until she walked away. *What the hell?*

As his throat was on fire and brow dripping sweat, Jon's whole body ached now, and he reached out to grip the door-frame as he turned to see Dan. The girl slammed the screen door on her way out.

He caught the sight of pink fabric in the bedroom the two had been in.

There's her pink hoodie! Kessy was here when I was . . . ? She had to have . . . ! Why couldn't she . . . ?

It connected on some level . . . the growing coil of white around the piercing green of that girl's eyes.

They were in the room with her. That girl Cassie was with her, but why did that guy think I was screaming for her this morning?

Had he missed something? The thought of being the first to know where she was . . .

Jon saw Josh near Dan at the edge of the living room and avoided eye contact purely out of fear for Kessy's state. His mind felt as frayed as his throat did.

Josh shoved Dan away. "Get away from me! Get the fuck away from me!"

Jon stood there, waiting for Josh to make his way down the hall.

Josh paused, then walked into the room with the pink fabric. Jon expected a range of reactions from screaming to a heavy thud of him falling to the floor. But he didn't hear anything. He took several deep breaths.

"Was he talking to you?" Dan asked as he walked toward Jon, followed by several people he did not recognize, sharing his dirty look.

Dan stood at the doorway, and placing both hands on the doorframe, stood in the way of anyone else trying to enter, including Jon.

"You were the one screaming just now, Jon! He thinks you were screaming at that other girl. They both went outside. Go see what he's talking about."

Jon didn't want to do this.

"Who is she?" Jon spoke with strain.

"Go find out!" Dan demanded.

It gave Jon the same feeling of being managed as when he was yelling for Kessy into the fog. He didn't want to go outside for this reason, but the attention was on him from screaming as he had that morning.

Taking a few steps that way, Dan reminded him where she'd gone.

"She's outside, Jon! Go see—"

"I heard you!" His blood rushed as he responded, gathering more dirty looks as he walked through the living room and to the door.

Jon found Cassie waiting for him with hatred in her eyes. They stared at each other, and the whites of her eyes grew, drawing attention to her piercing green eyes.

Like she's waiting for me to approach her!

A smattering of people had gathered behind her, as though setting up for another encounter between their cabins. The last time he was there he'd brought a lot of attention to himself by his screaming. Now he was back.

"All that screamin' and suddenly now you got nothing to say to her?" said the guy in cargo shorts.

Jon glanced his way and shook his head.

What the hell is he talkin' about?

It didn't make any sense to him, so he decided to walk away. But just as he started to turn, the same guy called out to him.

"Fuckin' coward! Screamin' for Cassie until . . ."

The guy continued talking about how Jon had found her and then had nothing to say to her.

Jon's open mouth and peering eyes brought mocking laughter from his audience.

"Ha! Ha! Ha! What the fuck is your deal, man?"

"Guy is fucking crazy!"

The guy shook his head at Jon and nodded toward the woman who continued to glare at him. "You finally found her, man! Screamin' her name like you wanted to kill her. Now you're standing there like you don't know who the fuck she is!" He took another drag.

Jon kept staring.

With his cigarette between his fingers, he finally pointed at her. "She's right there, the one you were screaming at—Cassie!"

He walked over and gripped the doorframe, feeling his stomach drop as he thought about this.

They have similar names. Cassie and Kessy.

Cassie appeared ready to put her cigarette out on his eye.

Oh fuck. What was she doin' this morning when she thought I was screaming her name?

"Cassie." Taking a breath, squeezing the frame, he spoke quietly and with a rasp from his constant screaming. "What did you do when you thought I was screaming your name?"

She appeared to retract slightly before constricting her eyes on him again.

Why couldn't Kessy respond when I was screaming her name?

Ready to ask the same question again, instead he let go of the doorframe and stood in front of her. "Why couldn't . . . she respond . . . when I was screaming . . . her name? Kessy Lane?"

Cassie was not listening to his words, more intent on maintaining her animosity for him now that he was in her face. They stared at each other for another moment until the sound of the screen door opening broke the silence.

Chapter 49

Tracy pushed Dan out of the way, taking his place at the door and pushing the people back in the process. He saw Josh for a brief moment as the smell in the room took his breath away. He had to see Kessy, but no sooner did he get a glimpse of her lying on the old worn carpet, hoodie covering her face, than he had to close his eyes. He hung his head.

"Josh, can she stand?"

"She's unconscious . . . I think," he responded, sounding incapable of doing anything about it.

Tracy had a good idea as to why. "Dan, get Jon away from that girl outside!"

"Why?"

"Because he's too unhinged!" Tracy said through clenched teeth. "If he engages her . . ."

Tracy didn't have to finish the sentence before Dan turned and left.

"Josh! Can she stand?" he asked again, realizing he didn't need to address Josh when Kessy was right there.

"Kessy . . . Sweetheart . . . We're here . . . We fucked up."

It was difficult to say the words as he took in the sight of her stained and dirty legs. They reacted ever so slightly, and he almost lost his mind at Josh for kneeling there.

"Josh! Stand her up!" he said, trying not to completely lose his composure. He felt his grip slipping on the doorframe from the sweat between his fingers.

"She's bleeding!" Josh said, a pleading note evident in his voice.

If I have to move from this doorway, all these people behind me, including Matt, are gonna get in here. That can't happen!

But Josh was in shock at seeing his sister like this.

I gotta go in there! If I don't I'm gonna lose my fucking temper, and I don't want to fucking do that!

He saw Trevor out the window and momentarily thought of having Trevor climb in through the window and take his place at the door, but the thought came and went. It wasn't going to happen.

He had to get Josh out of the room. He let go and could feel Matt shift in behind him. He grabbed Josh's shoulder and squeezed.

"Stand. Up."

His right hand squeezed Josh's shoulder again. Josh shook beneath his grip, in shock.

Still holding Josh's shoulder with his right hand, Tracy reached down slowly for the pink hood that covered Kessy's head and face with his left. As he did, he saw Matt from the corner of his eye, blocking the doorway.

"Josh. Stand up. Go to the window."

Josh tried to shake his hand off, twisting Tracy's arm in the process. He demanded, "Why?"

Tracy could hear the people in the hall.

"What the fuck is goin' on? Move!"

In that instant, he was thankful that Matt hadn't left the doorway, but he didn't feel done with the guy and his fucking take-charge attitude; there was a person lying on the floor in *his* uncle's cabin.

"You're not helping!" he growled at Josh. Reaching into his pocket, Tracy pulled the photo from his pocket. "Take this."

Josh was up in an instant, taking the photo and moving quickly over to the window. He pushed it the rest of the way open and threw himself right through the screen. Trevor helped him not to fall on his head.

At the sound of the ripping screen, Kessy curled into herself. She was finally reacting to something in the room. She appeared to regain consciousness. Tracy realized that she had not heard any of what had been going on.

I can't ask her now. She's not going to have her senses about her.

He was in a difficult position as her first friendly contact in days. He wasn't sure how she would respond to seeing him. He was almost afraid about what his first words with her should be, and whether she would understand.

It didn't feel right to stand her up immediately. It felt as though he was making first contact with a hostage victim. It seemed appropriate to take everything at a turtle's pace in his initial approach.

Where will her mind be, psychologically? This situation . . . the photo . . . the video . . . being in a new room. She probably won't even know if it's the same cabin! The sheer amount of yelling and screaming has probably made her experience here feel more like a nightmare.

He gently laid a hand on her side and leaned over her. He was ready to say her name as gently as he could when she turned her head. He didn't see her full face, but on the side he could see a red rug burn that immediately told a story.

"Matt!" Tracy demanded.

"What?"

"What happened?" Tracy asked, trying to speak quietly, so as not to upset Kessy. Her eyes squeezed closed, responding to the gentle sound of his voice.

"What?" Matt asked again, like he needed Tracy to speak up.

"What. Happened?" he asked, speaking a bit louder. Kessy turned away again. The sound of voices in the hall behind him pissed him off. He didn't want any more involvement from any more people than absolutely necessary.

"Matt!" Tracy demanded.

"I heard you! Some people in the hall saw what happened. They witnessed it."

Oh my fucking God!

He pulled his free hand through his short hair, feeling the oil coat his fingers as his teeth gnashed.

Witnesses?

He remained on his knees, by Kessy, waiting to hear this shit.

Fucking accounts? From people who have the courage only to speak up after the fact! After that hell in the attic footage? And why did she need to be moved?

He wanted to hear these stories and then punch them each in the face for standing by.

When Matt began relaying the first account, he couldn't believe it.

No fuckin' way.

It felt like bullshit as the story began with Matt continuing to call Kessy "your girl" and ended with Kessy pursuing Cassie. But he didn't interrupt, except to verify his understanding.

"She was seen doing this, following Cassie down the stairs?" When his suspicion was confirmed and the story continued, he gathered that Kessy had made her way down the hall and was going after Cassie before she'd been talked out of it and pulled away. It didn't line up for him.

"When was this? When was she 'coming down the hall'?"

"Sunday morning when you came up here, screaming after your buddy."

Kessy heard us! She heard her name and she reacted. When Jon let loose, it affected both of them!

Cassie had been told Kessy was after her, when she was probably after her brother and the rest of us in the den.

He could see it all happening in his mind's eye. Kessy had tried to make her way through a hallway full of people to reach the stairs. She'd recognized the girl from the attic and decided that she had to somehow get through her to get to her friends in the den.

For as long as we were down there, she wouldn't have had a lot of time to do that. Someone stopped her, forced her back to the room, and then they heard Jon screaming.

The rest of the story played out in his mind. Seeing the side of Kessy's face, red and bleeding, believing it was somehow a result of Jon's screaming through the cabin, his having a frightening effect on Cassie after she was told someone was coming after her. He imagined Cassie coming after Kessy, hearing Jon's screams, and reacting further against Kessy as his screaming continued.

Did she hear the discussion about the photo in the den?

He shook his head. It was not something that he wanted to dwell on, his having created some fear for Cassie just before Jon went after her. He'd seen the footage and the partial story, but his mind had filled in the details about Kessy's state as she lay on the floor. He'd thought he was seeing the second time these girls had been in contact with each other.

If these witnesses were in the hall, one of them had to have been in the attic!

"The attic on Friday night. That footage, there was a crowd. Someone saw that happen!" he asked the people crowding into the room.

He heard a guy's voice, a bystander, but couldn't make out what he'd said.

"That question was repeated?" Matt began.

"What question?" Tracy asked.

"The question, 'I didn't hear you. What did you say?'" was said by some fucking bystander.

As a variety of scenarios dotted his mind, he thought Matt might have been asking the same thing.

"What does that mean?" Tracy said quietly.

"What?" Matt said

Tracy spoke up, "Who said that?"

"Chris."

It felt like it was taking too long to figure this out.

"Did Chris talk to Kessy?" Tracy asked.

"I don't know . . ." Matt's sentence trailed off.

Tracy shook his head. "Someone does! The footage you showed me had a mess of people in it. Who was in the attic?"

Kessy stirred, curling away further. Tracy put his hand on her arm gently and she stopped moving.

"Matt, the attic. That footage! What happened?"

He heard the sound of whispering in the hallway.

"Matt!"

"Yeah, what I told you before, Tracy. Your girl was using!" The rasp of Matt's voice came through as he raised it in response to Tracy's prodding. "What they're talking about is what was said."

"What was said?" Tracy tempered his tone.

"She was asked if she wanted some more." Matt spoke confidently.

"Who asked her?"

"Cassie asked her."

The same story he was told outside, was being backed up by the people who'd watched it happen. Tracy shook his head in disbelief as he said, "She was actually *seen* using?"

"It was laid right out for her."

Tracy didn't want to believe those words, but he could envision someone gripping the back of Kessy's head and forcing her into it. He imagined she'd been singled out by that fucking girl as an easy mark, just to get her to do it.

Even though he knew the answer, Tracy asked anyway. "Why her?"

It was quiet for a moment, and Tracy felt his nerves twist. He wanted to hear from someone who had witnessed what had happened in the attic. Then Matt barked at him.

"It's my uncle's cabin, Tracy!" Matt growled at him again. "You *claimed* not to know that information, but I think your pink hoodie did! And your gang has been confronting us all weekend, all while leaving her here! Twice you guys used your fists instead of your mouths."

It was quiet for a moment. Tracy lifted his hand off Kessy to squeeze a fist. The thought of Kessy being helped inside and led up to their attic for a fix, as Matt and Cory had described, made him seethe.

Tracy was forced to dwell on his attitude at the time, and the one single detail about her name had launched such a physical tirade. Their perception of a threat was obscene to him.

Thinking about it made him feel like his head was going to explode.

Somehow it made him feel as though he had more in common with Jon. As the image of their clash on Friday at the front door floated back into his mind's eye, it forced him to remember how thoroughly upset Dan had remained through the next morning, over how out of hand the whole encounter had been. *I can't fucking believe . . .*

Chapter 50

That their encounter Friday night and Tracy's mention of a pink hoodie could have created such a destructive image of their group was heartbreaking. He didn't believe Kessy or anyone else in their cabin knew of this family aspect. But their assumption that Kessy did had served as a fuel for animosity for Matt and his sister Cassie.

Because of one fucking article of clothing!

He was astonished that the people trying to find Kessy were viewed as unhinged. But as far as Cassie was concerned, it was because of a family connection. This revelation caused Tracy to rethink through their conflicts with the niece and nephew of the uncle they'd rented from.

It had started with Tracy banging on the door, continued with Josh's attempted ambush, Tracy again leading a charge when he'd believed they'd attacked Josh, and ended with Jon screaming at them again. From their panicked beginning, the lot of them had approached this cabin as an enemy and had been labeled as insane, with Kessy at the center of it all.

Did she know the people in this cabin? Tracy shook his head; it didn't matter now. As he thought about the way he had to approach Kessy where she lay on the floor, he wanted to punish Cassie. The situation had become so tumultuous after Josh and Jon approached because of so much hate inspired by the photo. The combined efforts from their cabin had caused an equally callous reaction. Their insane and unrestrained efforts were being shoved relentlessly back in his face by the accounts of these bystanders.

When he closed his eyes, these thoughts bombarded him. When he opened his eyes, Kessy was still lying on the floor in front of him, bleeding and helpless, and he was too fucking scared to touch her. If he let loose as Jon had, it would scare Kessy further. He couldn't do anything.

They were still talking behind him. He'd missed most of what was said, as he was in his own head, but the sound of whispers in the hall still made him want to start throwing his fists again. Instead, he tried getting some information.

"Matt." He hesitated, not knowing what the hell to say, but he wanted to know what was being said and tried again. "What . . . ?" He trailed off again, unable to find the words.

Matt began, "She said . . ."

"What?"

"She said she was gonna do something in the attic."

Kessy's arms slid up to her head, as though she was trying to cover her ears. It suddenly became very clear to him that Kessy had been listening to all of this shit. The fact that she might have been reliving everything made him desperate to get her out of the room.

She's hearing this shit! Fucking people in that photo probably remember that fucking camera going off. He shook with anger; the desire to confront these bystanders was an enraging notion. When his leg bumped into Kessy as he swam in this hate, she pulled away. Seeing her react snapped him out of it, forcing him to take a breath.

I ran into her. She felt that. Tracy took another breath. *I need to know how she is . . . so I can handle this and approach her.*

He heard the explanation of Kessy's actions. "She was fetal on the couch in the attic. Her arms were wrapped around her waist and her hood was up." They were creating an effective image that Kessy had been under the influence and unable to handle it. That way whatever happened next would somehow be understandable because of her condition.

A bystander explained, "Chris and Cassie were watching her the whole time. They found a pink hoodie that you described just before you lost it and started throwing fists. We figured the guy with the tattoo around his arm was high because that was the only way to justify it, until we found a girl wearing a pink hoodie."

Matt spoke up, "Then there was no question. I was upset that our first night up included a fight and I really didn't want to believe you were staying in our uncle's other cabin! After I saw the photo you stole, I knew you guys got in several times and you were definitely still high because you came in ready to start another war."

They seemed to enjoy talking about just how out of his mind he, Tracy, had appeared. They had forgotten that he was in the room. They believed the girl in the pink hoodie, Kessy, was there to get high. The abundance of Tracy's blood was unavoidably part of their perception of him. He wondered about Jon's contribution to their perceived insanity.

It had been a mess of encounters that fractured Tracy's ability to find any fault with the people in this cabin. The explanation of why Kessy did what she did, from her supposed drug use to stalking her attacker from the attic, went back to Jon screaming her name that was one part confusion and one part that both women had similar names.

"Cass had her flailing in there. Her legs were flailing and pounding the floor pretty hard. Some guy in a black shirt had the presence to kick her," said the same bystander that had been in the attic.

"What?" Matt responded.

Tracy turned his head toward Matt's voice, shocked at the image of Kessy being brutalized then kicked.

"Someone kicked her while she was on the floor?" he asked but didn't get an answer.

He struggled to stay present as a bystander explained why Cassie had done this.

He discovered that while Jon was screaming, Cassie had been smothering Kessy.

"Everyone heard you guys screaming her name the whole time she was on that pink hoodie girl. I know that's why Cass reacted the way she did, because someone was screaming for Cass as though they wanted to find her and kill her. I think anyone would panic if they heard that." This bystander spoke as though Cassie's reaction were reasonable.

"Did the pink hoodie say anything to provoke Cassie?" Tracy asked, having picked up the title they'd given Kessy.

"Tracy, I told you what happened at the staircase!" Matt growled again. "You don't want to believe it, but—"

"What?" the bystander asked.

"This guy doesn't want to believe that Pink was after Cassie at the time! She described Cass as she tried to pursue her down the stairs instead of calling out to her friends. She was coming off a high and wasn't thinking clearly. Tracy can't stand hearing that!"

Tracy's fumbled attempt to question Matt's second account was just that. His heart ached as this explanation of Kessy's intention and drug-induced aggression against Matt's sister was hammered into the story.

"Is that Tracy? Do you know her, are you her friend?" The bystander asked Matt the first question then turned to him for the rest. He had a tremendous desire to thrust the guy's head at the wall for his blatancy.

How do you stand by while that's happening to someone? This question twisted in his mind each time he closed his eyes. But when he opened them and watched Kessy curl tighter in a fetal position, the feeling that he had to pick her up and leave without another word intensified.

He wondered how to respond. He was as stagnant as Josh had been; the only difference was he knew why Kessy had been treated the way she had. Remembering that he'd sent Josh outside with Trevor reminded him that he'd told Josh that he wouldn't leave his side.

Tracy assumed that when Cassie had "offered Kessy more" had had a heavy hand in the attic, motivated by panic. He vaguely understood why Kessy hadn't left this cabin on her own.

Picking Kessy up and moving her to the window would not only serve to get her out of this atmosphere but she also might see a friend to confide in. He wanted to hear what she had to say.

He moved his arms under Kessy. His body reacted to having kneeled next to her for too long, sending a rush of pain through his legs.

He maneuvered Kessy out the window, and she gripped the fabric on his sleeve. As Cristy helped her through the window, Tracy realized Cristy was standing where Trevor had been. As Kessy shifted into Cristy's arms, her hood fell from her head, and he noticed her disheveled hair was mashed together with its own oil. He wanted to make eye contact with her, to know that she was aware that she was being taken out of this situation. Most of all, he wanted to hear her voice.

It wasn't until Kessy came into contact with Cristy that she began to react.

"Mmmmm!" murmured Kessy.

Tracy maneuvered her as slowly and gently as he could. He was reluctant to let go until Cristy had a good hold on her. His eyes flitted between the two, waiting for them to speak to each other.

Are her eyes open? Is she making eye contact with Cristy?

When he did let go, he stood with half of his torso out the window. After a moment, he realized they were waiting for him to get through the window before they did anything. Then he heard the soft sound of Kessy's voice.

He couldn't quite hear what she was saying, but she'd spoken and that's what was important. Cristy's eyes were red and her face was flushed, as though she'd been through something emotional, but it wasn't about this. Whatever it was, it caused her to have a more empathetic reaction to what Kessy was saying.

When Cristy didn't immediately hug her, Tracy paused. Then a look of horror twisted Cristy's face, the whites of her eyes growing slightly. "He did that because he was worried about you! We all were."

Tracy immediately thought of Jon.

She'd heard him screaming.

Kessy's soft voice spoke again, again too soft for him to hear, even though he stuck his head out the window to do so. He had to know what she was saying. "Kessy, what d—"

"That's not what happened!" Cristy cut him off. "Jon was trying to find you when he did that!"

I need to hear what the fuck she's saying!

But he didn't want to take the time to maneuver through the window. It would take precious seconds during which Kessy would be saying something.

Kessy raised her voice slightly. "None of you were looking for me! And that was the best thing you could do? Because when you did, you only made things worse."

That he heard.

"We don't need you guys here."

"What?"

"I'm fine."

"No, you're not!"

A loaded, uneasy silence followed Cristy's words. Tracy wondered if Kessy might turn around and climb back through the window. He realized she was thinking that the people inside weren't bothering her, except when her friends showed up to clash with them and cause trouble for her.

She thinks that if we leave, she'll be OK. Holy God! The effect that that woman had on her.

"What happened to your contact lenses?" Cristy asked, but Kessy was silent.

"You washed the makeup off your face at some point and washed them out. Kessy, you got up at some point but you didn't leave," said Tracy.

Cristy glanced at him after he said this. His comment on her not leaving was one he wanted her to respond to. But Tracy was only connecting these dots out loud for his own understanding.

Acknowledging that Kessy had had the chance to leave this environment and hadn't was huge.

It meant he had to dig deep through years of psychology courses in college to remember the mental effect that he believed he and Cristy were witnessing. They were witnessing something he'd only read about.

What the fuck was it called?

Feeling like he was onto something, he finally made his way through the window, dropping next to them as gently as he could.

Something Syndrome . . . Sweden Syndrome . . . feels . . . feels close . . .

Standing next to Kessy, he pulled her hood back up over her head, covering the bruising around her eye and red scrape down her face. It took him a moment to realize that her hazel contacts were gone. The sense of conviction in her natural brown eyes was halting.

Being so accustomed to her hazel lenses, their burst of color now replaced by a deep chestnut, and her normally girly demeanor absent, Tracy saw a different girl than the one he'd driven up to the cabin with. The thought that the course of the conflict over the weekend had pulled some of her youth out of her was churning his desire to understand what had happened.

Kessy said "we." If she bonded with someone in this cabin . . . that woman. After the woman brutalized Kessy in the attic and the bedroom, leading Kessy to believe that her friends were the reason this happened, this was the only way Kessy was able to process it. This bonding . . . something syndrome . . .

Kessy's gaze didn't leave Cristy. The two were fixed on each other, and Cristy was having a near impossible time trying to comprehend what Kessy was telling her. As Kessy gave all of her attention to Cristy, it felt like the guys didn't matter; they weren't needed. Surprisingly, Cristy appeared as affected as they might have thought Kessy would have been. Perhaps this was the reason they were able to confide in each other.

Tracy waited for Cristy's next words.

"Were you in that bedroom the whole time?" Cristy asked Kessy.

What is she talking about? She knows that's not the case!

"I was in that room. He followed me down the hall and I ended up in there!" Cristy said, and tears flowed down Cristy's face.

"The girl that was in there, she wanted me out! She said it was my fault and she wanted me out!"

What the . . . ?

"Did she say the same thing to you?"

As she held Kessy, Cristy was trembling while she said these things like the memory scared her. She was losing composure.

Tracy realized there was more going on than he had understood. *They were both attacked in this cabin? And Cristy is trying to bond with Kessy over it!*

Tracy waited through a long moment of silence for Kessy to answer before he reached out to both of them, to gently begin the process of leaving this place. Pulling lightly, neither budged.

He felt a cool, tingling sensation as the blood drained from his face. *If Kessy thinks we're only making things worse, then leaving with us is not going to be an option! And Cristy's only going to leave when Kessy does!*

A feeling of helplessness dragged over him again. He had to talk about what he believed had happened, even if his words would fall flat.

"Kessy, you're right. We did make things worse when we were here." Kessy and Cristy's gaze didn't shift off one another as he spoke. "But we were looking for you the entire time. We—" The situation was unconscionable, but he was going to have to let it fully play out.

Josh's raised voice from the group on the other side of the cabin grabbed Tracy's attention.

"I don't know why you . . . ," Josh shouted. Tracy couldn't understand the rest of what he said. Josh was probably staring down Cassie after he'd seen the state of his sister, finding someone to blame for the photo.

Tracy thought about it further, deciding what to say. "Josh is at the back . . . the person who took the photo in the attic . . . he's by that person." Kessy didn't acknowledge his words, so he continued. "The photo that was taken the first time we were here. They laughed at us and decided we were only here for a fight, and I had spoken of a person in a pink hoodie." His head dropped as he choked it out for Kessy. "I started one. I was bleeding down the front of my shirt. We left you here."

He closed his eyes after saying these words. *This is such a fucked-up reasoning. But it's what Kessy will understand.*

"I spoke of a pink hoodie. Then I took a swing at a guy with a bottle—which he threw at me, and I walked away covered in it."

Kessy's gaze seemed to waver. Tracy waited briefly for her to comment, before realizing she was likely waiting for him to keep talking.

Chapter 51

The sound of Josh's voice careening through the woods accentuated the tension further. "Answer the fucking question!"

"Why'd you do it? He was screaming, and YOU reacted! Why the fuck—"

Tracy turned his head slightly in that direction. Jon was face to face with her. *I wonder . . . Did she threaten him for screaming her name?*

He imagined Jon squeezing his cousin's shoulder and then trying to explain the situation he'd created. Tracy heard the beginning of Jon's plea to Josh, but the rest trailed off. "When . . . I was . . ."

He's gonna try and explain what happened?

Tracy really hoped that neither of the girls heard what Jon had said. At that moment, he was thankful that Jon had no voice left on account of his screaming.

I don't want Kessy to know that . . . that Jon meant to engage her somehow.

"What the fuck does her name have to—" Josh demanded. Tracy knew the conversation they were having in front of Cassie.

He wanted to get Kessy out of the area. As he deliberated, he was sure she could hear their interchange, and he began to panic.

The photo! I still have the photo. It felt like the lesser of two evils at this point.

"Kessy," started Tracy, "the reason we clashed with this cabin . . . the reason we made things so much worse for everyone, was because Jon found a photo that was taken in this cabin." He paused, wondering for a second if she knew about the photo. If she didn't, this felt like a painful way to inform her of it. "It was the reason Josh came up on his own and why Jon went screaming through the cabin the way he did."

As he explained further, he could hear the strain of Jon's voice at the other side of the cabin. He wanted him to stop, so he could stop telling Kessy these things. Cristy seemed to be reacting to what he was saying more than Kessy was. She turned from Kessy and appeared to be fighting her emotions as he spoke of the photo.

"Everyone lost their cool because they thought you were in danger, with everyone surrounding you in the photo like that." Cristy's cheeks grew red as her eyes welled up.

"T-Tracy!" her voice pleaded as she cut him off. He glanced at Kessy, wanting to hear from her. It was obvious he was attempting to speak over the far more emotional conversation going on on on Joshes side of the cabin.

"No. I heard you! You searched over and over for Kessy through the whole cabin!" Josh yelled. Kessy's head turned slightly in the direction of her brother's voice.

"Kessy couldn't respond, because *she'd* put her on the floor!" Josh yelled. Tracy envisioned him pointing at Cassie, who fumed at the attention as he said these words. "Just like we saw in that photo you found!"

Seeing how Kessy withdrew into herself, he realized that the further they pushed it, the less likely she would be able to respond.

Now she knows where Cassie is. How is she supposed to respond while she still feels like she's in it?

The few words Kessy had spoken to Cristy had been all she'd said, and it felt as though that was going to be it.

Cristy found some composure. *Is she gonna talk to Kessy about this, or try and talk around it?*

Taking a deep breath, Cristy began, "I could hear her voice in my head the whole way back to the cabin. When I was in the room with Cassie, she remembered me from Friday night. Even after I was attacked, she got really angry when she recognized me and wanted to know what I was doing there."

Tracy desperately wanted to ask the question *attacked by Cassie?* but couldn't bring himself to interrupt. He stood, the blood boiling in his veins, clenching his fists, one by his chin and one at his waist, listening to Cristy.

"Being around a person like that, it's . . . she made me feel as though I'd done something wrong." She closed her eyes for a moment, finding her composure again. "The way that girl talks . . . if she talked that way to you . . ."

Cristy was having tremendous difficulty putting Cassie's character in to words. Kessy was barely responding to Cristy's difficulty. A sick curiosity made Tracy want to confront Cassie. The fact that this was exactly what Josh and Jon were doing now kept him from going after her. Instead, he waited to see if Cristy would find the gumption to say what she thought of Cassie.

She's afraid of that girl, Cassie! Cristy is still afraid of her! This realization made him hate Cassie even more.

This is a nightmare for Kessy and something else for Cristy!

"You're afraid of her." Kessy spoke so softly they both just stood in shock, waiting for more. Tracy felt a cold chill travel through his body, and his hatred for Cassie grew.

She sounds so fucking calm! She sounds like she's somehow siding with Cassie! How could she ever side with her after all she's done?

The possibility of Kessy suffering from that syndrome jumped back in to his mind, and it scared him. "Kessy, do you understand what happened to you?"

He spoke these words quietly. He had absolutely no fucking clue how she would respond, or even if she would. Asking her felt like a mistake, but it was necessary to try and understand the way he needed to approach Cassie. He remembered that Kessy had said she was fine. His heart sank as she continued to engage Cristy.

"Does she scare you?" Cristy asked her quietly, as though she didn't want Tracy to hear.

"You left because you were scared," Kessy responded just as quietly.

Cristy was quiet for some time, and when she did respond, Tracy had to lean into hear. "Did she say more to you after I left?"

He dragged the fingers of his left hand through his oily hair, waiting to hear what Cassie *might* have said. The heaviness in his chest gradually gradually began to burn.

Tracy glanced in the direction of the path. He looked at the front of Kessy's hoodie, feeling helpless, and said, "Kessy, sweetheart . . . look at your hoodie."

She still didn't respond to him, but Cristy's eyes slowly went down to the mess of dried blood that ran down the front of Kessy's hoodie. Her eyes drifted away, almost as though embarrassed by it. Tracy leaned in to try to get eye contact with her, hoping that seeing the state of her clothing might cause her to have some kind of reaction, so she could wake up from this nightmare.

It felt more uncomfortable than anything as she refused to talk to him. The steady realization that she wanted nothing to do with what he said to her made him feel a bit like a jerk for forcing her to notice these painful things. Kessy sounded so miserable as she talked to Cristy.

Cristy was scared of Cassie, and Kessy seemed to have formed some sort of bond with her. He reached a conclusion about Kessy's mindset and from there, determined his approach to Cassie.

While his proof was as frail as their conversation, he still felt as though he had to do something. Kessy hadn't given any indication that she was willing to leave the area, but it was the only idea he had. "Your brother's over by Jon."

He let his words linger, hoping Kessy would be willing to leave. He slowly reached out for them, hoping he'd meet no resistance from either of them.

Kessy turned, but he couldn't see her face. He subtly leaned forward, still wanting eye contact from her, but he didn't want to force the issue and instead led them away. He still wanted her to talk to him, to respond to the things he'd spoken of, or at least answer his question. As they both slowly walked behind him without another word, he knew he would have to engage Cassie without being certain of his conclusions.

Sweden Syndrome. The words drifted into his mind. His mind pushed and pulled at the idea, trying to work it into a theory so he could explain it.

He had no idea how he would bring it up or, if he could find a way to articulate it, how it would sound to Cassie. He wanted her to listen without walking away.

If she was gonna walk away, she would have been gone by now.

Coming around the back corner of the cabin, the path was in sight ahead of them just to their right. He glanced the other direction and saw a crowd gathered. Assuming Cassie was still there, he panicked, not wanting to let her near either of the girls again.

"Head for the path. We'll be right behind you."

Chapter 52

As Tracy broke away from the girls and headed for the gathered crowd, he nervously hoped that Kessy would not follow. When he heard only his own stride over the gravel, he felt a touch of relief.

He could see Josh and Cassie in the center of the crowd, surrounded as though another fight would occur. His slow stride over the gravel broke the silence and grabbed the attention of the crowd. As he approached, everyone was quiet. Those on the outside of the circle turned and stepped out of his way.

Moving past the crowd, he saw Jon and Dan. It was deathly quiet as he reached out for Josh, glancing at his red welling eyes. Only the sound of Josh's heavy breathing filled the air. Tracy gripped Josh's shoulder, but his attention didn't leave Cassie.

Josh and Jon had teamed up to discover why the girls' relationship had escalated.

The whites of Cassie's piercingly green eyes were so apparent, she'd surely been verbally sparring with both Josh and Jon. After berating her with what they both surely felt was a strong point— her reaction to Jon's screaming and the state Josh found his sister in—they were undoubtedly informed that their rental was owned by Cassie's uncle. It likely left them speechless as Cassie used this family connection to quell their hate toward her.

To this end, Tracy was ready for her to deliver this news to him in hopes he would back off as Jon and Josh were clearly forced to. Tracy wanted to explain to Josh what he believed had gone on, but he noticed the quiet and realized that Kessy and Cristy were watching from the corner of the cabin.

He still didn't want either girl to hear what he had to say, but he had to speak up. He had to ensure that Cassie not only heard him but paid attention. It didn't happen. She and Josh kept staring each other down.

"Josh, Kessy is conscious and able to talk." Tracy spoke loud enough for the surrounding group to hear. Josh and Cassie acted like Tracy wasn't even there.

They talked family.

Continuing became a bit more difficult. Tracy imagined Josh had been asked if when he'd rented the cabin down the path from her uncle, if he had ignored the family aspect that was shared with him as part of her uncle's sales pitch.

Some people believed that Kessy not only knew this, but purposely made her way up the path to use drugs in the uncle's other cabin.

Tracy knew Josh hadn't been able to process the circumstances surrounding his father's rental.

But in his efforts to shift the energy, Tracy didn't know how else to grab their attention other than repeating himself.

"Cassie, Kessy is conscious and able to talk."

Fixed on her green eyes, the words slid off his tongue. He tried to address her in a way that the others had not, like a person. That way she might listen. The anger that gripped her eyes appeared to coil just a bit, but she still glared at Josh.

"She was standing outside the cabin, talking about what happened."

He paused as Cassie glared at him. This was what he wanted, for her to listen.

Chapter 53

"This morning Kessy heard us yelling and fighting in the den just as you and the rest of the cabin did. She stood at the top of the stairs and was ready to follow you when she was stopped. That's where she learned your name," Tracy began.

Cassie's pupils slowly relaxed and she seemed almost pensive, like she wasn't sure where he was going with this.

"With all the screaming and fighting going on in the den this Sunday morning, you both panicked, and I don't blame you. Kessy and you were pushed back when we left, and Jon started screaming at what could have easily been perceived as either of you." He glanced at Jon.

"That's when you went back to the staircase; I remember seeing you, the same anger in your face. You wanted to see the guy who was screaming. But instead you walked away. You panicked. I get that. Instead of dealing with us, you dealt with the pink hoodie that you were told was moving down the stairs after you.

"But the screaming didn't stop, and that affected the way you dealt with her. The last time you were in the room was probably just now. She was unconscious; she didn't hear you."

His own words frightened him.

"She opened her eyes just now, after you left. She and her friend were attacked in this cabin. Both of them described the exact same thing.

"You believed Jon was screaming your name; she thought it was hers. From the marks on her mouth, I think you did your best to prevent her from screaming. Any noise out of her would have given you both away. There were witnesses, but no one said anything until now. From what was described by those that witnessed it in the hallway, her legs were flailing and pounding the floor pretty hard."

Tracy let this vivid image linger. He'd spoken around Kessy being the victim until that last part. It brought a snide slant to Cassie's face, an anticipating squint in her eyes.

"Kessy explained to her friend how much worse everything got when they came after her. Everything became unbearable with the amount of screaming and fighting that was going on when her friends were here. It started with your encounter that surrounded that photo."

He paused, thinking about it in his back pocket. As he debated taking it out, he remembered he'd handed it off to Josh. A feeling of uncertainty crept into his mind, as though without this proof his words lost their meaning.

"I've seen it. A person who is in the type of situation that results in that kind of photo feels as though the knockdown, drag-out fight like the one on Friday night isn't going to stop. All they understand is that a guy left covered in blood. And if that person mentioned a 'pink hoodie,' that's all you really need to create suspicion and, after that, fear.

"The excitement we caused didn't stop when we left. And as soon as we left, you wondered where we came from. You wondered if we were staying down the path in the rental. You assumed we must know your uncle.

"I think you found a person that fit what I described and it was enough to create the perception of a threat. From there on out, every response was out of fear."

Tracy paused, almost losing his train of thought, realizing he was recounting some of the argument he'd had with Dan. But what he'd heard from Matt was closer to the bone.

"Your brother said you used your uncle's Polaroid camera to take a photo of a girl wearing a pink hoodie. Whatever you said to her before you took it, you thought that she was as unpredictable as the guys who described her.

"Was that photo meant for Kessy's back pocket?"

The words slid off his tongue as though they had been resting in the back of his mind ever since he'd seen the photo. It didn't feel like blame, only asking about intent.

But Cassie didn't answer. She stared back at him as Chris cut in.

"You seem to understand how you came across when you were high and banging on our door. But you're leaving out the rest of your behavior as you maintained your high this weekend. You can't be that confrontational and not be high. But you've come up this morning and you come across a bit more level headed. I'm betting you don't got any left."

That was the same conclusion Matt had come to. Chris glared at him, waiting for Tracy to deny it.

Chris continued, "Yeah, you ran out. You mentioned the attic and Cassie taking a photo, but you're leaving out your girl's drug use.

"I was up there. I saw her on the couch and I saw what had been laid out for her. You're talking about what happened between the two girls in the attic after you started a fight with us at the front door. But you're talking around something you don't understand because you were high."

Tracy's attention slowly drifted back to Cassie's piercing green eyes. Hearing his explanation briefly brought to mind the memory of Trevor's footage where Chris had led the charge. The fetal body language of Trevor and the persistence of their questions in the footage, along with their combative approach, wasn't as mysterious as Chris had led him to believe.

Still, Chris spoke of how Kessy had used drugs in the attic and decided to stay even when the rest of her gang was at the front door.

"She pulled herself out of a fetal position and got up from the couch and ran into me as she was trying to get back to the table. Her nose was bleeding. I think it was her first time."

An awkward silence set in after he described Kessy bleeding her first time. Tracy didn't want to hear any more about this or

Kessy's supposed drug use from Chris; he wanted to continue engaging Cassie. But he had to stand there and listen, even if he thought the story was exaggerated or created.

"I'm not trying to call her out for it. Just telling you what she did directly influenced how she was treated. She used and had a real bad reaction to it, which happens, but she made a claim in a roomful of strangers. She said she was going to do something. I asked her to repeat it, but she wouldn't. The whole time I asked her to repeat what she'd said, she was bleeding from her nose."

"And it went south from there," Tracy concluded for him.

"She was called out on her drug use. I don't think she took a lot, but what she did caused her to have a serious reaction—"

Tracy cut him off as the image of Kessy being forced still sat in his head. "Someone grabbed her by the back of her head and shoved her into a—"

"Didn't happen." Chris confidently cut him off. "No one laid a finger on her to use. That was entirely on her."

"You said she was surrounded by strangers when she made some comment that she wouldn't repeat. That's called fear. That's not a threat. And you asked her to repeat it? That's called intimidation when someone doesn't respond."

"If she was so intimidated, she should have left when she had the chance!" Cassie cut in.

"I know!" Tracy declared.

But something happened to her between not walking out of the attic and not leaving after she left her contacts in your sink! She didn't leave when she had the chance.

He felt his heart pounding in his chest. As much as he wanted to throw these words into their back-and-forth, things would only become more of a clusterfuck of who was more at fault. It was enough of a mess already. He had to remind himself that it was largely over and he needed to say what Kessy had told him.

"I know. I get it. She shoulda left . . ."

Doing his best to stifle a nervous tone, he felt his body gradually relax as he continued. ". . . and you brought her to a separate room after your encounter in the attic so she could sober up. You cared about her enough to get her out of the atmosphere in that photo."

She stared at him, a touch of confusion in her eyes.

"You cared about her and had an impact on her of equal measure."

She cocked her head away from him slightly like she had no idea where he was going after the back-and-forth with Chris.

"Are you . . . thankin' her?" Chris asked awkwardly.

Tracy took a breath and spoke softly, "Well, when Kessy spoke to me, just a moment ago, she had an understanding of what happened. What she said to me was, 'We don't need you guys here; I'm fine.'" He let this statement linger for just a moment. "You are the 'we' in that assertion."

"What are you talking about?" Chris asked.

"What I'm saying is Kessy found a way to cope. She told me, 'I'm fine,' and told Cristy how bad things got when her friends were here. She was forced to find a way to cope.

"Kessy knows your name. She described you to a guy at the top of the staircase, and they called out to you and she learned it. Kessy could have called out to you at any time, and you would have engaged her differently than the way you did. She might not have been the girl in the pink hoodie anymore. When Jon started screaming, that's the part that was unbearable for both of you. You both panicked; you both reacted. You dealt with her, and she had to find a way to deal with you."

Chapter 54

Does he feel sorry for Pink and me after the chaos of the weekend?
Tracy spoke as though it affected them both and suggested as Matt had, that she'd cared for her. It was awkward to hear it again. The way she'd reacted to Kessy in the bedroom was a blur, but concern did not drive it. The only thing she remembered was trying to block out the screaming. It was unbearable. She distinctly remembered feeling flooded with rage at the guy who was screaming her name at the top of his lungs.

Chapter 55

Tracy broke the silence. "You can ask her. Or you can ask me."

Cassie shook her head at this, like she wanted nothing to do with it.

He glanced again toward Cristy and said, "I'll bring her over. You can—"

"No!" Her answer was resounding. Tracy knew this would be severely uncomfortable for her. That was why he'd suggested it, to force her to speak.

"She got singled out, because YOU singled her out." Cassie spoke with a definite disdain in her tone.

Tracy replied, "You went searching for a girl in the pink hoodie after I identified her that way, before the fight. You saw me leave with a bloodstained shirt. And that was your inspiration for what happened in the attic." It was like he was telling her exactly what she was going to say as part of her *right* decision.

He continued, "Then you cared enough about her to move her from the attic."

Chapter 56

Tracy suggested yet again that she'd cared for Kessy. He'd spoken with Kessy: he said this because she had. But when he offered to bring her over to discuss their time together Cassie thought of the bedroom. It was a jolt of panic she had to stomp. Cassie had planned to talk to Kessy about her drug, but when Tracy confronted her with the option, she realized she'd never intended to listen to Kessy.

She won't remember any of it! She did too much and crashed hard! The same thought she'd had in the bedroom, but one she couldn't voice now. Tracy would take it as her admitting to some involvement when it was strictly about Kessys own drug use. This position he'd put her in revved her irritation, Tracy was waiting for her to explain why she'd moved a paranoid Kessy from the room. When she remembered that beam of light searching the attic, it was a seething anger for Cory's deviant behavior with the video camera she'd seen in the kitchen that motivated her.

"She was gonna get fucking raped with Cory's video camera in that footage you saw. Where he couldn't get up the stairs."

Tracy grew pale. Knowing he'd seen that footage and did not know what the fuck was going on might inspire him to walk away.

Tracy spoke softly. "Jon stole the tape out of the camera after the fight. We saw Cory find her in the footage. He's the reason she wasn't left shivering in the cold." Cassie was getting vile, but she might have been right.

Cassie stared at him. He sounded like he was being *thankful* again.

You're fucking insane . . .

"What are you thinkin'?" Tracy asked, as though he wanted to draw more of these callous notions out of her.

"You're fucking insane."

"I told you, Kessy believes the reason things got the way they did is because we clashed with this cabin and made things worse."

"What else did she say?"

"She believes her friends have caused what's happened. She's developed a bond with you because of your encounters. It's a psychological effect that allows a person to cope with what's coming at them. It's called Sweden Syndrome."

What the fuck? That came out of nowhere.

Cassie was distracted by the term he'd used.

Tracy described how Kessy felt like she couldn't get out. And in order to cope with what was happening to her, she bonded with the person that was in contact with her during the most intense encounters, when her friends were present.

Cassie half-listened to his description of Sweden Syndrome, while her mind went into overdrive figuring out what he was actually describing. She felt the need to correct him, as she realized the coping that he was describing was actually Stockholm Syndrome.

Fucking guy failed psych class.

Her stomach dropped. She realized why he kept explaining how she'd cared. She'd let him in despite her efforts to put him off being near her. As soon as she found the correct term, she realized he was describing the weekends experience for the girls as though it were a hostage situation.

Like I was an emotional terrorist . . . The feeling in her stomach, the churn of the morning's soda and last night's booze, threatened to force its way out. Her forehead began to bead sweat, as her stomach caused her to hunch. *Where is he going with this?*

"Cory offered her warmth. You offered her some more . . . and you made sure she was with you."

He told her this, as though she'd offered the same thing Cory had. It was a twisted statement, as she knew he was using what she had said about Cory against her because he didn't know the guy.

He said warmth. I said he was gonna rape her with the camera.

I was looking at the table when I offered her more. He fucking told Chris that I grabbed the back of her hood to get her to use, like I'd already done it myself and I was talking her into it.

He thinks I used. That's why he was so quick to understand what happened, like he's accepted that pink hoodie used after I did. Like this Stockholm Syndrome shit makes sense if I was out of my mind on drugs like his pink hoodie was!

When Tracy talked about Cassie's belief that it was her name being screamed and not his precious Kessy's, and how it had such a profound affect on the both of them, she was back to wanting to crack her fist over his face, realizing what he was trying to do.

These encounters between the two of them depended on the severity of the girl's reaction to the drugs in her system. He was offering her a way out of her callousness by admitting to her own drug use, as though saying it was understandable if she had. Her stomach churned.

Waiting for his alternative version, she stared at him as the churn in her stomach gave her face a pained grimace, forcing her to fixate on him. Reacting that way when she wasn't using left the impression of a seriously unhinged mind, which she didn't think she had, but he made a convincing argument that she did. She lost her nerve to hit him.

Chapter 57

Tracy stopped talking. Cassie had grown pale moments ago as he'd described "Sweden Syndrome." He felt as though he was either resonating with her or really pissing her off. He realized after he'd said it that Sweden Syndrome was not the correct term, but he'd pushed on when he realized it had begun a mental process for her. He felt as though he'd given her an out.

All she has to do is admit to her own significant drug use. Then there would be a reason for her behavior.

Tracy had suggested drug use as a way to avoid verbalizing the other scenario, a pathic nature.

Chapter 58

Josh still stood in front of Tracy, intimidated into paralysis. As Tracy laid out the experience that his sister and this girl shared, he stared into space, attempting to understand what Tracy was saying.

His whole body shook as Tracy suggested Cassie cared for Kessy. It was heartbreaking to hear. He expressed an understanding of what Cassie had done and was OK with it, them both coping and using in reaction to the encounters between their cabins. It was like talking about Trevor's footage and the possibility of an organized fight involving Kessy.

He felt his face twist as he tried desperately to hold back the emotions that were pushing their way out.

He saw the state of my sister and he thinks Cassie cared for her? Why is he saying this? Is he making this up?

He could not make sense out of Tracy's words. He stared at the dirt and gravel. He had no fucking clue where Tracy was going with this.

Tracy sounded like he was exposing all of Cassie's impulses, and Josh was standing inches away from her. When Cassie shifted her weight and subtly put a foot behind her, Josh gently collided with Tracy, ready for a fist.

He'd attempted himself to throw blame at Cassie for his sister's state in the room. Josh didn't know what needed to happen for Tracy to be finished with her. He was drained, physically and emotionally. Though he tried not to, he felt himself leaning on Tracy like a support. So when Tracy's arm relaxed, he walked away from the group. Then he saw Kessy and Cristy standing at the edge of the cabin.

Her eyes not leaving Kessy, he pushed his way toward them. She was still wearing the same pink hoodie, and he could clearly see the mess down the front of it. She didn't notice him walking toward them at first.

As he got within fifteen feet of Kessy, his heart broke at the sight of the hateful marks covering her face. He opened his mouth to call to her when he saw she stared intently at Tracy. He felt that he needed to wait. It wasn't over yet. Tension grew as they waited for someone to end it.

"You look like you're gonna be sick." Tracy's voice wasn't loud, but they could hear his words clearly.

"That syndrome you described . . . it doesn't exist," Chris said.

Josh was tempted to turn around to see the reactions to this statement, but he couldn't. He needed to be there for Kessy. Or at least feel as though he were.

"Yes. It does. But it's not called, 'Sweden Syndrome,'" Cassie said under her breath.

That was the same thing Josh had thought but had given it no further thought. She apparently knew Tracy's terminology was off, as he did, but could not take it when that piece of shit, Chris, tried to discredit what Tracy had described.

She knows . . . She's thought about it . . .

At that moment, it felt as though she was just seconds away from confirming her effect on his sister.

"There's no such thing as *Sweden* Syndrome." Her voice was quiet, still moving slowly through her words.

"Stockholm," a guy behind him said softly, not quite loud enough to effect the conversation.

Now that she'd said this much, Josh desperately wanted her to say more. The quiet was agonizing. The desire to go back gripped him. He turned his attention back to Kessy but kept his right ear turned toward the crowd.

Chapter 59

"Your pink hoodie used; I didn't."

Cassie spoke quietly under her breath. The silence persisted. She would have the ability to explain what happened. Tracy had set it up this way, but she felt no need to give him anything.

Tracy began, "You decided that you had reason to panic from the beginning. Then you decided you were in . . ." he paused for a second, searching for the word, ". . . implicit danger when you thought it was your name being yelled, so you did what you wanted to do." Tracy continued, "And Kessy had to process all of it, us and more directly, you."

Cassie finally looked at Tracy.

You did what you wanted to . . .

These words felt like a conclusion of blame. They were strong enough to pull her mind away from the words "Stockholm Syndrome" and forced her to think.

Her stomach continued to churn. She could feel it spreading from her stomach to her chest and face. Like a building mass, the discomfort intensified the desire to be done with the questioning. She felt the same overwhelming hatred she'd felt when she'd had no idea why that guy was screaming for her.

***

Tracy stared down Cassie. Kessy couldn't take her eyes off her, and neither could Tracy. She found herself staring at the part in her hair and the side of her cheek with her face just out of view. The questions Tracy put to her were weird. He was acknowledging what she had just told him and was describing their encounters so vividly. He sounded as though he understood, but she felt like he kept pushing.

She was anxious about why he wanted to know these things and why he hadn't walked away when Josh had. These thoughts floated in then fell from her mind like dust in a breeze. She waited for the response to his questions, as though she were actually capable of listening, when all she wanted to do was go back inside.

Chapter 60

Cassie's face grew red then slowly lost its color, growing quite pale. Tracy and the others saw this.

I said what I thought she caused. The way she's reacting . . . it might be true.

Cassie's face grew pale and the whites of eyes recoiled when her words caught in her throat. Maybe Tracy was causing her agony with his persistence. He was still trying to appear as though he cared for her and that he believed she cared for Kessy, but he was uncertain how his confrontational words would land. And the fact that Kessy had heard it all was unsettling for him somehow.

Tracy would have to walk away to get any more out of her, if she was the type to need the last word. But he couldn't pull himself away just yet. He found some form of relief seeing her react, like something was coming out of her on a chemical level. Cassie's lack of response was stronger than a verbal response.

When Cassie walked away rather than responding, it somehow felt like the only real option he'd given her. She walked past him and back inside. The screech of the screen door broke the tension that had gripped the air, but it didn't feel like this was done. Tracy turned, as did some of the guys with him, to see where she went inside the cabin.

"Back to that same room?" Dan said.

Tracy didn't respond.

Dan spoke quietly. "How much further do you want to go?"

Tracy turned to him for just a second when he heard Cassie's voice through the screen.

"Hey." She spoke quietly, as though she wanted him alone.

Chapter 61

Tracy walked back inside. What they now had to say in private was heartbreaking for Josh when he just wanted this to be over. *What the fuck does she have to say to him in private?*

***

Tracy met Cassie near the kitchen. Glancing back and seeing that no one had followed him in, he turned to her.

As he waited for her to speak, he observed that her complexion had grown pale, as though something had begun to sink in. She asked, "She's OK?"

"I told you what she is."

Cassie's head dropped. Her eyes finally seemed to connect with the meaning behind Tracy's words. "You were serious," she confirmed quietly, as though it hadn't been real when they'd been standing outside. She'd gone inside because she couldn't remain guarded anymore. Her mouth opened a bit as she Hunched forward. *She does not know how to deal with being told that she'd cared for Kessy this whole time.*

"You look like you're gonna be sick." He turned to the door and began walking away.

"She's OK." Her words were confident, but the tone was pleading, as though she were really saying, *Tell me she's OK.*

Pausing briefly, he didn't turn as he spoke, "It's on film. You took her photo. Now you know what happened." He saw Jon and Dan out the screen door, listening as he reached for the handle.

Now it'll finally fucking resonate with her, he thought as he stepped back outside. He walked over to Josh, ready to answer his question as they left.

"What did she say?" Josh asked him, speaking slowly.

"She gets it," he said quietly.

"What did you say?" Kessy asked, Cristy's arm wrapped around her.

Tracy hesitated, realizing that all three wanted to know what those few seconds of conversation consisted of. "It's on film. She took your photo . . ." Tracy trailed off. Kessy asked, but still didn't seem to want to hear this as she turned away.

She doesn't understand why I said what I did. I told her that Kessy is experiencing this syndrome, but Kessy doesn't see it.

It felt like a subtle confirmation of what he'd been searching for. He glanced at Josh, who was still waiting for him to say more.

Josh doesn't understand it either.

Jon and Dan were walking toward them. Tracy guided the girls toward the path entrance. Kessy pulled away as he put his hand on her back.

Encouraged by the response he'd finally gotten from Cassie, he tried to make Kessy understand. "That woman sought you out based on your pink hoodie after we mentioned it."

Cristy glanced at Kessy's hoodie for a heartbeat before turning back to Tracy, her eyes wide, shocked that he was saying this again. His words brought back an uneasy energy when it felt like he wouldn't let this point go. Kessy didn't react.

She doesn't need to hear it; she knows it.

He glanced at Josh, who was just behind them, and made room for him beside his sister. Slowing his pace, he stepped in with Dan and Jon on either side of him.

Jon appeared exhausted, his face flushed and body frail. After screaming at Cassie again, Jon had no more control to lose.

Josh's arm was around Kessy, and her head leaned on his shoulder. She spoke quietly to Josh, "I'm gonna burn this fucking hoodie."